AN
UN

CHOICE

AN UNCERTAIN CHOICE

JODY HEDLUND

ZONDERVAN®

ZONDERVAN

An Uncertain Choice
Copyright © 2015 by Jody Hedlund

This title is also available as a Zondervan ebook.
Visit www.zondervan.com/ebooks.

Requests for information should be addressed to:
Zondervan, 3900 *Sparks Dr. SE, Grand Rapids, Michigan 49546*

ISBN 978-0-310-74919-6

Cover design and cover photography: Mike Heath / Magnus Creative
Interior design and composition: Greg Johnson/Textbook Perfect

Printed in the United States of America

15 16 17 18 19 20 21 22 23 24 25 /DCI/ 20 19 18 17 16 15 14 13 12 11 10 9 8 7 6 5 4 3 2 1

Chapter 1

Montfort Castle, Ashby
In the year of our Lord 1390

My slippered feet slapped the dirt road, and my heart hammered against my chest like a battering ram.

"Wait, Lady Rosemarie," my nursemaid called from the narrow alley far behind me.

But I couldn't wait. I lifted my silky gown higher and pushed my feet faster, straining to reach the town square before it was too late. I raced past the one-room thatched homes of the poor peasants, doors ajar and deserted.

Now I knew why everyone was gone, except for the bedridden and one lame beggar child who'd finally had the courage to tell me what no one else would. The entire town had gathered in the market square to watch several men receive punishment for their crimes. Only it wasn't the usual stocks or pillory, which I allowed. Nor even someone being placed in jail. No. This time, someone had apparently given the bailiff permission to boil the criminals alive.

Revulsion spread throughout my body. And anger. Why was the bailiff blatantly disregarding my law against cruel tortures?

I rounded the massive grain storage building and stumbled out of the dark alley and onto the cobbled street that led to the market. Almost immediately, I hit a wall of bodies—craftsmen and merchants who'd left their shops to watch the public punishment. My breath burned in my chest from my frantic run through town, and I gasped a lungful of the sourness that came from the unwashed bodies sweating in the merciless late-morning sun. The odor soon mingled with the stench of pigs and chickens brought to market, and the rottenness of overripe produce.

But fury mastered my nausea. I wouldn't tolerate cruelty on my lands, among my people. I hadn't allowed it in the years since the Plague had taken the lives of my dear father and mother. And I wouldn't start today.

With a flare of indignation, I stood on my toes, straining to see above the caps and wimples of all those who resided in my walled town. At the billows of black smoke arising from the center green, the ramming of my heartbeat doubled its pace. The smoke could mean only one thing—that an enormous fire had indeed been lit. And that a large cauldron had been suspended above it, filled with well water and set to boil ... with one of the poor criminals inside.

Panic rose to choke me as surely as smoke. "Cease this instant!" I cried. But amidst the clamor and shouts of those gathered, my voice only added to the confusion.

"I command you to release the criminals at once," I called again, louder.

My orders drifted into nothingness. At the back of the crowd, I was invisible. The townspeople were too intent on the cruel scene before them—some curious, others shocked. But mostly afraid. I could see the flickering lines of fear etching the weathered faces, the wrinkled brows, and the hunched shoulders. I needed to make my way to the front, to the bailiff, and demand that he stop the proceedings.

I tapped the back of one of the men standing before me. "Please. Let me pass."

Without a glance, the man shrugged away my touch as if it was nothing more than a pesky fly. I waited for him to turn around and see that it was I, Lady Rosemarie Montfort, the ruler of Ashby and all the many lands and estates beyond. If he would but take notice of me and realize who I was, he would fall to his knee before me. But he didn't budge. Like everyone else, he was too focused—too horrified—to see me.

With a breath of frustration, I stepped toward a group of women huddled together and attempted to wedge my way through their midst. But they only squeezed closer, blocking my way, shutting me out as effectively as the city gate.

With a desperate glance around the market, I caught sight of the steep steps that led to the guildhall's arched doorway. Bunching my gown, I worked my way around the edge of the gathering until I reached the large stone building. I wove through the children who crowded the steps, patting their bare heads tenderly as they bowed before me. When I finally climbed to the landing, the market spread before me. There, in the very heart of the green, was the bonfire. And suspended above the blazing heat was a large cauldron hanging from a metal tripod, with an old man cramped inside. The steam rising from the water told me it wouldn't be long before it began to bubble at an unbearable temperature. The old man's screams would soon fill the air as his skin blistered and flesh cooked. Even now, his exposed chest shone as red as freshly butchered beef. Beneath a mop of dirty gray hair, his eyes were wild.

To the side, another criminal was sprawled on the ground,

his hands tied to stakes above his head. Ropes bound his feet, and the petty constable was cranking a lever that was slowly stretching the man, nearing the point where his arms and legs would pull from their sockets.

I spotted the dark cloak and hat of the bailiff, and found he was adding more kindling to the fire.

"Bailiff!" I shouted. "You must stop this cruelty."

Only the children on the steps heard me. They lifted their faces to watch me expectantly. I cupped the cheek of the nearest urchin and smoothed my fingers over his filthy skin. He peered up at me with adoration, and I managed a small smile for him. He shouldn't have to witness such a display of inhumanity. No one should. Ever.

With a shudder, I crossed my arms over my chest and attempted to ward off the dark chill that came from remembering the torture I'd witnessed four years ago after my parents' funeral. The gruesome picture was stitched into my memory like embroidery threads within a tapestry. I wanted no more memories like that one.

"Stop!" I yelled again. "As Lady Rosemarie Montfort, your ruler, I command you to cease. Immediately."

This time, my declaration caused heads to turn my direction. The women closest to the guildhall began to whisper and grab the arms of those around them. Some of the men bowed. But the petty constable continued to crank the rope, and the bailiff tossed another log onto the fire, sending sparks shooting high into the air.

I uttered an unladylike cry of frustration and raised my eyes to the grand castle on the bluff that towered as a lord over the town. The outer walls rose as if one with the rocky cliffs, making the fortress impenetrable on three sides. A moat and the town provided the defense on the fourth side.

If only I'd thought to bring one of my guards. Even now,

I could make out the gleaming helmet of the soldier on duty at the gatehouse. But I'd never had need of protection in my town, among the people who loved me.

A glint of silver along the fringes of the gathering caught my eye. A short distance from the guildhall stood a war horse mounted by a knight. Dressed in his plate armor, the coat of arms on the horse's blanket was unfamiliar—red with a fire-breathing dragon emblazoned upon it.

How long had the warrior been watching the proceedings?

A shimmer of unease slipped up the veil trailing over my plaited hair and pricked the back of my neck. None of the neighboring lords had threatened Ashby. The land had been at peace. So who was this knight, and what did his presence in my town mean?

As if sensing my question, the knight shifted to face me. Through the narrow slit in his steel helmet, his eyes were dark and unreadable. Even so, there was something kind and respectful about his posture. He surprised me by bowing his head and paying me homage.

Then he lifted the long halberd at his side, dug his spurs into his horse, and charged forward toward the center green. At the heavy thudding of his steed and the sight of his weapon, those in his path fell back to make room for him. He thrust forward like a knight at a jousting tournament.

My muscles tightened. What did he intend to do? I wanted to call out, to question him, to demand that he explain his presence in my town. But as he made a direct path to the cauldron of bubbling water, I found myself praying he'd succeed where I had failed to bring an end to the torture.

With a precision and strength that no doubt came from years of training, the knight slashed the halberd's axe-head into the knotted rope binding the criminal on the ground, freeing first one hand then the other. Within seconds, the man was sitting and frantically working to unbind his feet.

The knight shifted to the bubbling cauldron. Again, he lifted his halberd, and this time swung around the fluke that hooked into the metal chain suspending the pot from the tripod. The knight gave his horse a kick that caused the beast to jolt forward. The swift jerk was all it took for the tripod to tip and then topple to the ground. As the cauldron crashed, boiling water splashed over the fire and onto the bailiff and other townspeople, who jumped back with cries. The poor old man who'd been inside, naked except for the breech cloth at his waist, rolled into a quivering heap.

"What do you think you're doing?" the bailiff called, brushing at the splatters of hot water soaking into his hose.

The knight steered his horse toward the newly freed criminal. The old man pushed himself up and held out shaking hands that were tied together at the wrist. His face was wreathed in gratitude. "Thank you, sir," he croaked.

Before the bailiff could protest further, the knight unsheathed his sword and slit the rope at the man's wrists. Then he reached down, clasped the old man's arm, and hoisted him onto the horse behind him. Though red and raw, the criminal wrapped his arms around the knight's armor and clung to him.

Only then did I dare to take a breath. The old man suffered burns and blisters from his ordeal, but he was free from his torture at last.

The bailiff pointed his dagger at the knight. "By whose authority are you disrupting this execution of justice?"

The knight said nothing. Instead he urged his horse away from the bailiff and trotted along the path he'd already made through the crowd. The townspeople were too stunned by his display of strength, just as I was, to utter a word.

With the pointed tip of his halberd, he caught the cloak

of a merchant in passing, lifted the flowing garment, and held it out to the criminal so that the man could shield his unclad body from onlookers.

The bailiff's indignation rose in the now silent square. But the knight didn't stop until he reached the guildhall. Only then did he sidle his horse against the tall stairway and help the criminal dismount so that the old man slid to his knees before me.

At the sight of me standing at the top of the guildhall steps, gasps wove through the marketplace, and soon every person, young and old, bowed to one knee. From atop his steed, the knight, too, lowered his head.

"Thank you, my lady," the criminal spoke through cracked lips. I recognized him as one of the men I'd recently pardoned. He'd been accused of stealing out of the parish coffers so that he could pay his rent and provide food for the numerous orphan children he kept in his care. I'd determined then, as I did now, that he didn't deserve punishment but rather benevolence.

I tucked the cloak more securely around his shuddering body before rising to my full height and straightening my shoulders with frustration. Who had dared to override my compassion? And why?

I narrowed my eyes on the bailiff and constable, who had knelt along with the rest. "Bailiff," I called. "I shall require an answer for this blatant disregard of my laws."

He lifted his head, and fear flashed across his countenance. "I was only carrying out the sheriff's orders, my lady."

My frustration fanned hotter. I should have known. The sheriff hadn't approved of my leniency among the populace. But with two recent outbreaks of a mysterious illness in outlying areas, the poor were dying, and I had no choice but to bestow more compassion.

"Tell the sheriff I request his presence at the Great Hall this very day. And you will accompany him."

The bailiff lowered his head in acquiescence.

Inwardly, I sighed at the confrontation that was to come. The sheriff had never liked me, even though he'd saved me from a plague-stricken peasant several years ago. He was the kind of man who thought women were useless. And now that I'd inherited Ashby, his dislike had only grown, as had his resistance to taking orders from me. Of course, I hadn't yet become full ruler of my lands. I was still under the guidance and leadership of Abbot Francis Michael until my eighteenth birthday. But in a month, I would be able to rule on my own, even if it would be from the convent as a nun. The sheriff would eventually have to learn to accept my decisions. No matter how much he disliked the idea of having a female ruler, I was the only and rightful heir to Ashby.

The warhorse in front of me snorted, shifting my attention back to the knight, who was obviously waiting, as he should, for me to speak first and acknowledge his presence.

"Sir," I started. "I owe you my deepest gratitude." Only then did he straighten. Through the eye slits, his guileless gaze met mine and radiated with approval. And somehow I knew he was a friend, not a foe.

"My lady." His voice echoed behind the hollow metal. "You owe me nothing."

If only he would remove his helmet so I could see his mouth, to know whether he offered me a smile. Although I wasn't sure why that should matter.

He shifted in his saddle, his steed tossing its head and growing restless.

I was tempted to order him to dismount and show his face. Who was he? A lord from one of the neighboring lands? But before I could speak, he shied back a step. "For one as fair and kind as you, my lady, whatever you wish shall always be my command."

With that, he bowed one last time. Then, tucking his halberd under his arm, he gave rein to his horse, allowing the beast to twist and rear away. Before I could tell him to stop, he galloped across the square and veered down the main street that led to the city gates.

Like everyone else, all I could do was stare after him until he disappeared.

Chapter 2

"The sheriff has gone too far this time," I said to the abbot, who stood by my side.

Abbot Francis Michael, taller than most men, bent low to speak into my ear, giving me full view of the bald spot on his tonsured head. "Don't be too harsh with him, my child. He's only attempting to keep order."

The sheriff and bailiff stood stiffly by the double doors of the Great Hall, flanked on either side by two of my soldiers. While the bailiff's expression contained the same fear I'd seen at the market square earlier, the sheriff's dark scowl reflected his irritation and none of the submission I desired.

"Think about the predicament from his perspective," the abbot continued in his calm and quiet tone. "If he allows a few to break the law without repercussion, then others will think they can do the same. Such lenience could lead to anarchy."

"You know I don't condone stealing," I said. "But if the poor are desperate enough to break the law, then we must increase the amount of their assistance."

The abbot rose and tucked his hands into the wide sleeves of his habit. Although a slender man from his many fasts, he was not weak. The reverent lines of his face radiated the strength I had come to rely upon over the past four years.

He didn't say anything for a long moment, and instead stared straight ahead thoughtfully and prayerfully.

I turned my own critical eye toward the view. The enormous hall with its high arched ceiling, palatial colonnades, thick tapestries, and glazed windows attested to my wealth. As did the elegant engraving on the golden chair in which I sat. What need did I have for such lavishness when my subjects languished? Selling or trading the opulent throne and tapestries could provide months of provisions for the poorest in the land. What need would I have for it anyway once I entered the convent next month?

The abbot finally sighed. "You have a soft heart, child. And you have already given more than you can afford."

My stomach cinched at the feeling of ineptness that weighed on me whenever I conversed with the abbot about the financial predicament of my lands. If there was one point of disagreement between the abbot and me, it was on the distribution of funds. Even though I supported the architectural plans for the cathedral and abbey he was designing, I wanted to remain generous to the poor. We seemed to be growing at odds on how to do so without draining the coffers.

"We must do more," I said more to myself than to the abbot. My parents had sacrificed their lives in order to help the people of Ashby. I'd vowed to do the same, to become the kind of ruler that my parents would be proud of, to do all I could so that their death wouldn't be in vain.

The abbot finally gave a resigned nod. He knew that I'd made it my life calling to rule my people with compassion. "In the meantime," he said, "you must show the same compassion to the sheriff that you wish to show to all of your people."

I glanced again to the swarthy face of the man in question, half concealed behind a full black beard. Across the distance, his eyes glittered with a hardness that had always unnerved me.

"But he knows I forbid the traditional methods of punishment in favor of more humane discipline."

"I'll speak with him," the abbot said with a nod at my guards. With curt bows, they ushered the sheriff and bailiff out the double doors. As much as I wanted to punish the sheriff and show him that he must obey me as his ruler, whether he respected my authority or not, I couldn't disregard the council of the one man in the world who often understood everything about me better than I understood myself.

The abbot rounded my dais and bowed before me, giving me a view of his shiny bald spot again. As he started down the long center aisle of the room with his slow measured steps, I wanted to call after him to stay. I wanted to talk about the problems in my kingdom. In fact, I would have been content to converse about anything rather than having to face the loneliness that had been growing in my life.

Lately, every time I entered the castle walls, I felt like I was returning to a deserted fortress. The enormity of the empty hall dwarfed me, reminding me of how alone I was. The long tables lining the walls had once been filled to overflowing, and the room had rung with laughter, the clink of goblets, the melodies of lutes, the songs of minstrels, and the chatter of the many guests who'd often visited.

But it was not so anymore. Few had stepped foot inside the Great Hall since that fateful night after my mother's death, when I'd found the parchment in her chest. It had been the first time I'd learned of the sacred vow my parents had made, the vow that said I must enter the convent upon my eighteenth year.

For a long while after that night, I hadn't wanted visitors. I'd decided it was useless to form friendships when I would have to sever them all too soon. Then after a time, word of my circumstances and my parents' vow had spread throughout the realm. Any potential suitors who had once considered vying for my hand in marriage no longer had reason to visit. The abbot encouraged me to continue to facilitate good relations with neighboring lords, but without my father, and having only a young woman ruler to contend with, the lords also visited infrequently.

After four years of isolation and missing my parents, I'd never felt as alone as I did now. It was only when I was outside the castle walls visiting my people and delivering goods among the poor that I could forget about the ache.

I released a long sigh that echoed in the emptiness of the hall.

As the guards opened the double doors for the abbot, my porter, James, entered the hall. He was a hulk of a man, with broad shoulders and beefy arms, and he stood a head taller than most, reminding me of a giant. At the sight of the abbot, James came to a halt and ducked his large, bald head.

"What do you need, James?" the abbot asked, eyeing the servant.

"I've a message for her ladyship." James's response came out in his usual gruff tone.

"Lady Rosemarie is distressed from a torture she witnessed today," the abbot said. "Step outside and deliver the message to me. Then I'll determine whether she needs to receive it."

James turned to do the abbot's bidding.

"No," I said, daring to defy my councilor. I wanted— needed—to talk with someone, even if it was only a servant.

The abbot's brows rose.

"I'm not too distressed to speak with James." I motioned him toward me. James lumbered down the aisle. Not long after my parents died, when I'd been alone, young, and vulnerable, the abbot had decided James would add another layer of defense to my castle as the one in charge of its main entrance, as well as be available as a personal bodyguard should the need arise. The first time I'd met James, when the abbot had brought him to the castle, I'd half expected the hulk to pull out an enormous club and bat away anyone who dared approach me. Since then, I'd come to realize James might look intimidating, but that's as far as the bravado went.

As he reached my golden chair, he bowed, revealing the abbot, who had followed closely behind him.

"Deliver your message, James," I said.

James kept his head bowed. "Your ladyship is to have guests."

Guests? The very mention of the word sent a ripple of surprise through me. "Do they come in peace?"

"Yes, your ladyship."

"It's been so long." The last visitor had been after the Feast of Epiphany months ago. And even that had been only because my neighbors to the south, the Baron of Caldwell and his wife, had been traveling to court and had been caught in a storm. They'd stopped to seek refuge for a night. Seeing them had brought back painful memories of their son, Thomas, and the last time we'd been together. Though I'd only been fourteen at the time, the attraction between us had been strong and our plans for the future had been so bright.

The vow had taken away all my dreams of a life with Thomas — or with any man. As a woman destined for celibacy, I'd had no right to hold on to love and plans for marriage. I'd let Thomas go, though it had been hard. And he'd done likewise. If Thomas had tried to cling to me, he would have put my life in danger, for the vow my parents made was unbreakable except by death.

I'd assumed that I'd long past buried my feelings for Thomas ... until Baroness Caldwell informed me that he'd finally married last autumn.

Why guests today? Why now?

James watched me, as if he had heard my unspoken questions and expected me to know the answers.

But I had no explanation. Thankfully, it was Midsummer's Eve. If I had guests this day, at least I'd be prepared to feed them. I'd already planned a lavish feast, as I did every year for all the servants along with the garrison of soldiers who worked within the walls of my castle. I always made sure the Midsummer's Eve feast was much more extravagant than necessary so that afterward the poor beggars who came to the kitchen door would have plenty to eat.

"Did they give word on when they would arrive?" I asked with a shiver of anticipation.

"The messenger said they're but a half day's ride away, my lady. They'll reach the town walls by eventide."

I nodded, thinking of the knight who'd rescued the criminals from their torture. Had he been the messenger?

As if thinking the same thing, the abbot's thin brows came together in a frown. "If this was the same knight who was in town earlier, dressed in his battle armor, then how do we know he comes in peace and not ready to wage war?"

James ducked his head and shied a step away from the abbot. "The messenger claimed he was riding with the Noblest Knight."

The Noblest Knight, the Duke of Rivenshire? I couldn't help myself—my heart expanded with a sudden bloom of hope. "Truly?"

James reached into his tunic and retrieved a ring. He held it out so that I could clearly see the cross at the center. The Noblest Knight's emblem. "He sent this to assure you of his goodwill and said he'll retrieve it when he arrives."

I took the heavy silver ring and traced the raised beams of the cross, reveling in the thought of having the company. The

Duke of Rivenshire had been one of my father's closest friends and my godfather. When they were younger, they'd served together in war campaigns and had saved each other's lives on more than one occasion. Although I hadn't seen the duke since my parents' funeral, I had no doubt I'd relish every moment of his visit.

The abbot peered at the ring. "How can we be sure it's his and not stolen by some crook hoping to storm Ashby?"

"'Tis his," I said. "There's no crook who could take this from the duke, not without severing his finger for it."

"Then would you like me to tell the servants to make ready for their arrival?" James asked looking between the abbot and myself as though he was unsure who was giving the orders.

"I think it best if we use caution, my child," the abbot advised. "Perhaps we can send out a regiment of our own men to survey the truth of the situation."

I held back a sigh. The abbot knew I didn't like to be overprotected and treated like a child. Most of the time, he held himself in check and tried not to smother me. But there were still times—like now—when he worried too much. It was for my good. I tried to remind myself of that every time he sheltered me. He'd had to bear a great deal of responsibility since my parents had died. He only wanted to ensure that I remained safe, and I was grateful for that.

Nevertheless, I was no longer a young, naive girl of fourteen who needed his advice and protection at every turn. I'd learned a great deal about running my lands in the last four years. And now that I was only weeks away from taking full leadership, I balked even more under the abbot's hovering.

"My dear Father Abbot," I said, giving him what I hoped was a grateful smile. "If I send out my own soldiers, the duke may think he's unwelcome here, and that's the furthest thing from the truth. I look forward to seeing him, and since we have only a few hours to make ready I suggest we put forth all our effort into preparing for his arrival."

The worried grooves in the abbot's forehead didn't smooth away. But after another moment's hesitation, he finally nodded.

In my chamber, I twisted a long strand of my blond hair around my finger. "How do I look?" I asked Trudy for the hundredth time.

Trudy swatted my hand away from the delicate but twirling curls that fell below my waist. "I say you'll look like a drowned cat in no time if you keep tugging at your hair."

I clasped my hands together at the front of my loveliest gown — a silk of purest pink, the color of the roses that grew on the trellises covering the stone walls below my chamber and in the gardens surrounding the keep. One of the maids had woven a crown of freshly cut rosebuds. It now graced my head, and matched my gown to perfection.

A trumpet in the courtyard outside my open window interrupted my moment of vanity. The excitement that had been building inside my chest resonated with the blast.

"The Noblest Knight has arrived, my lady," my oldest and most trusted guard, Bartholomew, called from the hallway.

Trudy stood back, planted her hands on her wide hips, and surveyed me. "I just don't know, my lady. I don't feel quite right about everything."

"Then you don't think I look nice enough to receive my guests?" I twirled in a circle so that my gown swished.

"You look too grown up."

I laughed, the echo of it wavering with both relief and nervousness. "You and the abbot make a fine pair, always worrying about me. It's about time, though, that the two of you realize I am grown up."

Trudy harrumphed and brushed at an invisible fleck of dust on my skirt. From beneath her plain head covering, her gray hair framed her plump cheeks. She was as dear to me now as she'd been in my childhood. And although I should have taken a proper lady's maid long ago, I couldn't relinquish this dear woman who'd been a second mother to me, especially in recent years when I'd missed the comforting arms and tender kisses of my mother.

As I crossed the spacious bedchamber, Trudy lifted the train of my gown to keep it from dragging in the fresh rushes the servants had strewn across the stone floor.

When one of the maids opened the heavy paneled door, it drew in a breeze from the window, bringing with it the sweet, familiar scent of roses. I let the air bathe my skin and tried to contain my excitement.

By the time I'd traversed the long hallway, descended the steep winding stairway in the stone tower, and reached the massive doors of the keep, my knees shook with anticipation.

James was waiting by the doors, wringing his large hands. "I think Abbot Francis Michael was right. The duke has brought other knights with him and they're all dressed for battle. What if he's come to attack you and take over your lands?"

"Don't be silly, James." I straightened the crown of roses one last time and then smoothed a hand down the front of my gown. "I'm sure the duke comes in peace."

"I think we should wait to receive them until the abbot returns," he whispered, his gaze darting to the shadows as though he wanted nothing more than to hide there. "I've sent a messenger for him so he's aware the guests are here."

"After a weary day of riding, we cannot keep them waiting. I shall receive them now." I nodded at the doors, the signal for James to open them, precede me, and announce my presence. He hesitated only a moment longer before bowing and

24

obeying. The doors squealed on their hinges as he swung them wide, making it obvious they had not been opened enough in recent years.

The fading evening sunlight poured into the hallway, beaming down on me. With Trudy's final fussing over my train, I glided forward, passing through the doors onto the wide, open balcony at the top of the front steps. The gleam of silver armor, the glint of weapons, the clanking of metal, and the stomping of horses greeted me. The knights were covered from head to toe in protective gear yet sat straight and tall on their steeds. They were followed by a small army: squires and groomsmen on horses behind them, along with servants on baggage carts.

A hush fell over the crowded courtyard, and every gaze turned to me. What if the abbot had been right about their intention? Had I rushed into a dangerous situation?

The peace I'd had only a moment ago fled, making me wish I could follow it back into the dark comfort of the keep. But I held still and forced the greeting required of me. "I am Lady Rosemarie Montfort, and I welcome you to Ashby."

The lead knight slid from his mount and tugged off his helmet and padded cap to reveal silver hair and the kind, regal face of the Duke of Rivenshire.

"Your Grace." I curtsied and bowed my head in deference. As a younger brother of the High King, the duke was my superior even if he'd been a family friend.

"Rosemarie?" His voice held surprise. He moved toward the bottom step, taking me in from the crown of roses on my head to the dainty slippers on my feet. A smile hovered over his lips.

"Yes, your Grace." I curtsied again, trying to quell the nervousness that sprang to life. What would he think of me after so many years?

"Of course I expected you to have matured since the last

time I saw you," he said. "And rumors of your beauty had reached us even to the far borders of the kingdom."

I could feel a heated blush moving into my cheeks.

"But I was not prepared for exactly how grown up and lovely you truly are."

"You are much too kind." I'd never paid attention to the whispers surrounding my beauty. I'd always believed the poor beggar children who admired me couldn't help it compared to the squalor of their lives. I'd never believed I was extraordinary, only that it was hard not to shine in such darkness.

The duke's smile widened, and he started up the stone steps. When he stopped before me, he reached for my hand and kissed it tenderly, his eyes crinkling at the corners and his face showing many more lines than it had the last time I'd seen him.

"And how are you, dear one?" he asked softly.

With his last words, I couldn't keep from envisioning the last time I'd seen the duke, the day after my parents' funeral. We'd stood in this exact spot saying our good-byes. Although he'd invited me to live with his wife in Rivenshire, I hadn't been able to leave Ashby and all the memories of my parents. My heart constricted with sudden longing—and sadness—for my father and mother, their love and companionship, and all that I'd lost when they'd died.

If only . . .

The moment the discontent whispered through me, I squelched it. There was no sense brooding about what could have been. I couldn't change anything now. I needed to accept my fate with the positive attitude I'd worked so hard to cultivate.

"I have fared well these past years," I said, through the ache in my throat. "And I'm delighted that of all the places to visit in the country, you've chosen to come to Ashby so directly. Surely after so long an absence, you and your knights are anxious to return to your estates."

For the briefest of moments, I allowed myself a peek at the retinue of soldiers the duke had in his service. Three knights were mounted directly behind the duke's steed, set apart from the others—obviously his most trusted men. I skimmed over two of them, but at the sight of the emblem of the fire-breathing dragon on the third, I stopped.

The slit in the man's visor was too narrow to see his eyes, but he gave me the barest of nods. And that was all it took to know that he acknowledged our earlier encounter.

Perhaps now I would have the chance to thank him properly.

The duke followed my gaze to the dragon knight, and his brow quirked. I quickly shifted my focus back to the fatherly figure standing before me. "After your lengthy absence, I'm sure your attention is greatly sought after throughout the land."

He released my hand, and his smile dimmed. "Yes, there are many cares that need my attention. But of them all, your situation is the most urgent."

"Most urgent? But of course not." I waved my hand toward the town and to the farm fields and forests beyond. "As you can see, my land is prosperous and at peace."

All was indeed well, except for the recent outbreaks of the strange illness in two neighboring towns. But thankfully it hadn't spread, as had happened when the Plague took the lives of my parents.

He studied my face and the seriousness in his expression stilled my racing thoughts. "I'd hoped to visit you earlier, and now I regret that we only have one month left until you turn eighteen."

"Have no regrets, your Grace."

The duke began to shake his head.

"It's all right," I assured him. "I've come to accept my parents' vow. And I've prepared myself for my future in the convent. I'll embrace the life set before me."

The duke's face tightened with an intensity that once again put me on edge. Something in his silver eyes told me that he was about to deliver life-altering news. The only trouble was, I didn't want to hear it if so. It had taken four years to adjust to the devastating revelation of my parents' vow. That recovery had been enough.

Should I send the duke away before he could say anything? I glanced to James, who peeked around the corner of the doorway before popping back inside. So much for having a club-wielding giant to protect me.

As if sensing my wariness, the duke reached for my hand to prevent me from leaving. "Please hear me out, dear one."

Maybe I needed to wait for the abbot to arrive so I would have someone to lean on. But as soon as the thought sifted through me, I pushed it aside. Hadn't I just lamented the fact that the abbot was still treating me like a child all too often? Maybe if I wanted him to respect me as an adult, I needed to act like one.

I straightened my spine and calmed the flutters inside. "Very well, your Grace. I'll listen. Please proceed."

The duke bowed slightly, and the seriousness in his expression did nothing to put me at ease. "After much investigating, my scribes have finally found an exception to your parents' vow."

Exception? To the vow? For a moment, I was speechless, unable to absorb his words. Was the duke jesting? If so, it was a heartless joke. "There's no exception. The Ancient Vow is one passed down from the time of Samuel the prophet, when his mother Hannah gave him to Eli the priest. It's unbreakable."

The duke's eyes were grave. "But, my dear, there is one exception, and only one."

At the seriousness of his tone, my knees began to tremble. I wanted to tell him not to say anything more, that I didn't need an exception, that I was prepared for the plans laid out for me from before my birth. But just as surely as I felt that, I realized a place deep inside needed to know of what he spoke.

I nodded at him to continue.

He reached for my hand. "If you find true love and are married before midnight on your eighteenth birthday, you will be released from the vow."

Chapter
3

"'Tis impossible." I paced in front of the spacious window seat where the Duke of Rivenshire sat watching me. He'd shed his armor, but he was still covered with the dust of travel. I knew I ought to allow the servants to escort him to the guest chambers and prepare him a bath, but he seemed as distraught as me and in no hurry to leave my company. At least we'd come inside the entryway, where we could have a modicum of privacy, although I was sure Trudy and James stood just inside the Great Hall listening to every word we spoke.

Outside the wide-open front doors, the men and servants who had accompanied the duke had begun the task of unloading their goods and caring for their beasts. They were surely hungry and tired and ready to relax. Especially as the scents of roasting geese, smoked hogs, and boiled mutton had drifted through the castle corridors all day. The Midsummer's Eve feast would soon be ready and my famished guests should be served without delay.

Even so, I couldn't turn my thoughts from the news the duke had delivered. I still couldn't believe him.

I stopped my pacing, knelt before the duke, and took his callused hands into mine. Even though my body was outwardly calm, my insides continued to resist, like a soldier defending a besieged wall. "Tell me all you know about my parents' vow, your Grace. I need to know everything." Of course the abbot had explained the vow to me after the death of my parents, after I'd discovered the scroll hidden in the secret chamber of my mother's chest. I'd realized then that my mother had tried to tell me about the vow from her deathbed, but hadn't been able to get the words out before she'd died. Over the ensuing years, I'd always wondered why my mother had waited until so late to finally try to tell me such important news. But I could only speculate that she hadn't brought it up because she'd wanted me to have as normal of a life as possible for as long as possible.

Even though I'd struggled through the questions and tried to make peace with them, there were still times that I wanted to discover more, to shed light on the truth.

Did the duke have more answers?

He smoothed his hands around one of mine and I settled back on my heels to listen to him. "Your parents were always very much in love with each other. And so it was easy during the first years of their marriage to ignore the fact that they weren't welcoming a new baby into their home. But as time passed, the emptiness of your mother's womb moved into their hearts."

His voice was soft, and his eyes had taken on a faraway look. "They wanted a child of their own very badly. And at last they became so desperate that they went to the convent and begged Abbot Francis Michael to pray for them ... and to give them a Tear of the Virgin Mary."

My pulse pattered with a strange rush that happened whenever I heard the story. The Tears of the Virgin Mary were very special. Whenever they were given for medicinal purposes, a miracle always seemed to happen. But they were also extremely rare and used only sparingly.

"As everyone knows, a Tear comes with a price," the duke

said. "And in the case of infertility, the price is always the Ancient Vow of Hannah, the consecration of the firstborn child to God for a life of service to him."

The duke's story was exactly the same as the one I'd heard four years earlier, yet I bowed my head and pressed a hand against my stomach in an attempt to calm the turmoil. Even though it had come as a shock and even though it had taken time, I'd finally accepted my destiny. I had no desire to question things now. "The Ancient Vow is unbreakable, unalterable. It must be fulfilled upon punishment of death. How can there be an exception?"

"After your parents died, I suspected that there was more to the Vow than they'd told any of us. I meant to investigate sooner, but the border wars kept me away longer than I'd anticipated." He reached into a pouch at his side and retrieved a rolled parchment. "Two months ago, I sent orders to my wisest scribes to have them search the ancient texts to discover if there were any exceptions to the Vow. Day and night, they did not stop reading until they finally located something."

Carefully, he unrolled the stiff, yellowed paper. "The one exception to the Ancient Vow is listed here." He pointed at a line of faded, handwritten text.

I read the words that were as exactly as he'd explained — that anyone bound by the Ancient Vow of Hannah could be freed from a life of celibacy and service to God if he or she found true love and entered the holy covenant of marriage by the age of eighteen. For long moments, I sat silently, trying to digest the facts. But it was all too much to try to grasp after resigning myself to a life of singleness. After Thomas left, I'd never again courted. I'd never mingled with men. I'd never even spoken to eligible young gentlemen. What would have been the purpose?

Now, with exactly one month until my eighteenth birthday,

what hope did I have of finding true love and getting married? It was a ludicrous notion. The only man I'd ever briefly cared about was already married. There were no other prospects.

"I cannot consider the exception," I finally said, lifting my face and speaking to the duke with all the earnestness I could muster. "I've already accepted that God wants me to go to the convent."

"I'm not convinced God wants you to lock yourself away and become a nun," the duke said slowly. "But at least we have a month left to determine his will in the matter."

"What difference will a month make, your Grace?" I rose, resignation coming easily to me.

"One month may not be long enough." The duke stood too. "But we shall pray that it's time enough to fall in love."

I gave a soft laugh. "Even if a month was sufficient time for falling in love—which it is not—I have no suitors. There haven't been any in years."

"'Tis no matter," he replied. "For I have brought you three of the finest knights in all the realm. They've proven themselves to be the strongest, bravest, most accomplished warriors."

Surprise and then embarrassment sifted through me. I couldn't keep from glancing outside to the knights now tending to their belongings. Even through their layers of armor, a certain nobility set them apart from the others. What would it be like to actually have a conversation with such a man and receive his romantic attentions?

Warmth curled through me. But I quickly shook my head. "Why would I have reason to break my heart or that of another if I'm destined to become a nun?"

"You aren't destined."

"Then why didn't the abbot tell me of this exception?"

"It's likely he didn't know."

At the mention of the abbot, my wise counselor burst

through the open front doors at a run, his plain habit flapping behind him like wings. He was breathing hard, and his bald spot glistened with sweat. The narrow line of gray hair that ringed his head was damp.

For a moment, I could only blink in surprise. I couldn't remember a time when I'd ever seen the abbot run. He always moved at the slowest, most devote speed—a pace he required of all his monks, a pace he claimed facilitated prayer and reflection on God. Whatever had happened to cause such uncharacteristic haste? Had he run all the way from the walled convent that sat on a hilltop a short distance from the town?

At the sight of the duke, the abbot came to an abrupt halt. He grasped his side and sucked in a deep breath. James walked out of the Great Hall and bowed to him, almost as if he'd been awaiting the abbot's arrival.

"James," the abbot quietly rebuked, "you should have called me sooner."

James kept his bald head bent. "I sent a messenger as soon as I could."

I stepped forward, acutely aware of the great breach in etiquette the abbot was making with the duke. "Father Abbot," I said, waving my hand toward our esteemed guest, "surely you remember the Noblest Knight? The Duke of Rivenshire?"

At my words, the abbot's face transformed into the calm, peaceful expression to which I was accustomed. He nodded at the duke. "Your Grace, how good of you to delight us with your presence after so long an absence."

"Happy Midsummer's Eve to you, Abbot Francis Michael." The duke bowed in respect to the man of God. "We were just speaking of you."

"Oh?" the abbot said, working to control his heavy breathing. Standing next to the muscular and bronzed knight, he looked like a tall, pale sapling that would snap with the slightest breeze. "I'm only sorry I wasn't here to greet you properly when you arrived."

"Lady Rosemarie's sweet greeting is all I needed," the duke replied.

The abbot tucked his hands under his long, flowing sleeves and met the knight's probing gaze. Something seemed to pass between them that I didn't understand.

"We were just discussing her parents' vow," the duke continued. "And I was telling Rosemarie about an exception to the Ancient Vow."

"There is no exception," the abbot said matter-of-factly without looking away from the knight. "The Ancient Vow of Hannah stipulates that Lady Rosemarie is to enter the convent on her eighteenth birthday and live her life in service to God."

"Unless she finds true love and gets married first."

"Nonsense," the abbot said. "How dare you come here and fill Lady Rosemarie's head with such false and dangerous notions—"

"His scribes have found the text that makes such a claim," I interrupted.

The duke held out the parchment to the abbot.

The abbot read the sheet quickly and then handed it back to the duke. His face was devoid of emotion. If the vow surprised him, he didn't show it. "You know as well as I do that if she breaks the vow, she'll die."

"Not if she finds true love first." The duke crossed his arms over his broad chest.

The abbot paused for a long moment. From the direction of the kitchen off the Great Hall came the clatter of lids and the shout of my cook, likely yelling at one of the scullion boys.

When the abbot finally spoke again, his tone was calm. "What could be more worthy than Lady Rosemarie honoring the Ancient Vow? Surely you don't think earthly married life is more desirable than a life set apart in union and service to God himself?"

"Haven't you puzzled, as I have, why the earl and countess never told Lady Rosemarie about the vow?" the duke asked.

"They would have eventually."

"Perhaps. But what if they knew about the exception? What if they fully expected Rosemarie to fall in love and get married before her eighteenth year? Did you ever consider that possibility?"

I started at the duke's explanation. Was that why my parents had been so encouraging when I'd been attracted to Lord Caldwell? Although I'd tried to bury the memories, I could still clearly picture the last hunting party, where Thomas had helped me from my horse and had lingered close to me. At the time my parents had both looked on with encouragement and not with the rebuke I'd anticipated.

Had they been hoping I'd fall in love with Thomas and marry him?

Outside, the sun had disappeared behind a cloud and the clatter in the courtyard had faded. The other knights, squires, and servants had moved to the stables. The eerie stillness reflected an unsettled silence in my soul. Only hours ago, the course of my life had been so certain and safe. But now, with the appearance of my erstwhile friend, my life had been turned upside-down. And I didn't like it in the least.

As if sensing my inner turmoil, the duke crossed to me and tucked a finger under my chin. He lifted my face so that I was again looking into his kind eyes. "I believe if your parents had known about the exception, they would have wanted you to have the chance to find a love like theirs."

"You could be right, your Grace," the abbot said. "But I also know that the earl and countess took the Ancient Vow very seriously. They assured me they would love and enjoy their daughter as long as they could have her, but they ultimately knew she belonged to God."

That indeed sounded like something my parents would have said. Perhaps they had waited to tell me about the Vow, hoping to shield me from my future a little while longer.

The duke squeezed my shoulder before taking a step back as though letting me know he understood my confusion. "I propose we give Lady Rosemarie the next month to test for herself the right course for her life."

"Test how?" I asked.

"You'll allow my three noble knights to court you and attempt to win your hand. And if you don't fall in love with one of them by your eighteenth birthday, then we shall take that as a sign from God that you're destined for the convent."

The abbot was silent but regarded me with concern. He'd witnessed my despondency in the days following the revelation of the Vow. He'd known how difficult it had been for me to truly accept the new course of my life. The compassion creasing his features told me that he didn't want me to get my hopes up only to have them dashed again.

"How can she make the decision to enter cloistered life if she has not yet discovered if she is more suited for married life?" The duke's eyes beseeched me to consider his request. "If she enters the convent, she shouldn't do so by default. Rather she should do so out of a knowledgeable decision made after testing earthly love and finding it wanting compared to her desire for union with God."

I nodded at the duke. "You're wise, your Grace."

"On the other hand, my child," the abbot said gently, "do you really want to put yourself through such a challenge? After you've already prepared your heart and mind for the convent? Think about the possible heartache."

What was I to do?

"Trust me, Lady Rosemarie," came the soft whisper of the duke. "I have nothing to gain from offering you this month of courtship with my men, except your happiness."

The abbot shook his head and began to speak, but I raised my hand to silence him. I couldn't make a decision at that moment, not with so many considerations. I needed more time to sort through all the information and the confusion swirling through my soul.

"Please, Father Abbot. I have great respect for both you and my dear friend the duke. I know you both have my best interests at heart. And I thank you for it. But now ... I must have some time to think about this important decision."

"For the love of the sun, moon, and stars," came the welcome voice of Trudy from the doorway of the Great Hall. Her cheeks were red, and a barely visible stain crept up her neck beneath her gorget—the wide bands of linen she wore around her neck and draped on her shoulders. I had no doubt my nursemaid had heard every word of our conversation. And now the dear servant waddled toward me on her short legs. "It's past time to get Lady Rosemarie ready for the feast."

All I wanted to do was race to my chambers, close the door, and block out all the confusion. But I managed a curtsey and smile, hoping to allay some of the tension radiating from their faces. "I shall think over the matter and deliver my decision at the banquet tonight."

But as I allowed Trudy to lead me away, I didn't know how I'd ever decide in such a short time. Not when my whole destiny, my very life, was the price I'd have to pay if I made the wrong choice.

Chapter
4

I knelt before the altar. The coldness of the chapel's stone floor had penetrated the prayer cushion as if to say I'd prayed long enough for one evening. And yet I couldn't make myself leave. Not even knowing that my guests were feasting without me on Midsummer's Eve.

There was something in my heart that demanded I seek God's guidance—even though I'd already made my resolution while Trudy dressed me.

In my chamber, with my nursemaid's advice echoing the abbot's, I'd decided to continue the course that had been set out for me these past four years. Why change things now? Not after I'd already planned and prepared for a life in the convent. Not after my soul was at peace with the decision. Not after I was so close to the time when I must go.

What did true love matter anyway? Hadn't I gotten along just fine without it? And besides, I was looking forward to my life of devotion to God in the convent, wasn't I? The abbot had already hired laborers to begin clearing land near the monastery to build an abbey. It would become a safe haven for un- wanted women, a place I could oversee. It would be an exciting new part of my life.

Certainly, I'd have to move out of the castle. And I wouldn't be able to take my wardrobe or many of my belongings, except for some of my personal items. But I'd decided that I would use the opportunity to sell many of my possessions so I could give more money to the poor. After all, everything would still be mine. I could do with my things as I pleased, especially when I turned eighteen and could make all the decisions on my own.

And yet . . .

I fingered my long strand of prayer beads and bowed my head lower. No matter my rationalizing, doubts lingered.

In the quietness of the chapel, without Abbot Francis Michael or Trudy or the duke advising me, I could finally hear the whispers within, the still, small voice of God that came when I blocked out everything else and listened for it.

What was he saying?

I couldn't deny that I'd been interested in the knights who had ridden along with the duke. Or that I was curious about what it might be like to speak with the men and get to know them. And in a deep place, I had to admit I felt longings from time to time to have a family again, to have a husband and children of my own. I'd simply never allowed myself to dwell on such longings. I'd known that to do so would only stir up dissatisfaction with the course set before me. Why think on what I couldn't change?

But the truth was that I suddenly had the power to change the Vow. At least that's what the duke claimed. What reason did I have to disregard his words? I trusted him like I would my father. He had no motivation for harming me.

Did I owe it to myself and my parents to participate in the duke's test before making an irrevocable choice? After all, I wouldn't want to live the rest of my days in the convent always wondering if I'd made the right decision. If, after the coming month, I failed the test, then I could begin my time as a nun without any doubts. I could embrace my future with a completely devoted heart.

At the clank of metal behind me, I raised my head and peered over my shoulder to the open door of the chapel. There stood the duke in his surcoat, and next to him, covered from head to toe in his plate armor, was one of his three knights.

With a nod at the knight, the duke stepped just outside the doorway so that in the darkness of the hallway his outline showed him standing guard.

After a moment's hesitation, the young knight started toward the altar, toward me, the steel plates of his armor jangling with each step.

I rose and brushed down my gown, my heart tapping a strange rhythm in anticipation of having a conversation with a man who wasn't one of my servants or the abbot.

"My lady," came the whisper of the knight from behind his helmet. "Please forgive me for disturbing your prayers."

"There's naught to forgive. I was almost done."

He stopped several feet away. Though his helmet was raised, in the dim light coming from the candle on the altar, I couldn't see past the shadows to glimpse his eyes.

"You're not at the feast along with the others?" I asked, trying to untie my tongue.

"No, my lady. I've just returned from visiting the bailiff as well as the sheriff." He spoke so softly that I had to quiet my thudding heart to hear him. "And I've discovered more information about this morning's torture."

At his news, my self-consciousness fell away. "You've visited my bailiff and sheriff?"

He nodded, his armor clinking again. "It was obvious that you hadn't ordered the boiling or the stretching upon the rack. That you, in fact, were opposed to torture. And after gaining the duke's permission, I took the liberty to investigate the matter further."

Was he the knight who had rescued the criminals earlier in the day? I wanted to command him to come closer, to reveal his face, to let me gaze on him. But he was keeping a respectable distance, and ordering him closer would surely be too brazen.

"Go on, sir," I whispered. "Please share anything you've learned."

He nodded and continued in a low voice. "I rode to the sheriff's estate and ... let myself in."

I held back a smile at the knight's chosen words. It was well known in my land that the sheriff kept a tight watch over his estate, the grand home my father had awarded him after he'd saved my life from the peasant with the Plague. With a heavy guard and vicious dogs, letting oneself in to the sheriff's manor was tantamount to breaching the walls of a well-fortified castle.

"I'm surprised you weren't torn to pieces in spite of your armor," I whispered, eyeing him for any signs of distress.

"I have a special way with dogs, my lady." His voice hinted at humor.

"You must."

"And I also have a special way of extracting information from sheriffs who decide to play mute." Again the humor in his tone belied the danger of the situation. I had no doubt he'd put his own life in peril to retrieve information about the sheriff's use of torture.

"You're a brave knight."

"Apparently, news of my expertise with various weapons had reached him ahead of me, so 'twas not difficult to gain his cooperation when he saw my fingers upon my dagger."

Not difficult? I studied him again through the dim lighting, wishing I could see him clearly. But in his armor, I could no more see him now than I could the knight earlier in the day. "And what did my sheriff reveal, sir?"

The knight held himself stiffly. "He said that once you're in the convent, he'll finally be able to do his job the way it's meant to be done, that he'll be able to handle criminals any way he wants without a girl telling him what to do."

At the bitter bite of the words, I sucked in a sharp breath. "And you agree with him?"

"Not in the least," the knight protested harshly. "Man or woman, you're his ruler and he ought to obey your orders whether he agrees or not."

I should have punished the sheriff earlier for his insolence. By showing him compassion, I'd apparently proven myself weak. "Once I'm of age, he'll learn soon enough that I'll rule as strongly and rightly as my father before me."

The young knight bowed. "I'm sorry that I had to bring you such news, my lady. I regret that I had to cause you even the slightest distress."

"You were noble to investigate the matter further, and I thank you."

I would need to speak with my sheriff again, although the idea of another confrontation filled me with dread. What would truly happen once I turned eighteen? I'd always thought I'd be able to rule just as my father had, even if it was from afar. But what if the sheriff did indeed have different plans? How would I be able to stop him if I was confined to the abbey?

If the sheriff felt that my power would decrease even though I'd come of age, how many more of my people felt the same way?

The duke had moved back into the chapel. He cocked his head at the door, signaling his young knight. The man bowed toward me and began to withdraw.

As he strode across the chapel, I called after him. "Wait." He stopped and turned.

"Thank you," I said. "You've done a hard thing in uncovering and bearing this news. And I admire you for your courage."

He gave a slight bow and continued toward the chapel exit. I could only stare after him, my heart thumping a strange rhythm at the realization that this was one of the potential suitors the duke had picked to woo me. If all of them were like this man, then the month would certainly not be dull.

"I'm sorry, Rosemarie." The duke crossed to me. "He didn't want to speak with you, since the sheriff's confession was insulting. But I encouraged him to see the task through to completion. For it is often the hardest tasks that build the most character."

I sighed. "Perhaps I've harbored false hope for what my rule will be like once I've entered the convent."

"You've been a compassionate ruler," the duke offered. "Your father and mother would have been proud of the way you've ruled this land, just as I am. No one could have done better."

The duke's praise was like a crown set upon my head. Whether he'd known it or not, he'd given me the highest compliment. "I'll rule my people justly, even from a distance," I said. "Once I have the power to make all the decisions, I'll do even more for my subjects."

He shook his head. "Although legally the power will be yours, I want you to think about how you'll know what your people need if you're closeted away from the world. Will you truly be able to govern justly?"

His words gave me pause and filled me with unease I wished I could ignore.

"I don't wish to sway your decision more than I already have," the duke said gently. "So I'll leave you to your prayers and trust that God will guide your heart and give you the best counsel."

"Then will you give me one more night to think and pray about the decision?" I asked.

He bowed his head in deference, causing the candlelight to reflect on the silver in his hair. "I shall tell my men not to expect you at the feast tonight and that you'll let us know of your decision on the morrow."

I appreciated that he wasn't pushing me to accept his test. But as he exited the chapel, I wanted to call after him to walk me to the feast. It had been so long since I'd joined in any festivities. And a small part of me wished to see the three men he'd picked to vie for my heart. Instead I resumed my spot on my prayer cushion and bent my head, as I knew I must. The decision was too important to make lightly without more prayer.

Even so, I couldn't keep from thinking about how the weight of my isolation had been growing heavy of late, of how much heavier it would grow once I committed myself to a place where silence was the rule and companionship was regulated. How could I bear the burden of seclusion for the rest of my life?

I hadn't wanted to raise the question before tonight for fear of stirring discontentment due to what I'd believed I couldn't change. But what if I could change it? What if my life didn't have to be so silent and secluded after all?

Chapter
5

I hesitated at the double doors that led to the Great
Hall and dug my fingers into the thick fur of my dog. My snowy
white companion was no longer a puppy and hadn't been in a
long time — ten years had passed since the day my parents gave
him to me for my birthday. Nevertheless, I'd always called him
Pup. It was the name that stuck when none else had.

I scratched his head and earned a lick upon my fingers.

"You're a good boy," I said, staring again at the closed doors
and trying to decide if I wanted to go in or escape back to my
chambers.

I'd been late in arriving for the morning repast. I wanted to
blame my tardiness on my slowness in dressing and in Trudy's
extra care in plaiting my hair and arranging it in a fashionable
twist. But the truth was that sleep had not come easily the
night before. Even when it finally arrived, it had been filled
first with blistered and boiled skin and then with visions of rav-
enous rats with sharp claws digging through human flesh. I'd
cried out in the night, and it was only after Trudy had allowed
Pup to climb into bed with me that I'd finally fallen into a fitful
sleep, this time seeing the four plain walls of a convent cell. The
utter aloneness of the tiny room had swallowed me.

Of course, I'd overslept and now had dark circles under

my eyes. And I was late in making my appearance in the Great Hall.

What must my guests think of me?

I touched the handle of the door and then stopped, startled to realize I did care what they thought. In fact, I cared very much.

Last night I'd finally understood I must give the duke's test for true love a chance. If not for myself, then at least for my people. They truly would benefit most if I remained available and continued to mingle among them instead of hiding away in a convent.

However, if I failed the test, I now realized that I'd have to find ways to be involved in their lives and understand their troubles in some other way. I'd also need to stay informed so that the sheriff and those like him couldn't ignore my authority. Surely I'd figure out some way to make it work. At least that's what I'd been telling myself.

In the meantime, I had to formally accept the duke's proposition. My nerves were jumping like grasshoppers at the thought of telling the duke and facing his knights.

Pup nudged my hands and peered up at me with his adoring eyes. His half-open panting mouth smiled and told me he would be there for me no matter what.

"Oh, Pup." I bent over and wrapped my arms around his neck, burying my face in his luxurious fur.

At that moment, the outer doors of the castle opened wide. The morning sunshine poured in, bathing the spacious hallway with glorious light. I quickly dislodged myself from Pup and straightened, but not before the visitor caught sight of my affection toward the dog.

"Good morning, my lady," came a strong, clear voice. I didn't have to look closely to guess it was one of the three knights who had come with the duke. Even without the armor from yesterday, there was no disguising the noble stature and bearing that set him apart as a knight.

As the knight glanced at Pup and then back to me, I blinked against the sunlight and fought off a wave of embarrassment at my most unladylike display with my dog. I braced myself for his censure, for everyone knew that good hunting dogs were not to be coddled. But instead of a frown, his lips twitched with a smile. He surprised me even more when he knelt, held out a hand, and gave a low whistle.

Pup wagged his tail and trotted across the hallway, lowering himself and lying before the knight in complete submission. The knight rubbed a gloved hand across the dog's back before scratching his neck. I gaped in wonder and then turned to study more closely the man who could so easily win the affection of my dog.

At the sight of his manly frame, his lean but muscular body, his strong shoulders, and the proud lift of his head, I drew in a shaky breath of nervousness. How did a young woman speak with a suitor? It had been years since I'd interacted with Thomas, and then I'd been only a girl. But now that I'd resolved to give the duke's test a good effort, I knew I must endeavor to know the three men who'd come to court me.

"Pup likes you." I spoke past the shyness that threatened to send me scampering back up the winding staircase.

The knight's eyes were the gray color of burnished steel. His hair was a hazy blond, not at all like my pure golden strands, but tested, tried, and weathered by battles and elements from which I'd always been sheltered. The muscles in his face were as taut and well defined as the rest of his body. The only imperfection on his face was a scar alongside one of his eyes — eyes that even now seemed to see past the walls that surrounded me and to the vulnerable young woman I really was.

I shifted my attention to the open doorway. Outside in the

fading coolness of the morning, the duke and his retinue were saddling their horses.

"You can't be leaving so soon." I started forward, my pulse lurching. I must stop them and inform the duke of my decision. Surely it wasn't too late.

The young knight released Pup with a pat to the dog's hindquarters and then stood. "No, my lady." He stepped aside to let me pass. "We're only making preparations for a hunting foray."

It was then I noticed his attire—his plain tunic and the leather belt at his waist containing his quiver of arrows, along with a long bow draped over his shoulder.

Even with the knowledge of the excursion, the urgent thudding in my heart didn't lessen. I hastened outside onto the upper landing. The inner bailey spread out before me a confusion of horses, hunting dogs, and men. "Your Grace," I called to the duke, who stood with his other knights conversing and laughing.

But my voice went unheard above the din of the barking dogs.

"Your Grace," I called again.

A long, shrill whistle sounded behind me. I turned to find that the young knight had followed me outside. With a curl of his tongue, he whistled again, the piercing sound penetrating the melee below us and bringing the men to the silence I desired.

For a long moment, I could only stare at the knight, at the confidence in his gray eyes, at the boldness of his manner. Was he the one who had so daringly rescued the criminals yesterday in the marketplace? And was he the one who had so bravely entered the sheriff's well-guarded estate and brought me information in the chapel?

His gaze was unswerving. And I could see that there was no pretense in him. He wasn't putting on airs or trying to be anybody other than who he was. Yet neither was he divulging whether he'd come to my aid before.

"Lady Rosemarie," the duke said, hastening to stand at the base of the steps and smile up at me. "You look lovely this morning. I trust all is well."

"Yes, your Grace," I answered, tearing my attention from the young knight. "I'm sorry to disturb your hunting preparations. But I would like to make an announcement."

"Anything for you, Lady Rosemarie," he replied with a bow.

"After much prayer and consideration ..."

The duke's eyes were warm and happy, as if he already guessed my next words. And suddenly I knew that no matter the outcome, my dear friend had been wise to present this option to me, even if the idea of courting three different men made me uncomfortable. Even if in the end I entered cloistered life anyway. At least I would be a stronger and better woman for taking this risk.

"I have decided to accept your challenge."

At my words, the two knights below stepped forward, surprise and delight registering upon their countenances. I could feel the other young knight behind me stiffen. I glanced at him again, hoping to see the same eagerness that the other two showed. I was unprepared for the glimmer of frustration I saw in his eyes before he shifted his focus to a nearby servant drawing water from the well.

"This is good news indeed," the duke said, drawing my attention. "I'm glad you're considering it. I'll make all the arrangements for the courtship and festivities. In fact, we shall begin the month with a dance."

"And I hope with proper introductions, your Grace," said one of the knights with a crooked but endearing grin.

"Ah, yes." The duke returned the grin. "Lady Rosemarie, let me introduce my three most loyal men." He waved his hand at the fair-haired man who had made the comment. The knight's skin was tan, his eyes an alluring green, and his face animated with a lightheartedness that made him appealing.

"Lady Rosemarie, may I introduce Sir Collin Goodrich."

With a gallant flourish of his arm, the young man gave a bow. Then he sprang up the steps, knelt before me, and reached for my hand. A sparkle in his eyes danced like leaves in the summer sun. "My lady, I look forward to winning your heart." And with that, he placed the gentlest kiss upon the tips of my fingers.

The sweet warmth of his words and kiss was unlike anything I'd ever known, and it seared a trail up to my cheeks.

"You may not monopolize her attention, Collin," said the other knight standing at the base of the steps.

"And this is Sir Bennet Windsor," the duke said, nodding at the one who had just spoken. He was slightly taller than the others, with wavy raven-black hair and features of chiseled perfection. The overall effect was as if a master artist had crafted him after an ancient Greek god. Even though his midnight eyes twinkled, there was a determination on his face that made me blush again.

How strange it was to be desired by these men and to entertain their attention and flattery. After the past years of solitude, it was disconcerting, but not unwelcome.

"I look forward to getting to know you, my lady," Sir Bennet said, his eyes speaking the truth of his words.

Sir Collin shot his friend a grin. "First, you'll have to fight me away from Lady Rosemarie."

"Oh, I doubt I'll have to fight you away," Sir Bennet jested with a smooth smile of his own. "Especially when she realizes just how dull you are."

"And how unsophisticated you are," Sir Collin countered, bumping his friend good-naturedly.

"I'll look forward to seeing a little competition between you men." The duke chuckled. "But rest assured, I'll give you each fair time to win Lady Rosemarie's hand."

A prick of doubt assailed me. "I wouldn't want to be the cause of discord between good friends."

"This competition will serve to strengthen their character," the duke replied. "And while I hope they'll fight hard to win your hand, I know they'll do so with the utmost integrity, honor, and kindness toward one another."

The knight behind me on the upper landing hadn't spoken or moved since his whistle. I glanced at him again, suddenly conscious of his presence nearby and the fact I still didn't know his name.

"Sir Derrick Harding, my lady," the duke said, as if reading my mind.

"Sir Derrick." I curtsied. His gray eyes clashed with mine again as they had inside, and they probed deeply. The frustration from a moment ago was gone, making me wonder if I'd only imagined it.

"My lady." He bowed.

I waited for him to say something witty or flattering, as the other two had done. But he only straightened and reached out to stroke Pup, who'd taken a seat at his side.

At the sight of Sir Derrick with the dog, the duke raised his brow. Sir Derrick shrugged his shoulders. "He likes me. At least that's what I've been told."

I smiled at the picture he made standing against the massive stone keep with the dog by his side, almost as if he were already master over the dog and the castle.

"At least the dog likes you," Sir Collin called. "Be happy with that, because that's about all the affection you'll have the chance to win."

"I'll have something to speak about, even if it is a mutt."

Sir Derrick's response was quick. "Which is more than you'll be able to say for yourself."

Sir Collin laughed, clearly appreciating the witty exchange. I could only watch, feeling suddenly breathless and completely out of sorts. I wasn't skilled in speaking with men or flirting or carrying on intelligent conversations. I had absolutely no idea how to relate to them.

How would I ever be able to participate in this contest for true love? Especially without making a bumbling fool of myself in the process?

When the men made ready to depart on their hunting foray, I went directly to my garden, to the beds upon beds of flowers I'd cultivated over the years. I buried myself in their sweet fragrances and gentle colors, all the while thinking about the men and wondering what it would be like to spend time with them.

"Here you are," came the voice of a man behind me. From where I knelt among the hedgerow roses, I peeked over my shoulder. The tall, dark-haired knight stood several feet away, freshly groomed in finely tailored breeches and matching shirt of a royal blue that only served to highlight his features. The waves of his hair had been brushed into submission, and he looked like he was about to venture into the king's court rather than depart on a hunting excursion.

I wiped the dirt from my fingers, suddenly conscious of how grimy I was compared to him. "Oh, you're not hunting, Sir . . ."

"Bennet. Sir Bennet," he supplied. "We've already returned, my lady. Sir Collin shot a stag with his longbow within the first five minutes of the hunt, and we decided we were done."

I stood and shook the weeds from my gown. "I didn't expect you to return so quickly."

"We were a little too distracted to hunt today." He smiled meaningfully.

I stared at my dirt-encrusted fingernails, embarrassed once again. I didn't know how I would ever become comfortable with the attention and kind words of the men. Even when I'd met Thomas, I'd not had much practice before he'd gone away.

"Besides, the duke is anxious to start planning a month full of activities and events to delight you." He stepped closer, bridging the distance between us.

"And you? How do you feel about staying for a month?" I forced myself to make conversation even though my insides were squirming like a puppy. "Are you not ready to return to your own home and land after so many years away?"

"I've been gone from my home longer than I ever lived there, my lady," he said wistfully. "Like most nobility, my parents sent me away when I was but a young lad to prepare me to be a knight. Fortunately, I had the privilege of living with the Noblest Knight first as a page then later a squire."

"'Twould indeed be a privilege to live with him. I'm sure he was a good master."

"He has become like a father to me—to all of us. He's taught us not only how to wield our weapons, but more importantly how to use our minds."

I wasn't surprised that the duke had invested in educating his pages, although there were some noblemen who thought it a waste of time. "There's no one better in the land. If you become half the man he is, you'll indeed do well."

"I agree." Sir Bennet was only a hand's span away. His gaze traveled languidly around my face, feasting on my features. When he reached my nose, he paused, lifted his fingers, and brushed at my skin.

Even though his touch was light and innocent, it made my stomach tremble.

"The rumors didn't lie to us," he spoke softly. "You're the fairest in the land, my lady. Even with a smudge of dirt on your nose." His smile—revealing even, white teeth—made his noble face devastatingly handsome and lit up his eyes.

There was a hint of magnetism about his natural dark looks that would turn the head of any young lady. While he certainly had distracted me now, would he continue to hold my attention over time? Or would it take more than outward appearances to draw me to a man?

I searched his face. Was he the one who had rescued the criminals and come to me in the chapel last night?

The question rested at the tip of my tongue, but when he thrust out his hand from behind his back and held out a bouquet of wildflowers of the most stunning display of colors, the question fled.

"I found them during our hunt," he said. "And their beauty reminded me of yours."

I took them and breathed in their fragrance, letting the array tickle my lips. "Thank you, Sir Bennet. They're lovely."

"As you gaze on them today, I hope they'll remind you of me."

I fingered one of the silky petals. "I'll think on you, sir," I said somewhat breathlessly.

And as he bowed and left me with another one of his heart-stopping smiles, I realized I would indeed have no trouble keeping my promise to him.

Chapter
6

I slipped through the gardens toward the back of the keep, hoping to enter the castle undetected. I would need a bath to wash away the dirt and grime of my gardening before I was presentable to the knights. As I walked, I pressed the bouquet from Sir Bennet to my nose and breathed in deep. Delight rippled through me—whether from the flowers or from my encounter with the handsome knight, I knew naught.

All I knew was that my interactions with the men were affecting me more than I'd anticipated.

"Lady Rosemarie, wait," came a voice from near the well. I turned to find Sir Collin striding across the edge of the courtyard toward me by way of the stables. He wove through squires and servants busy at work and dodged hens and geese that flapped about the inner bailey. His hair gleamed in the summer sun, turning it the pale gold of ripened wheat. He was not quite as striking as Sir Bennet, but his face was just as pleasant to look on.

The duke's claim yesterday had been no exaggeration. He had brought three very fine suitors. He was determined to give me the chance to fall in love, as he believed my parents had wanted.

"Oh, fairest one," Sir Collin said, falling to one knee before me and bowing his head.

I couldn't keep from smiling at his theatrics.

"I have been searching for you high and low, through city and state, even to the sun and back." He peered up at me with his dancing green eyes.

"Have you now? Then 'twould seem you have neglected to look for me in one of my favorite spots in all the world." I was surprised at how easily I bantered with him.

"What a fool am I," he said, taking in my bouquet and playing along with me. "How could I have neglected the gardens in my search for the Rose among roses?"

Should I hide the bouquet behind my back? Surely Sir Collin would know one of his friends had bestowed it upon me.

But seemingly indifferent to the flowers, he held out his hand. "For you, my lady."

I opened my palm and he laid an exquisite diamond pin there—a pin in the shape of a spiraling rose. "A small token of my affection," he said more seriously, his eyes turning a darker forest green.

Small token? I stared at the glittering jewels, the intricate and gilded pattern of silverwork. Perhaps it was small in size, but it was in no way a small token. It was beautiful and extravagant. "Sir, I cannot take this—"

"Consider it my bouquet to you." He folded my fingers around the pin. "Perhaps it's not as colorful as what you've already been given, but a flower nonetheless."

He stood and only then did I notice the fine linen of his apparel, the wide gold belt at his waist, and the jewel-encrusted mantel across his shoulders. Everything about his clothing spoke of riches. Although I'd inherited a great deal of land and wealth from my parents, he apparently had much more to his title, enough to give away diamond pins as one would flowers.

"Whether or not you choose me as your true love, I want

you to have the pin always. At the very least, it will help you remember this month and the great fun we are about to have."

I hesitated.

"You'll have to get used to lavish praise and lavish gifts, my lady." He gave me a smile of encouragement. "What is chivalry and romance without it?"

"I'm finding it a bit difficult to adjust to," I admitted, fingering the diamonds. After having two meetings with my suitors in short succession, I hoped I was reacting appropriately.

"Then I shall make it my goal to help you adjust." He winked. "Perhaps I shall resort to giving you a new jewel every day until you're accustomed to the lavishness?"

"'Tis often the rarity that makes something so precious, wouldn't you say? If I were to have such extravagance daily, then I might begin to think the jewels and the praise are ordinary rather than treasure them as I do."

"You are wise, my lady." Admiration shone in his eyes.

Was he the one who had stopped the public torture yesterday? I tilted my head and studied him. He was certainly carefree enough to attempt the deed.

"I guess I'll have to restrain myself around you," he said in a low voice. "I wouldn't want you to think me or my gifts ordinary."

A call from the stables demanded his attention, and with another grin, he bounded away. Lost in a dizzying cloud of emotions, I wandered toward the back of the keep admiring both the flowers and the diamond pin. I had to admit that my anticipation of the next month was growing.

When I reached the far side of the keep and the entryway that led down into the kitchen, I stopped short. There by the door stood a ragged group of beggar children waiting patiently while Sir Derrick handed out slices of bread and Cook ladled soup into their tin cups. At the sight of me, the children gasped and elbowed one another, until finally one of the youth remembered to kneel, as was the custom. Once the older children began to pay their respect to me, the littlest ones followed suit.

"Children." I smiled and started toward them, recognizing many of their faces. They were from among the poorest of the poor in my land, many having parents who had died or fallen prey to the Plague. Some of the children supported younger siblings. Others were homeless.

I mingled among them, touching a cheek here or patting a head there, bestowing a smile upon each one. As I did, my back warmed under Sir Derrick's watchful eyes as he followed my every move.

When I finally turned from the children to face Cook, my gaze collided with Sir Derrick's. Although he didn't offer a smile, there was something in his expression that said he was pleased with my kindness to the little ones.

I didn't say anything to him, but I hoped he could read my approval for his own kindness. Rather I spoke to Cook. "I thought they would be given extra this morning out of the plenty from the Midsummer's Eve feast."

"'Twere all given away last eve, my lady," Cook replied. "Every last crumb from every last plate."

"I thought you would save some for the children. You have in the past." I didn't mean to rebuke my faithful cook, who always went above and beyond to oblige my grand plans for feeding the masses, but I couldn't keep the disappointment from my tone.

Cook glanced sideways at Sir Derrick and then lowered his voice. "We didn't have as much left as we usually do, my lady." He turned to check on a great kettle of soup.

"I see." I certainly couldn't begrudge my honored guests and their servants the feasting they deserved. But I could only imagine how disappointed the children were this noon to come for their usual bread and soup, expecting to also receive out of the bounty of the leftovers from last evening's feast only to be sent away without any extra.

Sir Derrick gave a thick slice of bread to an urchin with a bare head and feet, whose face was thin and dirty. Then he paused in his work. "My lady, let the children have the food that was intended for my noon meal."

The wafting scent of onion and garlic rose from the steaming pot as Cook stirred the floating chunks of carrots and turnips and bits of wild goose. My stomach growled in response. After a morning working in the castle gardens, my appetite was hearty. But I was sure it couldn't compare to the appetite Sir Derrick had gained on his hunting expedition earlier.

"I wouldn't think of asking you to go without a meal," I started.

"You're not asking, my lady," Sir Derrick interrupted as he placed bread into the hands of the next child. "I'm offering. After last night's overindulgence, the sacrifice won't hurt my body in the least. And if it would help these children and make them happy …"

For a moment I was at a loss for words.

"I have no doubt the duke and my two companions will willingly sacrifice their portions as well, in order to fill the bellies of these children to overflowing." His gray eyes held the intensity I was coming to expect from him.

"You're very kind, and I would indeed be grateful for your sacrifice."

"Although I would do anything for you, my lady," he replied softly, "I'm doing this for the children's sake, not yours."

I didn't quite know how to respond. My vanity suggested I should take offense, but the deeper part of me was relieved — relieved that he was noble enough to want to make such a sacrifice from his heart rather than from his desire to impress me.

In the end, I said nothing at all. For some time, I worked with Cook and Sir Derrick to distribute the loaves, pastries, cheese, and cuts of meat Cook had prepared for the noon meal. When the last of the children had skipped away with an extra bundle, I leaned against the cool stone wall near the kitchen door and wiped the perspiration from my forehead.

Sir Derrick had disappeared into the kitchen and now stepped out of the dark interior with a mug in hand. "For you, my lady." He held it out to me. "A cool drink of ale."

"Thank you." I offered him a smile and then took a sip of the spicy drink, letting the coolness of it soothe my parched throat.

He glanced to the high noon sun and then rested his back against the stone wall as well. He soon began watching a few remaining children nearby petting Pup.

In the shade, I took another sip, and peeked at Sir Derrick sideways. In his sun-bronzed face, the scar near his eye stood out starkly white and lent him a ruggedness that his companions lacked. Strands of his hair stuck to his forehead. And he wore his hunting clothes from earlier. But even without clean and fancy apparel, he was still as fine-looking as the other two knights.

I waited for him to start a conversation like his companions had. But he only crossed his arms over his chest. The movement pulled his tunic tight against his muscular arms. From the rippling set of his jaw, I had the feeling he wasn't planning to be the first to speak.

Very well. Perhaps he wasn't as outgoing as his friends. "You must be glad to be free of your hot armor and ready to have a break from the fighting."

The muscles in his jaw flexed before he cast me a sideways glance. "I'm a warrior, my lady. It's what I've been trained to do."

"Why, sir," I said with a half laugh, unable to keep from

baiting him. "Surely you enjoy other things too?" I waited for his declaration that he was looking forward to spending time with me. But it never came. Instead he pushed away from the wall as if to leave. I held the mug out to him. "You must be thirsty. Would you like a drink?" I wasn't sure why, but I didn't want to part ways yet.

He hesitated but then reached for the mug, careful not to brush his fingers against mine. He took a long drink and over the rim of the mug, his gaze captured mine.

What should I do? Pretend I didn't notice him staring? Or stare right back? My heart fluttered, and I peered at the bouquet I'd discarded on the wooden serving table. The flowers were long-past wilted.

He wiped his mouth on his sleeve. "I see my friends have already been hard at work wooing you."

I wanted to deny it, but the pin burned in the pocket underneath the layers of my gown. "Yes, they've both sought me out."

"And given gifts?"

I nodded.

"Then it appears I'm lagging behind." There was something hard to his tone I didn't understand.

"Shall I go away, sir?" I said lightly. "And give you the chance to seek me?"

He smiled at my small jest, and I found that I rather liked the curve of his lips and the unguarded softness that came over his stony features. "You can't hide from me for long. I'm good at the hunt."

For some reason, his words sent a tremor of warmth through me. And the longer he held my gaze, the warmer my insides grew, until I was tempted to press my hot cheeks against the cold stone of the wall behind me.

He finally set the mug onto the serving table. There was

something in his eyes that told me he was every inch a man and that he wasn't playing a child's game. "I regret to say I've already done all the hunting today that I should."

"Done?" I didn't like the dismissal in his tone. How could he not want to woo me the way the others had? I'd not mistaken the attraction in his eyes, had I?

"I cannot hope to compete with Bennet's winsome ways and whatever gifts Collin may give you." He gave a small bow and then started away.

I wanted to reach for him and stop him. But I could never be so brazen as to touch a man of my own accord. "Perhaps you're afraid." I said the first thing that came to my mind. "Perhaps you lack the courage to pursue me as your friends have."

At my words he halted and spun around. His brows came together in a fierce scowl. And before I could react, he strode back to me, closing the distance between us with quick, decisive strides. He didn't stop until he was mere inches away.

My breath caught at his closeness. What had I done? Had I made him angry? Somehow, I felt as though I ought to blame myself for goading him. But he'd been so aloof, I hadn't been able to resist.

He lifted his fingers to my cheek, and his callused thumb drew a gentle line down my jaw. I sucked in a sharp breath at his boldness but found myself melting under his touch.

When his thumb reached the end of my jaw, he cupped my chin, tilting my head up. "My lady, people may say many things about me," he whispered hoarsely. "But I pray they never say I lack courage. God forbid it."

His face was near enough that the warmth of his breath fanned me.

Never had I looked so deeply into someone's eyes. I was helplessly lost.

"I'm not and never will be a coward." His gaze fell to my

lips, and my chest contracted with a frightening yet excited swoosh. Surely he would not be so audacious as to take a kiss from me. Not here. Not now.

I wanted to reply, but even if I'd been able to think of something to say, I doubted I'd be able to make my tongue work to speak.

"And I am most certainly not afraid to kiss you, my lady." His lips hovered all too close, and my breath stuttered. The steel in his eyes darkened, and I felt as if all time were standing still.

But then slowly, deliberately, he let go of me and took a step back. He locked his hands behind his back and put several steps between us, leaving me suddenly cold. I wrapped my arms across my chest to fight off a shiver.

"Please rest assured, my lady, that if I resist pursuing, it's certainly not because I'm a coward."

"You have convinced me, sir." I wished I could control the waver in my voice and the strange, overwhelming desire to stand close to him again.

Even though he'd put a safe and proper distance between us, his eyes wouldn't let me go.

Sudden angry shouts from the inner courtyard at the front of the keep drew my attention. Before I could make sense of the commotion, Trudy appeared from around the corner, hustling toward me.

"Rose, you come with me this instant," she called, shaking her head, her portly frame heaving with each step.

"Whatever is the matter?" I asked as she flew upon me as fast as her short legs could carry her.

"The sheriff has come with several of his men." Trudy grabbed my arm and began to steer me toward the open kitchen door. "And he's very angry."

The swift sound of metal rasping against metal was followed

by the glint of Sir Derrick's dagger as he unsheathed it from his side.

The strength in his face and the steadiness of his stance should have calmed me. But dread crept into my heart. After learning that the sheriff was resistant to my rule, I wasn't sure I was ready to face him again. And yet, how would he learn to take my rule seriously if I cowered away?

"Why is the sheriff here this time?" I asked while trying to tug away from my nursemaid.

Trudy swatted my backside, urging me to continue toward the arched doorway. "He's accusing you of sending one of the knights to break into his estate last night."

I glanced again at Sir Derrick. One of the knights had undeniably done the deed. Had it been Sir Derrick? His gray eyes glinted, but his face was like iron, giving nothing away. If it had been him, I couldn't tell.

"Let me go to the sheriff." Once again, I tried to break free, but Trudy's grip was strong. "I'll set the matter aright."

"No, my lady." Trudy huffed, and her ample chest rose up and down in her distress. "We need to wait for the abbot. He knows how to calm the sheriff."

I needed to learn how to put the wayward lawman in his place once and for all. But part of me hesitated. The sheriff had already sent me an unspoken message with his disregard for my laws banning the old torture methods. He'd made a mockery of my compassionate approaches. What if I faced him and he only mocked me further? What would I do then? I would only make myself look weaker and frailer.

Perhaps for now my best move was to let the knights confront the sheriff on my behalf.

I sighed and let Trudy lead me into the castle, into safety. As much as I wanted to be seen as a strong leader, there were times when I didn't want to face my growing responsibilities.

Chapter 7

SWEAT TRICKLED DOWN MY BACK BETWEEN MY SHOULDER blades. Even though the doors and windows of the Great Hall were wide open, my body was tense and hot.

The altercation in the courtyard with the sheriff's men had been swift. Although the sheriff had come with the intent of forcing the duke to leave the castle, no blood had been shed. The mere sight of our weapons had persuaded the sheriff to solve any differences through peaceful methods rather than might.

I turned my attention to the front of the Great Hall, where Lady Rosemarie sat in her golden chair on the raised platform. With the long room open before her, she remained still and regal: her chin held high, her shoulders straight, and her gaze never swerving from the sheriff at the doorway.

Even so, I could see a flicker of anxiety in her eyes and wished I could reassure her that we would keep her safe no matter what happened.

The duke stood guard next to her. He laid a hand upon her shoulder and gave a gentle squeeze.

The abbot entered behind the sheriff and moved with slow, measured steps down the center aisle toward Lady Rosemarie. He tucked his hands in the long sleeves of his flowing brown habit. His expression was serene, as if he were getting ready to lead Matins. Apparently he was unruffled by the altercation with the sheriff, and with Lady Rosemarie's decision to give the duke's contest a try.

The duke had reminded her only moments before that neither he nor the abbot controlled her destiny. Whatever the future held was in God's hands, and it was his will she must seek above all else.

Nevertheless, something hot slid around me, blanketing me and making me sweat.

What if she changed her mind about the contest? What if she decided she didn't want to go forward with the month of courtship?

The thought was more unwelcome than I cared to admit.

A part of me pondered the irony of my thoughts. My friends and I had been reluctant when the duke had first broached his plan to us. He'd explained Lady Rosemarie's situation and her severe time constraint of having only one month to fall in love or become a nun. He'd wanted us to compete for her affection, to do everything within our power to win her love. Not only for her sake, but also for ours. He'd been firm with us, telling us we were long overdue to settle down and get married.

And yet we were the closest of companions, and on the trip to Ashby had discussed how uncomfortable we felt competing with each other for the affection of a woman. In fact, when the duke had informed us of the contest to court Lady Rosemarie, I'd already had trepidation about the entire idea. A contest was a frivolous way to find a wife. If I must settle down, I'd much prefer the more traditional way—having the duke make an arrangement for me.

Despite our reservations, our leader had brought us to his goddaughter. And when Lady Rosemarie had stepped outside that first day, with her golden curls streaming past her waist and the loveliness of her smile, it had been easy to set aside our reservations. After a few slaps on the back, we'd resolved to keep the contest friendly and civil.

I'd agreed to go along with the duke's plans, but not because of her outer beauty; rather because I'd witnessed her consideration toward the tortured criminals in the market. She'd shown kindness when no one else had. I had been unable to stop admiring her, even though I tried.

And now I was frustrated by my conflicted desires. On the one hand, I wished my fearless leader hadn't pushed me into the frivolous contest. But now, after meeting her, my heart and actions betrayed me. I couldn't deny that I hoped I'd have the chance to get to know her better this month.

After what felt like an eternity, the abbot finally reached the front of the Great Hall, only feet away from me and my two companions. "Your ladyship," he said, giving Lady Rosemarie a small bow of respect. "I've talked with the sheriff, and he offers his pardon for disturbing you."

I studied the sheriff. Even from across the chasm of the room, it was clear from the sheriff's scowl and stiff shoulders that he was still angry. Did he recognize me as the knight who'd accosted him in his home? My helmet and armor had concealed me, mostly. But the sheriff was staring back at me, as though he'd guessed I was the one.

"If you give him your gracious pardon," continued the abbot, "he's agreed to leave peaceably without pressing charges against any of the knights."

"Perhaps I should speak with the sheriff myself," Lady Rosemarie offered.

The abbot leaned in and lowered his voice, but even so his words still carried to me. "His pride is wounded, your ladyship. And 'twould not do to harm it further."

The conflict raging across Lady Rosemarie's face gave way

to resignation. "Very well. Send him on his way. But tell him I don't wish to see him in my court again anytime soon."

I wanted to urge her to question the sheriff further. The man had an attitude of rebellion that didn't bode well. But I held my tongue. Clearly, Lady Rosemarie was young and inexperienced as a ruler. She still had much to learn, and it wasn't my job to teach her.

When the guards urged the sheriff to turn and leave, the man's gaze clashed with mine one last time. My pulse sped and I gripped the hilt of my sword. I didn't know much about the sheriff, but from the derision in his eyes, I could tell I'd already made an enemy.

Once the sheriff was gone, the abbot spoke to Lady Rosemarie. "Word has reached me regarding your decision to participate in the duke's courtship plans."

"And are you agreeable?" She watched the abbot expectantly.

His face remained placid, but his eyes brimmed with concern. "I just hope that you're not setting yourself up for heartache, my lady."

Indecision rippled across Lady Rosemarie's face.

"I shall support whatever you decide to do, my child," he continued, "but I'm concerned that after experiencing such revelry for a month, you may find it more difficult to enter the convent and be content there."

"I'm concerned about that too," she admitted. Her gaze slid to the three of us. I had to keep myself from sighing at her indecisiveness. Something in my expression must have caught her attention, for she looked at me a second longer than at the others as though I'd spoken my chastisement aloud.

"It is a risk," the duke said from beside her, his expression turning grave. "But is it a risk you're willing to take?"

She didn't respond right away. And I found my muscles

tightening at the thought of her saying no, even though I knew I should feel relieved instead.

"My other concern," the abbot said, his forehead furrowing so that his tonsure dipped near his thin eyebrows, "is that I would not want the duke's men to unduly tempt your ladyship. You're pure and undefiled, and I only want to make certain you remain that way—"

A growl of protest rose in my chest, and before I could stop myself I stepped forward. "Your words insult Lady Rosemarie. She would never dishonor herself. And we would never seek to harm her, only to honor her in every way possible."

Even as the words left my lips, I thought back to the moments earlier in the day when I'd been alone with her, how beautiful she'd been. Was it possible we could unintentionally harm Lady Rosemarie with our affection and desires? My gut cinched. God forbid it.

My companion laid a steadying hand upon my arm, silently urging me to use caution.

The duke nodded at me and then turned to the abbot. "I understand your concerns, Father Abbot. My knights are but men, at the prime of their youth. They've been denied the pleasure of a woman's company for too long."

Lady Rosemarie's eyes widened at the duke's admission and a rosy hue colored her cheeks. I fastened my attention on the abbot, unwilling to let Lady Rosemarie know just how true the duke's statement was. Although I was reluctant to leave behind my warring ways, I couldn't deny my need to experience the love of a woman or the draw I'd felt toward Lady Rosemarie. And yet, was my attraction toward her special, or would I find myself drawn to anyone at this point in my life?

"Nevertheless," continued the duke, "I'll be overseeing all the events and outings, the dance and the jousting tournament. I'll make certain Lady Rosemarie is chaperoned at all times when she's with my men. We'll do our utmost to cherish and protect her purity."

"And that's exactly why I'm here today," the abbot said, getting to the point he'd obviously wanted to make all along. "I don't wish to see her pushed by you into the arms of one of your men so that you can gain control over her and her lands."

At the words of insult toward the duke, I tensed and stepped forward again. "My master has absolutely no need for gaining control of Lady Rosemarie's lands. Not when he's already the lord over his own lands and estate, too numerous to count, and is bound to receive more gifts from the High King for his valor in the border skirmishes."

The strong hands of both my companions reached out to caution me, but I shrugged them off. I might have rash tendencies, but during my many years training with the duke, he'd made sure I had learned to control them. My friends should know that, I thought with irritation.

Lady Rosemarie had been watching me with wide eyes and now held out a hand to the abbot. "Father Abbot, I invite you to stay here at Montfort Castle for the duration of the month. Then I shall have your wise counsel along with the duke's."

The abbot pressed his lips together as if he'd like to say more. Then he bowed his head—in prayer or acquiescence, I knew not.

Lady Rosemarie's expression was conflicted. I could only imagine what a surprise the duke's news about the exception had been and how difficult it was to reverse her plans to enter the convent when she'd already mentally prepared for a future as a nun. But still, she needed to make a decision and then stay the course.

"As always, Father Abbot, I shall covet your spiritual guidance. And I shall covet yours too, your Grace." She turned to the duke.

The duke nodded with understanding.

"As much as I respect the guidance of you both," she continued, her voice growing stronger, "I'm coming of age, and this is a decision I must make for myself."

I silently applauded her brave stand. This time when her glance slid to me as though to gauge my reaction to her words, I gave her a slight nod. Perhaps she would learn to be a strong leader in time after all.

Silent screams tore at my throat. I thrashed, trying to wrench my attention from the awful sight before me. But as hard as I willed it, I couldn't look away from the starving rat in the bottomless cage latched to the prisoner's stomach.

"No!" I cried. My eyes flew open to the darkness of my chamber and the bed canopy overhead. With a deep gasp I bolted up, my body trembling with the lingering horrors of the nightmare. It was the same one that had plagued me these past four years.

The bed curtains were open, letting in the cool night air.

I untangled from the sheet, crawled to the edge of my four-poster bed, and slipped my legs over the edge. The scratchiness of the rushes pricked my bare feet. Hugging my arms across my chest to calm the quaking in my limbs, I glanced around the darkened chamber lit only by the moonlight spilling through the open window.

"Pup," I whispered. "Come here, boy."

I waited for the usual soft patter of his paws. But the only sound was Trudy's heavy breathing coming from her sleeping pallet near the window.

I slid off the bed. "Pup?"

A loud snore from Trudy filled the stillness of the night.

I glanced from the shadows of my bed to the twisted sheets

and the haunted dreams that awaited me if I climbed back in there. I needed Pup. His warm presence next to me in the bed always calmed me.

I crossed the room on my tiptoes. When I reached the door, I grabbed my cloak from the peg, slung it over my nightdress, and then lifted the latch.

The door opened soundlessly. Even so, I paused and held my breath, waiting for Trudy's sharp command to return to bed.

But after a moment of the same rumbling snores, I slipped through the crack and into the hallway. The light of the oil lamp in the sconce outside my door illuminated the hunched shoulders of the soldier on guard—Bartholomew.

"My lady," he said, rising quickly from his stool and standing at attention.

I put a finger to my lips, bidding him to be silent. "I'm looking for Pup," I whispered. "Have you seen him?"

The wizened face cracked into a grin that revealed gums where many of his front-most teeth had once been. "He was pawing to get out, my lady," he whispered back, albeit too loudly. "I thought he needed to ... you know ..."

I nodded.

"But apparently he's made a new friend."

"I don't understand."

"He's down in the Great Hall, my lady." Bartholomew shuffled forward, still grinning. "I tried to call him back. But he wouldn't come."

"Take me to him, Bartholomew. Please."

Through the dimly lit passageway, I followed the old guard's labored footsteps. We went down a winding back stairway so that we entered a narrow door next to the buttery, where the ale and other beverages were stored.

The Great Hall was dark except for the low light of the

fire and a shallow candle on the table closest to the hearth. Many of the duke's men slept on pallets and rushes on the floor throughout the main gathering place. Of course I'd given the duke the largest guest room, and I'd assumed Sirs Collin, Bennet, and Derrick took turns sleeping outside the door of his chamber and guarding it as was the custom. I'd also assumed they'd long past retired for the night.

But to my surprise, the duke sat at the table pulled before the hearth. On a bench across from him was one of his knights. A chessboard was spread before them, and the duke was staring intently at the pieces.

The knight across from him stretched his arms above his head, fiddled with a spot of dried wax on the table, and finally slouched on one elbow, giving the chessboard a cursory glance. Seemingly without thought he moved one of his pieces and then backed away, leaving the duke to study the board again. This time, the knight let his hand dip down to scratch behind the ears of the dog lying at his feet.

"Pup?" I whispered.

Pup raised his head, cocked his ears in my direction, but then turned back to the knight, whose fingers moved to the dog's flank with long, scratching strokes.

"I told you he made a new friend, my lady," came Bartholomew's laughter-filled whisper by my side.

The darkness of the room shadowed the knight's face, but when he bent closer to the candlelight to take another turn, I caught a glimpse of his straight, sandy-brown hair and the scar next to his eye. "I should have known it was Sir Derrick," I whispered, remembering Pup's attraction to him earlier in the day.

Sir Derrick took no time at all in moving another piece— this one his queen. Even from a distance I could see that he didn't have many left on the board and that he'd placed his queen into a dangerous situation. I could only assume he lacked any strategy or was entirely too reckless and impatient for the game.

"You want me to go over and fetch the dog, my lady?"

Bartholomew's too-loud whisper reached across the distance and brought Sir Derrick off the bench, dagger in hand. He peered into the darkness that surrounded him. "Who goes there?"

Bartholomew shuffled forward several steps. "Just me, sir. Come to get the dog for Lady Rosemarie."

Pup rose and wagged his tail. Yet he still didn't leave Sir Derrick's side.

Bartholomew waved at the dog. "Come on now, Pup. The lady needs you."

Pup didn't budge.

"She needs him?" Sir Derrick asked, stuffing his dagger back into the sheath belted at his waist.

"Yes," I said, stepping out of the dark shadows. "As a matter of fact, I do need him."

At my appearance, the duke rose and Sir Derrick bowed. "I'm sorry, my lady," he said as he straightened. "The dog came to me and has stayed. I would have sent him back to you had I known."

"'Tis all right." I bent and stretched out my arms to the dog. "Come now, Pup."

Pup lifted his face toward Sir Derrick, his big eyes seeking the knight's permission.

I let my arms fall to my sides, surprise washing over me. "Sir, it looks like you have won the undying devotion of my dog."

He grinned, gently rubbed Pup's nose, and started across the room toward me with Pup trailing at his heels. He stopped several feet away and nodded at my dog to continue. Pup bounded the last of the distance, eagerly rejoining me and licking my outstretched hand.

"How quickly your loyalty shifts, Pup," I admonished, sinking my fingers into his thick hair.

"'Tis not any reflection on you, to be sure," Sir Derrick said. "The dog is merely affectionate."

"No. He's rarely affectionate with anyone but me or the village children. You must have a secret way with dogs."

"Perhaps I do." His voice was mysterious, and I thought back to the knight who had visited me in the chapel and what he'd said about the sheriff's dogs.

"You must share the secret with me." I nodded toward the abandoned chess game. "Then perhaps I shall share my secrets regarding chess with you, for it appears you have need of them."

"Have need?" Sir Derrick's brow shot up, and his lips quirked. "I was doing quite nicely, if I may be so bold as to boast."

I laughed softly. "Then I should like to see you play when you're doing poorly."

His grin inched higher. "I would enjoy engaging you in a chess match, my lady. I think you'd be in for a surprise."

Behind us, the duke cleared his throat, reminding us of the late hour and the inappropriateness of being together under the circumstances—especially in light of the abbot's concerns earlier. I took a quick step back, relieved at the darkness that could hide the heat infusing my cheeks.

Sir Derrick took a step after me. "Wait, my lady," he whispered, glancing over his shoulder to where the duke still stood, seemingly studying the chessboard. I was sure he watched our every move.

Sir Derrick lowered his voice. "I wanted to beg your forgiveness for my forwardness earlier today."

My mind flashed back to the encounter outside the kitchen,

to his soft caress on my cheek and the warmth of his mouth near mine.

"Will you forgive me for my boldness?"

"Of course." I didn't harbor any ill-will for our encounter. Quite the opposite. But I couldn't very well admit I'd liked being near him.

"I don't know what came over me, and I promise I shall do better in the future."

Did I want him to do better?

I nodded and ducked my head to hide my own confusing desires. And then, before he could sense the conflicted emotions within me, I retreated into the darkness of the hallway that was untouched by the light of the candle and hearth.

"Goodnight, Sir Derrick."

"Goodnight, my lady. Sweet dreams."

With Pup in my bed and thoughts of Sir Derrick on my mind, perhaps I really could forget my nightmares and have sweet dreams.

At that thought, mortification crashed through me. Now who was being the bold one? How dare I think about Sir Derrick in my dreams?

I moved swiftly up the spiral stairway, leaving my faithful old guard far behind. I suddenly needed to put as much distance as possible between the handsome knight and myself.

Chapter
8

The next morning, I awoke to a flurry of activities.
My dear friend, the Noblest Knight, the Duke of Rivenshire,
had begun making arrangements for the courtship process. He
announced that over the coming weeks he would host a hunting party, a dance, and a jousting tournament.

In addition, he wanted to give each of the young knights
the opportunity to plan an outing of their own, something special that would give them the chance to spend time alone with
me—with a chaperone, of course.

Sir Collin was the first to orchestrate his special event: a romantic dinner for two in my rose garden. Dressed in a doublet
threaded with what appeared to be real silver, he held out my
chair with a flourish. "For you, my lady."

Strands of his blond hair dipped over his forehead, and his
grin rose on one side in an adorable quirk. As he helped push in
my chair, I took in the elaborate decorations on the long table.
The biggest bouquet of roses I'd ever seen graced the center
amidst crystal goblets and gold platters loaded with delicacies
of all kinds. The garden itself had been transformed with candelabras glowing among hundreds of roses garnishing hanging
trellises, their petals fluttering gently in the summer breeze.

"I'm speechless," I said, drinking in the beauty.

He took his seat next to mine, and his grin widened. "I hope that means you like it."

"I love it."

"Before we start our meal," he said, his smile disappearing and his expression growing serious, "I have something for you." Sir Collin reached into his pocket and retrieved a small pouch. He drew open the strings and took out a gold bracelet. It was a plain band, devoid of jewels and instead engraved with a spiraling rose pattern.

He held it out to me. "I had this especially made for you by the local goldsmith."

It was stunning. But I couldn't accept such a gift, could I?

"Since I gave you something too lavish before with the diamond pin," he said, his smile returning with a teasing glimmer, "I thought this time I should keep it simpler."

He reached for my hand, and as his fingers grazed mine, my breath caught. Gently, he slid the bracelet on until it reached my wrist.

"It's beautiful," I whispered, hardly seeing the bracelet. Instead I watched his fingers twist the gold band, relishing the faint brush of his fingertips.

At a soft cough from a corner bench, Sir Collin let go of me and sat back in his chair. Tucked in a nearby corner of the garden sat the abbot, his head bent over a thick prayer book. Even though he was reading, I had no doubt he was well aware of every word we spoke and every move we made.

"Thank you." I felt like a little girl caught in the kitchen sneaking a sweetmeat.

"It's not nearly enough for you," he replied, "but I'm trying to show restraint, as hard as it may be."

A servant appeared at the table to pour spiced ale into our goblets and to hold out the heaping platters that contained more food than the two of us could ever eat. Taking my first bite of a sweet roll crusted in honey, I couldn't stop thinking about all the poor children this meal would feed. I could appreciate that his extra food purchases and hired help for the feast had provided work and money for many in my town. But as the meal progressed through various courses, the thought of the extravagance kept growing until finally, as the servants cleared away the excessive remains, I had to speak my mind.

"What will you do with all that remains from the feast, sir?"

Sir Collin sat back in his chair with a lazy, contented grin. "What would you have me do with the delicacies, my lady? Invite my friends to partake?"

He'd already given orders for the servants to begin erecting a stage in front of us, and I watched for a moment without answering, uncertain how to explain the deep concerns of my heart. Until now I'd had no trouble keeping up my end of the conversation with Sir Collin. He was easy to talk with and made me laugh more in one meal than I had in many months.

Nevertheless, I found it difficult to speak more seriously with him, especially about matters that were important to me.

"Would you have me feed your hunting dogs, my lady?" Sir Collin asked. "You need only say, and it shall be done."

"Oh no, not the dogs," I said, horrified at the thought of wasting all the food on animals alone. "I was hoping that we — or I — could distribute the excess among the poor."

Sir Collin's eyes widened at my suggestion. Thankfully, I saw no disapproval there, but neither did I see excitement at the prospect. Instead he shrugged. "If it means that I'll get the chance to spend more time with you, my lady, then I shall be more than happy to oblige you in handing out the food."

His answer was satisfying enough, and I rewarded him with a smile that lit up his summery-green eyes.

Later, as the jesters, jugglers, and even a dancing bear made their appearances on the stage, I tried to forget my hesitancies and just enjoy the evening. After the past few years of simplicity and solitude, I was bound to feel uncomfortable from time to time with normal life and relationships.

At least that's what I told myself as the evening came to a close and Sir Collin walked me back to the keep amidst the chirping of crickets and the winking of stars overhead.

He stopped before the stone steps leading to the massive front doors. "I had a magnificent time with you tonight."

"You did?" The thought was slightly intimidating. I wasn't all that exciting to be around. In fact, I was rather shy, didn't always know what to say, and still felt completely inadequate relating to men.

Sir Collin started to reach for my hands, but at the sight of the abbot ten paces behind me, he clasped his own behind his back. "I hope you had a good time too."

"It was lovely," I said. "I can't remember having so grand an evening before either." I was surprised by how much I meant it.

With my declaration, his grin made a quick but dazzling visit. Then before the abbot or I could object, he reached for my hand, brought it to his lips, and pressed a soft kiss there.

My heart swelled within my chest. And for the first time since I'd heard the news about the exception to the Ancient Vow, I realized that perhaps it was more possible than I'd believed to fall in love with one of the duke's men.

The next day, Sir Collin rode with me throughout town as I gave away two cartloads of leftover food among those who were most needy. I was grateful for his company, but erelong I could see Sir Collin was growing bored. And as his yawns and yearning glances toward the castle increased, I knew it was time to wrap up my ministrations for the day.

When we returned, I was surprised at my reluctance to

part ways with him. After spending the previous evening and now a second day in his presence, I'd finally begun to feel more comfortable around him. I'd found myself basking in the many conversations as well as the companionship.

Although I would have preferred another day in Sir Collin's easy-going presence, on the duke's encouragement I decided I had to be fair to all three of the men. I had to give them each a chance to win my heart.

Thus Sir Bennet's special day arrived. I dressed in my finest, donned a smile, and did my best to enjoy his planned activities, especially when he'd gone to so much trouble to arrange an art fair outside the castle grounds. Local artisans, as well as those from neighboring lands, had arrived to display their crafts, including pottery, beaded jewelry, and woven tapestries.

After the first awkward moments, Sir Bennet's utmost politeness and chivalry made me forget about everything but the displays that spread out in the open tents around me. We walked from canopy to canopy appreciating the fine workmanship, watching demonstrations, and discussing the merits of art and creativity.

"You have an eye for quality," I said as we left the tent of a glassblower.

Sir Bennet's raven hair shimmered almost blue-black in the sunshine. His dark blue eyes regarded me thoughtfully. "My parents have spent their lives collecting rare treasures and relics. I suppose it's only natural that I should have an appreciation for art as well."

The duke followed us a safe distance away. Since we were the only ones attending the fair, we'd been able to talk freely, and I'd found myself appreciating the more serious conversations that I could have with Sir Bennet. He was clearly intelligent and the topics steered toward issues of history and science, which fascinated me.

Sir Bennet stopped suddenly, and his dark brows furrowed over his flawless, handsome face. I took in his beautiful eyes with long lashes, as well as his perfectly straight nose and chiseled jaw. "I know a rare treasure when I see one." His voice dropped. "And you are one of the rarest, my lady."

"You're too kind, sir. I'm not without flaws—"

"If you have any, they are most certainly hidden beneath your beauty."

His praise warmed me to the tips of my slippered toes. It was indeed high praise from one so handsome and schooled in discovering treasures.

"Lest you think me vain," he continued, heedless of the artists and tents around us, "I believe that you're made more beautiful because of the sweetness of your inner spirit."

What was I to do with such compliments? I simply didn't know. I glanced down at the grass, which had been clipped to form a level plain for Sir Bennet's art show.

As if sensing my discomfort, he politely held out his arm, his expression once again dignified and calm. "I have a surprise for you, my lady."

I slipped my hand into the crook of his arm, conscious of his hard muscles beneath my fingers. Sir Bennet matched his step to mine, and we strolled leisurely toward the last tent, one we had yet to visit.

Underneath the canopy, in the middle, stood a painter, his palette already filled with paints, his paintbrush in hand. He bowed to Sir Bennet and then to me. Then he waved at a chair placed in an area of soft light. I was surprised to see that it was my golden chair, the one from the Great Hall. It was elaborate, due to its elegant carvings, but I had no particular fondness for it. In fact, most of the time it only served to remind me of how much I had and consequently how much more I could be doing for my people.

"I don't understand," I said. "You're commissioning a painting of my chair?"

"It is a very fine chair." Sir Bennet's ready smile was heart-stopping. "But I would much rather have a painting of you, my lady."

Finally, understanding began to dawn.

"I would be greatly honored if you'd sit for a portrait, one that I might take with me and have forever."

"Of course," I said. But what if I didn't choose him as my husband? Then what would he do with the portrait? Or was he so confident that I'd fall in love with him that he disregarded all else?

"I thought the chair would make a remarkable backdrop." Sir Bennet led me toward the chair. "Although it could use a bit more polishing."

At Sir Bennet's declaration, the painter spoke quietly to his young assistant, a boy not older than ten. The child rushed forward with a rag. It wasn't until he reached the chair that I saw his fingers—or at least what was left of them. Most were nubs of varying lengths, and those left were masses of flaking, peeling skin.

Compassion stirred in my chest, making me all the more ready to sit for this portrait and by so doing provide the painter and his assistant a purse of coins they likely hadn't encountered in years.

But the moment the boy lifted his rag to the chair, Sir Bennet held out his hand. "Don't touch it." The knight's attention was fixed on the rotting flesh still left on the boy's few fingers, and his eyes registered first shock, then revulsion.

"I don't mind if he polishes my chair," I said, hoping to allay Sir Bennet's concern.

The handsome knight swallowed hard, looked away from the assistant's deformed fingers, and then cleared his throat. "I think the chair is just fine after all. It will not require additional polishing."

Thankfully, Sir Bennet was quiet about the matter for the remainder of my portrait. Mostly he ignored the boy's presence and focused the whole of his attention on me and on the likeness that was growing on the easel. Nevertheless, I was determined to double the painter's payment. It even crossed my mind that maybe I should just give him my chair.

But with the growing delight I witnessed on Sir Bennet's face as the portrait neared completion, I soon lost thought of the chair and couldn't keep from wondering: What would it be like to be married to a man who adored me heart, body, and soul? Was that man Sir Bennet? He certainly seemed like it.

If I had to pick between him and Sir Collin, how would I ever be able to make the choice? They both seemed like the kind of men who would cherish me — unlike Sir Derrick, who hadn't spoken with me since the night I'd chanced upon him playing chess with the duke.

I frowned at the mar to my otherwise perfect week. Although I'd caught Sir Derrick watching me a time or two, I'd sensed his silent challenge — a challenge to stand up for myself and be a stronger leader. At times, I even wondered if he really wanted to be there at all, that perhaps he was simply waiting things out until it was time to leave.

I wasn't sure why the thought bothered me, except to blame it on my vanity. I couldn't expect that every man would find me attractive and wish to woo me.

Chapter
9

Sir Collin's hearty voice rose in the air above the braying of hounds, making me smile. His song was silly and light and cheerful. As the bright noon sunshine glittered through the arches of branches and leaves overhead, I hummed along with him. Our hunting party rode through the lush forest, the coolness of the shade a welcome relief from the heat of the summer day. Our pace had long since slowed, the dogs having lost the scent of the game several times during the chase.

I couldn't remember a time when I'd felt quite as carefree and happy. Perhaps since the Plague had taken my parents, since that last hunting party when my life had changed forever. The beauty of the forest was something I'd missed — the dense green, the lush moss, the rushing of the river. But more than that, I'd missed the companionship, laughter, and conversations that were all but a distant memory, as if of another life altogether ... and I realized how much more I would miss if I chose to enter the convent.

Could I willingly relegate myself to a life of quiet and solitude? I'd always thought I could. It would be a noble service and sacrifice to God. But could I do it? And did I even want to anymore?

I was disconcerted by how quickly over the past week I'd

adjusted the thoughts of my future. Where once I'd resigned myself to the idea of life as a nun, now I wasn't sure I'd be able to endure it. And that was more than a little frightening, for what if I failed to fall in love and had to go to the convent after all?

Sir Collin finished the last words of his song and then grinned from his steed next to me. "Do you think I missed my calling, my lady? Should I have become a minstrel instead of a knight?"

I laughed, once again noticing how little I'd done so in recent years. I suppose I'd had little to be merry about. "Your songs have brought me great cheer this day."

"Are you sure Sir Collin's songs haven't soured your appetite, my lady?" Sir Bennet jested from my opposite side, where he'd been riding for most of the hunt. "I usually lose mine when I have to listen to so many."

"Then perhaps I should switch to my stories," Sir Collin countered. "Since I know how well you enjoy those."

"Please. Spare us all. Your stories are the worst kind of torture imaginable, worse than a skinning alive."

At Sir Bennet's words, my stomach did indeed sour. I'd suffered too many nightmares of late, especially of gruesome torture.

Upon seeing my subdued expression, Sir Bennet's laughter died away and was replaced with concern. "I'm sorry, Lady Rosemarie. I pray you will forgive me for speaking so glibly about torture methods."

I shivered and nodded. "You meant no ill will, sir."

Both of the knights grew silent and exchanged looks over my head. Did all of them know about my aversion to torture and the incident with the criminals in the town square?

I still hadn't discovered which of them had been the one to dash to the rescue. If only they or their horses wore their family emblem. The coat of arms with the fire-breathing dragon would certainly identify the rescuer and put an end to my curiosity. As the days passed, I longed to acknowledge how much I'd admired the knight's courage, and properly thank him for his daring deeds.

I could simply ask which of them had done it. Today was the perfect day to pose the question, while we were all together.

If only we were all together.

My gaze strayed to the forefront of the hunting party. I could barely see Sir Derrick from where he rode at the head of the group. Nevertheless, the rigidness of his back and the broadness of his shoulders made him easy to recognize.

A tiny prick of irritation needled me as it did every time I thought about the fact that he hadn't yet planned his special day for me. After Sir Collin's garden dinner and entertainment and then the art fair with Sir Bennet, I'd begun waiting to see what Sir Derrick would plan for me. I didn't know how he could devise anything more lovely than what I'd already experienced.

It had been two days, but surely he would plan something. He wouldn't be so cold that he'd do nothing at all with me. Would he?

He certainly didn't appear eager to single me out and spend time with me. Of course he was always polite whenever we were together, but he lacked the enthusiasm of Sir Bennet and Sir Collin.

Had I done something to offend him, to make him dislike me? Part of me whispered that I shouldn't care, but for a reason I couldn't explain, I did.

"My lady, this looks to be the spot the duke has chosen for our picnic." Sir Bennet reined his horse as we broke into a clearing.

I halted next to him and smiled at the scene that met me. In a meadow dotted with the most beautiful array of wildflowers, a canopy had been erected. Underneath the canopy were blankets for us to sit upon. And upon those blankets lay an arrangement of platters of fruits, cheeses, breads, and pastries.

"It would appear that our leader is a romantic at heart," Sir Collin winked.

Sir Derrick had already reached the picnic spot and dismounted his horse. As we got closer I could see him handing the reins to one of his squires, who led the steed away to a distant area where the rest of the hunting party would relax and eat. We spurred our horses into a trot and arrived at the canopy laughing and breathless. Sir Bennet helped me dismount and led me into the shade of the tent. He situated me on the center blanket as carefully as if I'd been one of the colored glass creations we'd seen at the art show.

"Thank you, sir." I smiled up at his eager face. My heart fluttered at the nearness of his presence, his strong muscled jaw, the smooth shaven skin, and how every wavy strand of dark hair stayed in its proper place.

He hovered above me, taking in my appearance as I'd just done to him. "I didn't think it was possible for you to become any lovelier than you already are. But every day that I see you, you grow more beautiful."

His words caressed me, making me want to curl my toes. His gaze dropped to my lips and blue heat flared in his eyes. He licked his lips, and my pulse fluttered at the thought that perhaps he was seriously considering kissing me. He wouldn't, would he? So soon? So publicly?

My heart raced. Did I dare let him?

"No fair, Bennet," Sir Collin said while ducking under the canopy. Even though his words were lighthearted, something hard flashed in his eyes as he glanced at his friend. "You can't whisper endearments into Lady Rosemarie's ear. I'm the only one who gets to do that."

I bestowed a smile on Sir Collin as he tossed himself onto one of the three blankets that surrounded me. His fair hair flopped over one of his eyes endearingly and his grin cocked higher on one side.

What would happen if I fell in love with them both? Was it even possible to fall in love with two men at the same time? And how would I know if I was truly in love and not simply infatuated? A sudden rush of confusion swirled through me, and I tried to take a deep breath and remind myself that I didn't have to make any choices today. I still had three weeks until my eighteenth birthday.

Sir Derrick bent under the canopy, and as he made his way past me his smoky eyes snagged mine. I waited for a smile, for warmth, for some kind of interest to appear in his eyes, just as I'd seen in the other two men. Instead, he merely gave me a nod, moved on, and then lowered himself to his spot on the last empty blanket. I could only stare at his back, at the taut leather of his jerkin, and will him to turn around and say something to me.

As if hearing my unspoken request, he tilted his head and stared at me boldly while reaching for an apple. All the while holding my gaze, he took a crunching bite and a small smile tugged at his lips, as if he'd sensed my reaction to him and was pleased with it.

I snapped my gaze away from his, flustered and irritated at the same time. I plucked one of the wild strawberries from the dish. "All the activity this morning has made me ravenously hungry." I nibbled the berry and tried to ignore Derrick's hard-muscled, intense presence that was entirely too noticeable.

I wanted to tell him to hold his pride in check, that I wasn't enamored with him the way I was with the other two. But since saying so would have been presumptuous of me, I determined to show him that I didn't long for him, that it didn't matter to me whether or not he made any effort to win me as Sir Collin and Sir Bennet were doing.

During the leisurely mealtime, I allowed Sir Collin and Sir Bennet to monopolize me and entertain me with their lively banter. I entered into their jesting, all the while trying to pretend I didn't notice Sir Derrick reclining lazily and not minding in the least that he wasn't the bearer of my attentions.

But in reality, the more standoffish he remained, the more annoyed I began to feel and the more I wanted to show him I didn't care. I knew it was irrational to be insecure about one knight's inattention, but I didn't have the power to stop it.

As the noon hour passed, Sir Derrick soon excused himself with some of the leftovers and headed toward the hunting dogs lying in the shade of the nearby glen. Sir Bennet also took his leave at the beckoning of the duke. The knight's parting glance to Sir Collin was dark and filled with warning. I wasn't sure what his warning was, but I sensed a growing rivalry that caused me to fidget in unease.

Sir Collin smiled more cheerfully at his friend's departure, juggling several grapes like a court jester. "You didn't know I had such talent, did you, my lady?" he asked, letting the grapes fall into his lap save for one he caught between his teeth.

"You are indeed a man of many talents," I replied. I felt suddenly weary, ready to lie back upon the blanket and close my eyes in slumber. The troubled sleeplessness of the past few nights was beginning to assail me.

He chewed the grape but then paused in his eating. "I see my antics are only putting you to sleep."

"'Tis not you, sir. You've brought smiles and laughter back into my life after too many years without. And I thank you for it."

"But . . ." He paused, his green eyes gently probing me.

Had he heard about my nightmares? Had he heard my screams in the night?

The abbot and Thomas had been with me that day four years ago when I'd unknowingly ridden upon the gruesome sight on the outskirts of town. I'd known that the Plague must be contained, that we needed to punish anyone who broke from the quarantined areas. We couldn't risk it spreading any further than it already had.

But I hadn't expected the sheriff to exact such swift and severe punishment upon the two men who'd disobeyed. In fact, I'd become violently ill at the sight of their tormented bodies displayed outside the walls of town for all the land to see.

Since that day I'd outlawed the use of torture devices. Even if I'd been able to eradicate torture from my land, I had been unable to erase the memories from my mind. The visions still haunted me. And seeing the criminals in the boiling pot of water and stretched on the rack had unleashed the memories again …

"I haven't slept well the past week," I finally admitted softly to Sir Collin, who still awaited my answer.

"I'm sorry." He studied me, his expression serious, as if he sensed the depth of my turmoil.

Even if torture was an accepted method of punishment throughout the realm, I was convinced that there were kinder, more humane ways to dispense discipline when it was needed. I could only pray that the sheriff wouldn't disobey me again in such matters, although I had the sinking feeling that the battle had only just begun.

Sir Collin broke into a grin. "I have the perfect solution to not sleeping well."

I waited expectantly for him to share his deep and profound secret. He plucked another grape, tossed it in the air, and then caught it in his mouth with a widening grin. "You simply need to stay awake, and we shall dance and sing all the night through."

I tried to muster a smile at his jest, but at that moment I wanted more than playful antics. Maybe there were no easy solutions. But at the very least, I needed someone to listen and understand how I felt.

Before I could continue, something suddenly flew by in my side vision. A sharp whistling noise rent the air, followed by a thud and a pained cry from Sir Collin. I turned to find him fallen onto his back against the blanket with an arrow sticking from his shoulder.

Sir Collin's face first rounded with surprise and then crumpled with agony.

The sight was so unexpected and disturbing, I couldn't contain the scream that slipped from my lips. An arrowhead had embedded into his body—altogether too close to his heart. Blood had already started to flow out of the puncture and seep into his fine linen shirt, staining the area around the shaft a deep crimson.

Sir Collin gasped as if breathing his last breath and grabbed at the shaft.

The spot of blood on his shirt widened, and I cried out. "Help! Please help! Sir Collin has been shot!"

Already, I could hear the commotion and yells of the others reacting to my previous scream. Urgency prodded me to my knees next to him. I grasped one of his hands and found it slick and sticky with blood. At a loss for words, I whispered the beginning of the Lord's Prayer. "Our Father in heaven . . ."

Sir Collin's green eyes dulled with pain and yet shone with apology. "You'll have to forgive me, my lady. I'd hoped to provide you with excitement and adventure today. But I didn't quite plan to have it happen this way."

"Oh, sir," I whispered, holding his hand. His eyes closed and his face tightened with obvious pain.

The duke was the first to arrive and kneel next to Sir Collin, breathless. The lines in his regal face grooved much deeper than usual as he gently touched the arrow. When his fingers probed the point where it had entered Sir Collin's flesh, the young knight bit back a groan.

I held my breath, praying the shot wasn't fatal.

The duke then raised his worried eyes to me. "Are you hurt, dear one?"

I shook my head. "I'm untouched, your Grace. But Sir Collin ...?" Fear clogged my throat, preventing me from asking if he'd live.

The duke's expression turned grave. "'Twould appear that someone has murder on their mind."

Chapter
10

"What have you discovered, your Grace?" I asked from the chair my servants had placed next to the large cano-pied bed where Sir Collin reclined against mounds of goose-feather pillows.

"My men have scoured the forestlands for clues." The duke stood at the foot of the bed, his faced lined with weariness. He was dusty and grimy, and dressed in his hauberk and surcoat, proof he'd likely slept little if at all over the past several days. "We still have no trace of the man who might be responsible for the attempted murder."

Sir Collin's normally tan face was pale, but thankfully, after three days abed, the liveliness had returned to his eyes. Whatever culprit had thought to take the knight's life was ap-parently not an expert bowman. He'd missed Sir Collin's heart by several inches.

I shuddered again at the thought of how close Sir Collin had come to dying. Not only had the arrow come too close to vital organs, but he'd also lost a great deal of blood during the ordeal.

The gloomy thoughts only added to the grayness of the day. Even with the open window, the clouds that covered the sky had shifted inside and filled the spacious guest chamber I'd given to the duke.

"Perhaps we need to question some of the known criminals." Abbot Michael Francis sat in a chair on the other side of the large bed. The flicker of light from the candle on the bedstead cast strange shadows across his thin face. I was grateful he'd been willing to act as a chaperone every time I came to sit with Sir Collin—which had been nearly constant since we'd brought him back from the fated picnic.

The sheriff stepped out of the shadows, his features creased in a scowl. "With a little persuasion, I'd sure enough glean some information that would lead us to the culprit."

"No, sheriff." I spoke quickly, my body tightening at the implications of his words. "We cannot arrest men on suspicion alone. We must have some proof first."

"We have proof in their character." The sheriff's voice was as sharp as the arrowhead the physician had dug out of Sir Collin. While I appreciated that the sheriff was helping with the investigation, I certainly couldn't condone arresting criminals based on character alone.

What could I tell the sheriff that wouldn't stir more antagonism between us? My muscles tightened, and even though I knew I should handle this matter on my own, I couldn't keep from looking at the abbot.

His hands were folded in his lap and hidden in his sleeves. His face had a pinched quality I knew came from his worry over my safety. He'd been the first to mention what might have happened had the arrow missed Sir Collin and hit me instead.

I wanted to ask him for his advice, but I had the sudden picture of Sir Derrick watching me with disapproval, his steel eyes challenging me to grow up. With a deep breath, I shifted my attention back to the sheriff. "I insist we have more physical proof before making arrests—"

"We know they've already given themselves over to the devil," the sheriff said, "and usually that's all the proof we need."

The duke wiped a hand across his brow. "We'll continue to make inquiries. Sir Derrick and Sir Bennet are still investigating. I'm sure, with time and due course, we shall find the guilty one."

"I cannot understand why anyone would want to hurt Sir Collin," I said, studying his face against the pillows. Of the three knights, I was sure he would have the least number of enemies. He seemed like the kind of man who would have a difficult time making them even if he tried.

He gave me a half grin. "Likely someone is jealous of how winsome I am."

"Perhaps it's possible one of the other knights is jealous of Sir Collin," the abbot said. "Since he seems to be winning Lady Rosemarie's heart the quickest, perhaps they decided to eliminate their competition. Maybe one of them hired someone to assassinate Sir Collin."

The duke and Sir Collin both erupted with protest, defending the other two knights vehemently in their absence. I shoved aside the abbot's accusation too. I didn't know Sir Bennet or Sir Derrick well, but I couldn't imagine either one of them resorting to such tactics.

"I'm not worried about who's responsible," Sir Collin said after he'd resumed his calm. He reached for my hand and his long fingers wrapped around mine, their warmth encompassing me. "I should think that I'd like to get injured more often since I'm in heaven to have you by my side all the day long."

Even if his touch was forward and made me slightly self-conscious in the presence of everyone else, I didn't pull away.

"I would take an arrow in my body any day if it meant I'd get to enjoy your undivided attention all the more."

"'Tis not necessary to gain my attention so drastically, sir."

His grin and the twinkle in his eye shared his jest. But before he could tease me further, the abbot stood, scraping his chair so that it grated against the floor. My wise counselor cleared his throat and gave a pointed look at Sir Collin's hand holding mine.

I rapidly withdrew my hand.

The abbot pursed his lips before speaking. "Perhaps the knight's injury is a sign from God that he's displeased with all these activities."

I sat forward. A sign from God?

I hadn't considered that possibility. Was it possible that God was displeased with my intention of breaking the Ancient Vow? After all, my thoughts had been centered less on God lately and more on the young knights. In fact, I'd been so busy the past week, I'd hardly had time for my charity work.

A sick feeling swirled in my stomach.

"Sir Collin's injury is most definitely not a sign from God." The duke spoke directly to me as if he'd heard my anxious thoughts. "God himself instituted marriage when he created Adam and Eve. He designed the basic attraction between men and women. 'Tis natural, good, and right when young people begin the process of finding mates."

"Perhaps right for those who cannot resist temptation to the world," the abbot replied. "But for those who are stronger, like her ladyship, God offers a chance to do so much more for his glory."

"Marriage doesn't put an end to one's ability to serve God and bring him glory." The duke remained unruffled. "In fact, I've seen many married couples who have done more for God together than was possible as individuals."

"You raise a good point, your Grace," the abbot said, bowing slightly to the duke before facing me again. "Your parents worked well together, my child. I cannot diminish all of the good they did."

I nodded my gratefulness to the abbot for his words to

allay my concerns. However, a new anxiety had taken root within my heart. I'd vowed to be a compassionate ruler, to do even better than my parents. Would marriage and love distract me from my mission?

"Come now, Lady Rosemarie." The abbot started toward the door. "We shall go to the chapel and pray. Prayer is always the solution for our troubled spirits."

"You're right, Father Abbot." I rose, letting my gown flutter around me on the humid breeze that blew through the window.

"You'll offer a prayer on my behalf, will you not?" Sir Collin sat up, his gaze following me as I made my way around the bed. "I want to be back on my feet by the time of the dance."

The abbot stopped abruptly and frowned at the duke. "You have no intention of going forward with plans for a dance, do you? Not now that one of your own has been hurt."

"Collin's strong. He'll recover in no time." The duke smiled at the young man lying within the shadows of the canopied bed. "And even were he bedridden, he wouldn't begrudge Lady Rosemarie the opportunity to have a dance."

The sheriff stepped forward. "I agree with Father Abbot. With a murderer still on the loose, I cannot guarantee her lady-ship's safety if you go forward with the festivities."

The duke cocked his brow and met my gaze. "Lady Rosemarie, we'll do whatever you wish. After all, it's your future."

I appreciated the duke's deference to me, but I didn't know what to do. What was the safest choice for everyone involved?

I resisted the urge to glance again to the abbot. The sheriff already thought I was weak, and I would only confirm it in his eyes if I asked the abbot what I should do. In fact, the sheriff's hard gaze was trained on the abbot as though waiting for his command. He likely thought I was incapable of deciding any-thing for myself.

Although the thought of contradicting my wise counselor made me uneasy, I squared my shoulders. "We will continue with the dance."

The sheriff glanced at me quickly, but I caught sight of the irritation in his eyes before he could hide it. While the duke nodded his approval, the abbot's shoulders seemed to sag and his face creased with wariness.

"There's no need to cancel the festivities over one incident, Father Abbot," I hurried to explain. "Besides, we shall be inside the Great Hall and well guarded."

The abbot stared at me for a long moment. "If that's what you wish, my child." His expression had resolved into one of calm resignation. Nevertheless, I couldn't help feeling I'd somehow disappointed him.

The door banged open and Bartholomew barged in, breathing heavily as if he'd been running as fast as his old legs could carry him. "My lady," he said between gulps of air. "I beg your pardon for disturbing you."

The worry in his aged face set me on edge. "What tidings do you bear?"

"There's been a new outbreak of the strange illness," he gasped, "in town."

Dread dropped like a ball and chain in my stomach. "Here? In Ashby?"

Bartholomew nodded solemnly.

For a moment I was too weighted down by the news to move or think. Then panic sent me into motion. "Send word to the steward to prepare a cart of food and medicinal supplies. I must go into town at once."

"No, my child," came the abbot's reply. "You cannot go. It would be too dangerous."

"I have to agree," the duke said, his chain mail clinking as he crossed toward me. "It's too dangerous. We don't know enough about this illness yet. And you cannot chance exposing yourself. Your people need you too much to risk catching the illness."

My heart urged me to rush down into the walled town to help the people I loved. My parents had risked their lives to help the sick during the Plague. But the truth was, as the only heir of Ashby, I couldn't afford to die. If I were to perish now, my lands would be divided among the neighboring lords, including the cruel Lord Witherton, who was rumored to use torture regularly simply for entertainment. I had to stay alive for as long as possible in order to assure that my people were governed kindly and fairly.

"Allow one of my men to take the provisions and medicine," the duke continued, "but please use caution for yourself."

The abbot nodded, his gentle eyes admonishing me to accept the council.

"Very well," I said. "Send the cart without me."

I hurried out of the gatehouse and onto the drawbridge, glancing behind me to make sure none of the guards had recognized me. In one of Trudy's plain cloaks and with a basket underneath adding to my girth, I hoped I passed for my plump nursemaid.

"I've neglected my visit to town long enough," I said to myself, trying to push away my guilt. "Besides, I didn't promise the duke I would refrain from visiting. I only told him to send the provisions without me."

Although I'd sincerely wanted to obey the advice of the abbot and the duke to stay out of town, the need to visit had been growing all through my prayer time with the abbot. I wanted to reassure the people myself that I cared about their plight. I wanted to make sure they were being taken care of. And a curious part of me wanted to discover how the illness had started in town, especially after the sheriff had reassured me that he'd made great efforts to quarantine and contain the disease to the already infected outlying areas.

I'd also felt a strange need to mingle among my people and prove that I wasn't changing, that I was still as devoted to God as I'd always been. Besides, I'd promised myself that I wouldn't get too near the infected, that I wouldn't put myself in harm's way. Surely a short visit would do no harm.

I glanced heavenward to the clouds, to the angry, swirling black and gray. Was God angry with my people or with me? The question hadn't stopped needling me all afternoon. Why else would he allow such outbreaks throughout my land?

With the heavy basket underneath my robe weighing me down, I was breathing heavily by the time I made my way to the area where the poorest of the poor lived. A makeshift fence had been erected at one end of the deserted alley and a guard was posted in front of it to effectively keep anyone from entering the infected zone. More likely, the guard was charged with prohibiting anyone from leaving.

I ducked into a dark side street. How would I approach the area and the guard without revealing my identity?

I leaned against the side of a ramshackle hovel that had somehow escaped the illness. I drew in a deep breath, wrinkling my nose at the sourness of waste that was a constant stench in the poor district—not only from the dogs, cats, and chickens that roamed freely, but also from the human excrement that was slovenly dumped from those too busy or sick to carry it to the ditches outside of the town walls.

Down the street, a group of children played a game of chase among the refuse. 'Twould not be long before they noticed me and came closer to discover the reason for my visit.

My mind whirled, trying to formulate a plan. But before I could move, a form darted out of the shadows of the huts, and a hand slipped around my neck, quickly covering my mouth. Strong fingers clamped across my lips, blocking any sound I might have been able to make if fear hadn't rendered me speechless.

The grip pulled me back into a solid chest, not roughly but firmly nonetheless. My captor began to walk backward, dragging me along several steps.

I tried to struggle, but the man easily pinned my arms. I knew I ought to scream, to scratch, to kick, to do anything to free myself, but the fear pounding through me was paralyzing.

What was happening?

"So you're safe, are you?" came a soft question near my ear.

The voice was familiar, and even before my captor's fingers fell away from my mouth and released my arms, I knew who it was.

"Sir Derrick," I said, spinning around to face him.

He reached for my arms and steadied me, but I wrenched free and scowled at him. "How dare you frighten me in such a manner?" My body shook as much from relief at seeing him as fear at what had almost happened.

"My lady." His face was grave, and his gray eyes mirrored the stormy clouds overhead. "I saw that you left the castle without a chaperone and only thought to offer my services."

"If that's your idea of how to behave as a chaperone, then I must ask that you leave me to my own endeavors."

"'Tis not safe for you to be out on your own."

"It was safe—it still is—"

"And what if I'd been someone more menacing, my lady?"

I couldn't answer. Indeed, I could only stare at him.

Like the duke, he was dusty and worn from the travails of searching for Sir Collin's attacker. But even with the grime of the past few days, his face was ruggedly appealing, the layer of scruff on his chin and cheeks darker than usual and his eyes more brooding.

"Even if your nursemaid were with you, I think it unwise for you to be wandering about town without the protection of several armed guards."

I swallowed the lump of anxiety that rose again at the thought of what might have happened had he been the same culprit who wounded Sir Collin.

"My people wouldn't think of hurting me." I squeezed the words past suddenly dry lips.

"What if I'd been a man from a distant land who had no affection or respect for you?"

I couldn't formulate a response.

Without waiting for my agreement, he parted my cloak, unhooked the basket from my arm, and took the heavy burden upon himself. Only then did the hard lines on his face soften. "I'm sorry for frightening you, Lady Rosemarie. But I wanted you to see how easily and quickly someone could accost you, and thus how important it is for you to have the proper protection when you venture outside the castle."

I waited for him to rebuke me for coming to town following the outbreak of the illness. But his gaze held no censure this time. "I regret any distress I caused you ..."

I got a faint impression from the glimmer in his eyes that somehow I'd gained his respect for my actions. "You only thought to teach me a lesson — one I apparently deserved and, in my stubbornness, likely wouldn't have learned any other way."

I glanced around the shadowed alley to the faces peeking through cracks in doors and the children who'd stopped their game to watch my interaction with the knight. None of them gave me the usual happy greetings or smiles of welcome. Instead, they watched Sir Derrick with mistrust.

"Then you'll forgive me?" he asked.

His expression was sincere. He had not a trace of the

mockery I'd glimpsed in him from time to time over the past days. And although I wanted to remain irritated at him for ignoring me too often, I couldn't muster any anger. I was only relieved — relieved that he was speaking with me, that he'd apparently cared enough for my well-being to follow me.

In fact, I couldn't resist teasing him in repayment for his scare. "I can't begin to think about forgiving you ..."

His brow shot up.

I resisted the urge to smile, doing my best to pretend solemnity. "I can't forgive you ... unless you agree to help me deliver the supplies."

A smile twitched his lips, but he too did his best to hide it. "Very well, my lady. I shall bind myself to you as your slave the rest of the afternoon. I shall do whatever you wish."

"Whatever I wish?" I couldn't keep from smiling then.

"Absolutely anything." He lowered himself to a knee in front of me, laid the basket aside, and reached for one of my hands. Much to my surprise, he lifted my fingers until the warmth of his breath brushed my knuckles. His gaze held mine as my heart began to stutter. Finally, he brushed my skin with an exquisitely soft kiss, the touch of which went straight to my knees.

"Whatever you wish shall always be my command."

Chapter
11

My breath caught. The boldness of Derrick's words taunted me.

"You're the knight," I said. He was the one who'd rescued the criminals that day in the marketplace.

He released my hand, stood, and retrieved the basket. "Yes, I am indeed a knight." And when he finally turned his gaze on me, they were filled with innocence. Too much innocence.

"Then you won't take credit for your rescue in the town square?"

With the basket in hand, he started out of the side street. "I have nothing for which to take any credit, my lady. Except for rescuing you just now from the most villainous and barbaric attack by the most hunted criminal in all of Christendom."

I hurried to catch up with him. He was grinning.

"Then I shall have to think of a great reward for this rescue. What could I possibly bestow upon you that would make you happy?"

His grin widened. "I shall think on it, my lady."

"And you'll let me know?"

"Yes, in due time."

The rumble in his voice made my insides quiver. There was something about Sir Derrick that was raw and real and altogether too hard to resist. It unleashed confusion within me and reminded me of how little time he'd spent with me, of how seldom he had sought me out.

I stopped and waited for him to face me. He took several more steps before turning and raising his brow at me. "My lady?"

"You haven't planned your special day with me yet." I was unable to keep the accusation from my tone.

He studied my face. "No," he finally spoke quietly.

"Why? Have I done something to offend you? Something that makes you hold me at arm's length?"

"I would think you'd be completely satisfied with my two friends." There was an edge to his voice I didn't understand. "Are they not giving you enough flattery and attention to equal that of ten men?"

"They're both very attentive." I toed a rock with the tip of my slipper. I didn't quite understand why I wanted to spend time with Sir Derrick. Certainly, Sir Collin and Sir Bennett made my heart flutter with strange new feelings.

But ... it was becoming undeniable that there was something about Sir Derrick that drew me in a different way. Maybe it was only the fact that he held himself aloof and I needed the satisfaction of drawing him out. Whatever it was, I wanted to be honest with Sir Derrick. I had the feeling he would settle for nothing less.

"Yes, I like your friends," I admitted. "But I would like the chance to get to know you too."

His eyes held mine. He seemed to peer into my soul to test the weight of my words. I glanced away to the guard by the quarantine fence, who stiffened to attention as he'd finally recognized me. For a long moment, I waited for Sir Derrick to respond, to put me at ease with flattery, or something. When I finally looked at him, he was wearing a cocked grin. "If you insist, my lady. Then I shall give you a day you will not soon forget."

"I won't insist." I'm sure my cheeks had turned to flames. "If you'd rather not spend a day with me—"

"Only if you think you can put up with me for an entire day." His eyes twinkled.

My indignant retort faded. How could he be so irritatingly arrogant one moment and entirely endearing the next? I couldn't contain my smile. "It might be difficult to put up with you for that long, but I shall endeavor to try."

"Then you're a brave woman." He held out a hand. "Now, shall we get to work? After all, I've promised to be your slave for the afternoon. And I don't wish to break my word."

I crossed toward him and hoped I didn't appear too eager.

"What shall I do first, my lady?" He offered me the crook of his arm.

I slid my fingers against his strong flesh, hoping he couldn't feel me tremble at his nearness. "I don't suppose you'd be willing to find a way for me to cross into the infected area so I can check on my people?"

He started to shake his head, but when I turned the full force of my pleading eyes upon him, he stilled and studied my face. "I cannot do that, my lady. But what if we were to have the guard allow those who are well to come out of their homes so that you can talk to them from this side of the fence? Then you might encourage them from a safe distance."

His plan was fair and level-headed. In no time, he'd convinced the guard to allow me limited access. For a short while I was able to offer words of comfort and pass out the medicines I'd brought in my basket.

When we were done, Sir Derrick didn't oppose me when I stopped to visit some of the bedridden elderly who weren't in the affected area. I was surprised, but not displeased, when he joined me inside the dark huts. Although he didn't speak much, he was kind and attentive to the people and seemingly in no hurry to leave.

By the time I made my way out of the last home, a slight drizzle had begun to fall. I fell into an easy step next to Sir Derrick as we retreated toward the town gate that would lead to the castle.

"I thank you, sir, for your kindness in accompanying me today."

"'Twas my pleasure." He swung the basket in a carefree manner.

"I suppose it wasn't the most exciting afternoon you've ever had, especially compared to the tournaments and hunting and skirmishes you participate in."

"Exciting isn't the right word to describe the occasion," he said, earnestness hardening his face. "There's nothing exciting about seeing the suffering of others."

I nodded in understanding.

"But it was an amazing afternoon," he continued, observing me with an intensity that made me squirm. "You continue to surprise me. To feed the poor from your kitchen is one thing. But I hadn't expected that someone like you would trouble herself with visiting among them."

Even if his words weren't high praise, I still basked under his half-admission that I'd finally done something he liked. "And why wouldn't I visit among them, sir?"

"Because you certainly have more important things to do, like wear fancy gowns and enjoy dinner in the garden." The mockery in his tone was barely concealed.

"Shall I don rags and roll in the dirt?" I retorted. "Will I meet with your approval then?"

He didn't respond. Except for the slap of our steps, silence crept around us. And I couldn't help thinking that even though the three knights were in a contest to win my approval, somehow things had gotten turned around so that now I hoped to win his.

I chanced a sideways peek to see if I'd offended him. He glanced at me at the same moment and gave me one of his cocked grins. "Don't worry, my lady. If you want to roll in the dirt, there's no need to don rags. You can do it in your current attire." He glanced then at the dirt that caked the road and was now turning muddy in the mist.

"I'll do it, but only if you'll join me."

His grin quirked higher and his eyes flashed with appreciation for my wit.

I tried to hold back a smile of my own but failed dismally. I was surprised by how much I liked him, and I could no longer pretend indifference.

He stopped suddenly and faced me, his smile fading and a new seriousness taking the place of his mirth. "You've shown yourself to be a kind ruler. I can see now why your people love you."

"I only wish I could do more for them."

"Yes, there's a great deal more you can do."

His blunt honesty took me aback and left me speechless for a moment. I was used to the abbot reminding me of how much I already did and how my people couldn't possibly expect more.

The rain began to fall harder, and we resumed walking.

"The duke said that I'm a compassionate leader, that no one else could rule them better than I. Are you contradicting him?"

"No, my lady. Not in the least. They're blessed by God to have so kind a ruler."

"But you still think there's more I can do for my people?"

The rain pattered against the dirt road and sent splatters

of mud against my gown. The wimple covering my hair was beginning to grow damp.

"The kind acts you perform are very necessary. And they most certainly please God. But … you've been putting small bandages on a large, festering wound. Perhaps you must now consider how you might eliminate the wound altogether — or at the very least diminish it."

Again, I was unprepared for his honesty, but I couldn't fault him for it.

When the rain turned into a complete downpour, he lifted his face to the sky and let the drops pelt him. I could only watch him with wonder, trying to grasp the implications of all he'd spoken. Was there more I could be doing to help my people? If so, what?

As if realizing where he was and that I was garnering a soaking too, he reached for my hand and wrapped his fingers around mine in a strong, warm grip. "Come. We must make haste. I must deliver you back to the castle before you're drenched."

I didn't resist as he tugged me along. I had to half-run to keep up with him, but for a reason I couldn't explain, I was utterly happy. With my fingers against his and the loveliness of our time together warming my heart, I felt happy and free.

By the time we raced across the drawbridge, we were both breathless and laughing. We didn't stop until we crossed into the gatehouse. Finally out of the deluge, we could only stand gasping for air. Sir Derrick's brown hair was plastered to his head, and rivulets of rain ran down his face. His clothes were soaked and dripping. My gown was likewise, and strands of my hair stuck to my cheeks and neck.

Even though I surely resembled Pup after one of his baths, I wasn't self-conscious. I wasn't sure whether it was because Sir Derrick still held my hand or because he was smiling down at me. Whatever the case, I didn't want to break the contact with him.

As our breathing finally steadied, I could hear the rain pattering against the stone gatehouse with a lyrical rhythm. He dropped the basket to the ground and lifted his hand to my cheek. His fingers hovered for only a moment before he gently peeled a blond strand from my skin. My pulse sped to the same beat as the rain.

His smile faded, replaced by an intensity I couldn't understand but that filled me with greater urgency to know this man standing before me, to discover his deepest longings and fears, his past struggles, his present enjoyments, and his hopes for the future. I had the desire to reach out to him and comb a wet strand from his face, just as he'd done to mine.

But the sudden calling of my name from the outer bailey startled me. I stepped away from Sir Derrick, breaking the contact and forcing him to release my hand.

"Lady Rosemarie," called my porter as he ran through the downpour toward me, the rain pelting off his bald head and wide shoulders.

Even though I'd broken the physical contact with the knight, I couldn't break the hold his eyes had on me. His eyes, the color of the solid stone walls, encompassed me, drew me in, and refused to let me go.

Only when James stood next to me, his hulking frame towering over me, did I force myself to glance away.

"Your nursemaid has been sick with worry, my lady," James said with a bow. "She sent me to fetch you and bring you directly to your chambers."

"You may tell her I'll be along shortly." I wasn't ready to leave Sir Derrick just yet.

"She said I wasn't to return without you." James hunkered away from the castle as though he expected Trudy to come running after him with a broom in hand. "She's concerned that you may take a chill from being out in the rain."

Now that he mentioned it, I felt the cold dampness of my gown pressed against my fair skin, and I couldn't hold back a shudder. I crossed my arms, hugging myself for the warmth I lacked.

Sir Derrick frowned. "I agree with your nursemaid, my lady. You must hurry along and change out of your wet clothing."

As I allowed James to lead me away, I could feel Sir Derrick's gaze following me, blazing a trail of heat through my insides, regardless of how cold I was on the outside.

Chapter
12

I peered out the open window of my chamber, trying to get a glimpse of the arrival of another set of guests. But the inner wall of the castle stood in my line of vision, preventing me from viewing the arrivals that had been ongoing since morning.

"I really wish you and Abbot Francis Michael would stop worrying about me so much." I turned away from the window to Trudy, who had hovered at my side since I'd returned from town wet several days ago. I'd heeded her instructions to remain in bed, secluded from my guests, only because the abbot had insisted on it as well. When he'd discovered I'd gone near the infected area, he became concerned that I might fall ill. All it had taken was the mention of spreading disease among my guests for me to willingly seclude myself. The last thing I wanted was to bring the illness into the castle among the knights, and now the other nobles who were arriving for the festivities.

Trudy clucked her tongue as she finished pressing the last wrinkle from the gown I planned to wear to the dance that evening.

"We're only worried because we love you so much and don't want to see you hurt in any way by this whole grand scheme of the duke's."

I gave an exasperated sigh, just as I had done numerous times since I'd been confined to my room. Their protectiveness stemmed from love, just as my parents' had. But still, I longed for them to treat me more like an adult. Like Sir Derrick did. Perhaps that was one of the reasons why I had been unable to stop thinking about him since our walk home from town. He was kind, but he didn't treat me like I was fragile or breakable. Rather he seemed to push me to be better, to do more, and to rise higher. And I liked it.

Dare I say, I liked him?

"I only want what's safest and best for you." Trudy spread the pink gown out over the bed, its sheer layers and softness similar to so many of my gowns.

No one could deny that a life behind cloister walls would be the securest and most peaceful course for my life. "But what if what is safest and what is best for me require walking two divergent paths?"

Trudy shook her head, her flushed cheeks wobbling. "There you go again, speaking in a manner far above me."

"Did my parents do what was safe?" We both knew the answer without my saying it, but I answered the question anyway. "They chose the risky road, Trudy. They could have stayed back in the castle, locked themselves away, and let the people fend for themselves against the Plague. But instead, they went out and were willing to sacrifice their very lives if needed to do what they thought was right."

I paced across the room, treading the path in the rushes I'd already made during the afternoon of restlessness in my chamber. After days of solitude, I'd begun to feel like a caged songbird and I was ready to be set free again.

Trudy pressed her fisted hands against her hips, watching me and shaking her head. "Come sit down this instant. You're wearing me out with all your prowling."

But I couldn't stop. A peculiar need was driving me, the need to test the new feelings inside me. Somehow I knew I wouldn't be satisfied until I'd tested them to their fullest and found them wanting.

"Sometimes we have to take risks, even put our lives in jeopardy to do what's right."

"Oh, Rose," Trudy said, using my childhood nickname. Her face crumpled with concern. "More than anything, I want you to be happy. Whatever you choose, as long as you're happy, then I'll be happy."

I stopped in front of her and grasped her hands. "Then will you help me, Trudy? Will you help me discover what all these new feelings mean?"

"I don't know—"

A knock on the door echoed hollowly through the chamber. Trudy rushed to respond, and I again padded to the window and listened to the cheerful calls of men and women arriving and being escorted into the keep where my servants had guest rooms prepared.

When Trudy finally closed the door, she held a large bundle wrapped in a silver cloth. "The duke has sent you a gift for the dance tonight, my lady." She crossed to the bed and deposited the present. Slowly, she lifted the cloth and unveiled a luxurious, shimmering gown of deep crimson, glittering with pearls and diamonds embroidered on the sleeves, neckline, and waist.

We gasped together at the beauty and stared at it with open mouths.

"Did his servant say why he chose to bestow such a fine gift upon me?"

"He said the most beautiful woman in the kingdom deserves the most beautiful gown tonight." Trudy reverently brushed her fingers across the full skirt.

"It's magnificent," I whispered. But did I dare wear

something so fine and regal? I glanced at the pale pink gown I'd planned to don. Next to the red creation, it seemed plain and childish.

"He wanted you to know it's exactly the kind of gown your father would have given you for your first dance." Trudy's voice cracked. "He said your father would have wanted you to make your first public appearance looking like the woman you're becoming and not like the little girl you once were."

Another knock on the door interrupted us. Trudy bustled to answer and again spoke to a servant in the hallway before stepping back inside holding out a small box. "Another gift," she said, her eyes wide with wonder. "This one from Sir Collin."

I took the box, untied a pretty ribbon holding the lid shut, and then opened it. This time, Trudy's gasp was louder, echoing my inner wonder. There, enfolded in silk, was a necklace alternating diamonds and pearls from clasp to clasp.

"I can't accept this," I said in swift protest.

"The servant said you must have it. If you return it, Sir Collin will only send it right back."

I lifted the necklace from the box, letting it dangle from my fingers. The jewels sparkled in a dazzling array.

Something inside whispered that I couldn't accept such a gift from Sir Collin. As much as I'd enjoyed Sir Collin's bantering and easy ways, as much as I liked his goodness and generosity, my feelings for him weren't yet deep enough to take something so extraordinary.

"You must wear the necklace with the gown." Trudy bustled to the bed and spread out the rustling layers of the gown. "It matches so nicely."

A third knock sounded on the door and brought a smile to my nursemaid's face. "Another gift, my lady? Which knight do you think it's from this time?" She answered the door and talked with the servant in the hallway. "I was right," she said a moment later as she closed the door. Her ruddy face beamed as she brought forward a box. "Another gift."

Would it be from Sir Derrick? My heartbeat skittered forward at the thought. What would he send me? How would he choose to favor me?

The box was longer, and when I opened it I understood why. It was a long, sheer veil attached to a crown of red rosebuds interspersed with the purest white baby's breath.

"Oh, my lady." Trudy's words came out a reverent whisper. "How lovely."

It was exquisite. But I couldn't seem to summon the pleasure I knew I ought for such a gift. "It's from Sir Bennet?"

"Yes, my lady. How did you know?"

I couldn't quite say, except I had the feeling a gift from Sir Derrick would be different somehow.

I cast aside my strange disappointment and attempted to conjure appreciation for the headpiece. Sir Bennet was as thoughtful as always and certainly had an eye for beauty.

As Trudy began the process of preparing me for the dance, I couldn't stop waiting for the final rap on the door, the one that would bring Sir Derrick's gift. But as the hour passed silently, without any further interruptions, my heart filled with uncertainty. Surely he wouldn't neglect to send me something, not when his friends had taken such trouble to bestow such fine gifts upon me. Especially after the way we'd bantered in the rain. Had he misplaced his gift? Or forgotten?

But as the afternoon wore into evening, my heart pinched with the truth: he had not forgotten to give me a gift. He'd simply chosen not to.

Chapter
13

"*Are you ready, dear one?*" *The duke tucked my* hand more securely into the crook of his arm.

I stared at the massive doors of the Great Hall and swallowed hard. "Yes, I believe so."

Dressed in a knee-length doublet with polished silver buttons, the duke stood tall, his face clear of worry, his eyes brimming with pride. "Your father and mother would have been delighted to see the beautiful young woman you've become."

I glanced at the full crimson skirt, at the tight-fitting waist and bodice that shaped me perfectly, and at the diamonds and pearls that sparkled brilliantly. "I know I've already said it a hundred times, but thank you for the gown. I've never worn anything like it."

He smiled down at me. "You deserve something special to celebrate this occasion."

"Thank you, your Grace." I stood on tip-toes and kissed his cheek as I would have my father. "I don't know what I'd do without you."

"Then you've forgiven me for throwing your future plans into disarray?"

"There's nothing to forgive. I've realized I can't shy away from this challenge out of fear." I'd opened my heart to the knights, I'd made myself vulnerable to love. I didn't want to think about what would happen at the end of the month if I wasn't in love with one of them. Even worse, what if one of them didn't fall in love with me?

"Shall we proceed?" the duke asked.

I nodded, swallowing my nervousness once again.

As the duke signaled the guards standing at attention to open the doors, I resisted the urge to let my fingers flutter to the diamonds and pearls that circled my neck or to the veil of roses gracing my head. Instead, I once again felt the sting of Sir Derrick's slight. I lifted my chin, though, and hoped he would see the gifts the other two had given me and realize his mistake. At the very least, I'd determined to thank Sir Collin and Sir Bennet generously by paying them all my attention. If Sir Derrick was making it clear that he didn't want to court me, then why should I spend my remaining time considering him? Especially when I only had two weeks left.

The doors swung wide and a sudden hush fell over the guests. The duke squeezed my hand and together we started into the large room with its high vaulted ceilings, arched stained glass windows, lush tapestries, and a long strip of gold carpet that had been rolled down the center of the room for my entrance. I could feel all eyes on me, curious yet admiring. I kept a smile on my lips and glided forward through the room, grateful for the strong, steady presence of the duke at my side.

He delivered me regally to my place, and then, after pushing in my chair, he took his seat next to me. The three young knights joined him that evening as guests of honor at the head table.

Throughout the dinner, Sir Collin and Sir Bennet carried on a lively conversation with me. Although I was tempted to glance at Sir Derrick positioned farther down the table, I refrained. He seemed disinclined to enter into my discussion anyway. I tried to pretend that I didn't care, that I was completely happy speaking with and spending time with Sir Collin and Sir Bennet. Why should I not be? They were both entertaining and thoughtful. And I truly harbored fondness for them both.

Nevertheless, after the time with Sir Derrick in town earlier in the week and the moment in the gatehouse when we'd been dripping wet but happy, I'd expected him to begin showing me more attention and making an effort to seek me out. But he seemed content to sit back and converse with those around him without so much as a glance in my direction.

I tried not to admit how much it hurt.

After the feast, the duke escorted me around the room and introduced me to the guests, many whom I hadn't seen since my father and mother had died. I was pleasantly surprised at how much I enjoyed mingling among them and was secretly relieved the Baron of Caldwell and his wife weren't there. I wasn't sure I could have endured thinking about Thomas and the possibility I could have been married to him by now if only I'd known about the exception much earlier.

By the time my servants had cleared the remains of the meal and the musicians began to play, I'd grown more relaxed, so that when the dance started I only had to fight a few nervous tingles.

Sir Collin and Sir Bennet fought over me for each of the dances, at first good-naturedly. But after several dances, I sensed a growing tension between them. As they grudgingly took turns twirling me and making me laugh, I told myself I wasn't disappointed that Sir Derrick hadn't come to claim at least one dance. I only hoped he would look on from time to time and see that I was happy with the other two men. And secretly, I wished him to be jealous, even if just slightly.

"May I have a dance with the queen of the hall?" The duke

smiled at me over Sir Collin's shoulder, which fortunately was healing well and now only required a bandage.

"Only one dance, your Grace." Sir Collin relinquished me with a wink. "I can't bear to be apart from Lady Rosemarie for longer than that."

The duke took Sir Collin's place, towering above me, his eyes gentle as he gazed down at me.

"You look like you're having a wonderful time tonight," he said as the musicians started another tune.

"I'm having a delightful evening." I smiled up at him. "I cannot thank you enough for giving me this experience—even if only once in my life. I shall remember this night always."

The duke's brow wrinkled. "Then you're not taking a liking to any of the three knights? I thought for sure you would have some developing affection for at least one of them by now."

"Oh yes, I like them all very much."

He studied my face as we danced.

"They're all very kind and sweet," I reassured him.

"But none of them are stirring deeper feelings and interest within you?"

I hesitated in responding, wanting to be truthful with the duke. Had I begun to experience deeper feelings for any of the men?

My jumbled thoughts returned to the moment in the gatehouse with Sir Derrick, when we'd returned from town, to the desires that had swelled in my chest to be with him longer and know him better. The longing had been keen—and yes, different from anything I'd felt so far when I was with Sir Collin and Sir Bennet. Even now, I couldn't keep from stealing a glance in Sir Derrick's direction.

The duke followed my gaze. "Ah, I see."

I snapped my attention back to the duke.

"You're interested in Sir Derrick." He stated it so simply that I couldn't help but believe him.

Even so, a denial quickly pushed for releases. "Oh no, your Grace. He has no interest in me. He didn't even give me gifts like the others."

"Perhaps his gifts are different than theirs."

"And he hasn't planned a special day for me yet."

"He told me he's working on it."

I shook my head with mounting frustration at myself for caring so much. Why couldn't the attention of the other two be enough? "I shouldn't complain," I said, forcing a smile. "I'm perfectly content with Sir Collin and Sir Bennet. They're both wonderful men."

"But ..." The duke held my gaze, demanding honesty.

I sighed. "But I don't understand why Sir Derrick hasn't sought me out like the others. Perhaps he doesn't like me."

The duke smiled. "Knowing Sir Derrick as I do, I have no doubt he likes you. He just may need slightly more convincing that you do indeed want his company."

Suddenly, I knew with certainty that I not only wanted his company, I longed for it—perhaps more than the others. But I could hardly admit that to the duke, could I?

The music began to slow, signaling the end of the dance.

"Shall I inform Sir Derrick of your desire to dance with him next?"

The duke's question shot a streak of panic through me. "Your Grace, I couldn't possibly—"

"Have courage, Lady Rosemarie," my wise friend gently admonished. "Besides, I shall be discreet in relaying your desire to him." He didn't give me the chance to protest further, but instead stalked over to the head table.

Sir Collin was at my side in an instant, claiming me for the next dance. Sir Bennet was close behind.

"You had the last dance with Lady Rosemarie," the dark-haired knight spoke stiffly behind Sir Collin, his blue eyes shimmering with barely concealed anger. "It's my turn now."

Sir Collin's fingers at my waist tightened and his smile turned brittle. "You're mistaken, my friend. Lady Rosemarie has been waiting to dance with me again, haven't you, my lady?" I could hardly muster a response. My stomach was too aflutter and my hands damp. My focus was on the duke as he approached Sir Derrick. He interrupted the young knight's conversation with the two men standing at the side of the table, whispered something in Sir Derrick's ear, and finally stood back, crossing his arms over his chest and smiling with satisfaction.

Sir Derrick slowly turned to look at me, his gaze immediately spanning the distance, crashing into mine and taking my breath away. One of his brows lifted, as if questioning the truth of whatever the duke had whispered to him.

I rapidly dropped my gaze and pretended to focus on Sir Collin. But Sir Collin had grown quiet. Behind him, Sir Bennet's brows had come together into a scowl. At first I thought they'd witnessed the duke's interaction with Sir Derrick, but then I realized they were too busy glaring at each other to notice anything else.

The music for the next dance began, and this time the tune was slower. I smiled at Sir Collin and Sir Bennet as brightly as I could. "We have plenty of dances left."

But neither returned my smile. Their usual lightheartedness had dissipated. Instead their features were taut, their bodies tense.

"You're not being fair," Sir Bennet ground out between his teeth.

"You know as well as I do there can only be one winner to the contest," Sir Collin replied lightly, although his eyes were hard.

Sir Bennet took a step toward Sir Collin and placed a hand on his shoulder—the injured shoulder.

Sir Collin winced but shoved Sir Bennet's chest.

Sir Bennet squeezed Sir Collin's shoulder before letting go, a warning in his eyes. "Play by the rules."

Sir Collin's grip on my waist didn't lessen. "I didn't know we had any rules." With that, he smiled and spun away from Sir Bennet. But before he had the chance to complete the rotation, he bumped into Sir Derrick.

Sir Derrick ignored Sir Collin and Sir Bennet. Instead, he looked at me and said nothing, as though he were waiting for my acknowledgement. The other two knights would have flattered me to put me at ease. But he was different, somehow bolder and requiring boldness of me at the same time.

My heartbeat tripped like a bumbling dancer. I didn't know what to say, especially in front of the other two men. I could only offer Sir Derrick a tentative smile and hope that he could read the welcome in my eyes.

As if seeing what he wanted in my unspoken message, he offered Sir Collin an apologetic nod. "I hope you'll forgive me for cutting in on you, my friend. But I couldn't let the evening pass without claiming at least one dance with Lady Rosemarie."

Sir Collin gave a short laugh and nodded toward Sir Bennet, whose scowl had darkened. "I suggest getting in line." He started to pull away from the two, but Sir Derrick's thick arm shot out and blocked his friend.

The steel in Sir Derrick's eyes was suddenly sharp. "Why don't we leave it up to Lady Rosemarie to pick which of the three of us she wants to dance with next?"

I could feel Sir Collin stiffen at the challenge. I certainly didn't want to hurt any of their feelings, but I didn't know how it was possible to choose one of them without creating more tension.

"If she chooses you," Sir Derrick continued, "then Bennet and I will bow out of your way and won't offer a word of protest for the rest of the night."

Would Sir Derrick relinquish me that easily? I caught a glimmer in his eyes that was almost taunting, as though he knew I would pick him over the other men.

His overconfidence stirred my ire. I ought to turn my back on him and hold out my hand to Sir Bennet. From the way the young knight had stared at my mouth during a couple of the dances, he was bound to steal a kiss from me before the night was over. Maybe I'd let him do so at a moment when Sir Derrick could witness it.

But as soon as the thought rushed through my mind, I silently chastised myself. I wasn't planning to give away my first kiss out of spite. But I would show Sir Derrick that I wasn't pining away after him.

I took a step away from Sir Collin and lifted my chin. "Very well. I shall give Sir Derrick this next dance. I can do nothing less since he finally gathered the courage to ask me."

I'd questioned Sir Derrick's courage once before and earned his quick censure. So I wasn't surprised when his eyes narrowed and his nostrils flared. He brushed past Sir Collin and took his place in front of me. Without waiting for my permission, he placed his hands upon my waist as the dance required.

I sucked in a breath at the contact, at the strength of his fingers, and at the closeness of his body. Then, catching myself, I placed my hands upon his arms and prayed he wouldn't feel the trembling in my fingers.

For several minutes we danced silently and stiffly about the Great Hall, mingling with the other couples. He kept a proper distance between us, but nevertheless, I felt as though I would be scorched under the heat of his hand at my waist. Part of me whispered that I needed to apologize for insulting his courage.

JODY HEDLUND

But I couldn't seem to find the words, and even if I could, I wasn't sure I'd be able to force them past the constricting bodice of my gown and the tightness of my jeweled necklace.

"You dance well for your first dance." He finally broke the silence between us.

"Thank you, sir. You dance well too."

The words were as stiff as our movements. We might have been marionettes held by a puppeteer's strings.

I had wished to dance with him, to be near him. And now that I was, I was ruining the moment with my silly pride. I struggled to find a way to bring about a peace between us.

He finally sighed, his warm breath caressing my forehead. "My lady," he started, his voice soft, almost apologetic.

I couldn't resist glancing up into his eyes. The candlelight that shimmered from the wall sconces reflected warmly there. I could see that he was making a noble effort at a truce.

Relief sifted through me and relaxed my muscles.

"I'm glad you chose to dance with me," he admitted in almost a whisper. He glanced off for a moment before taking a deep breath and making another confession. "I'm not sure how much longer I could have held myself back."

My heartbeat sped forward. "I didn't think you noticed me in the least."

"How could I not?" His voice was low with an intimacy that whispered across my nerves.

I had to work hard for several seconds to still the thrumming of my heart before I could respond. "I know you don't lack courage, sir," I said, offering my own apology. "So if fear wasn't holding you back, then what was?"

He didn't speak for a long moment. Instead he glanced away to the other dancers. "I cannot rightly seek out your attention, my lady, especially when it's not mine to gain."

"Of course it is."

Regret pooled in his eyes, a regret that did nothing to ease my inner churning. "I've already determined I shall not stand in the way of my friends winning your heart."

At his confession, we glided in step to the dance for a few silent moments. But questions clamored through my mind. Why did he feel thus inclined? Why would he acquiesce to his friends so easily?

"I don't understand." I struggled to keep from sounding desperate. "Why would you not want to participate in your master's plans? Have I done something to offend you? Have you found me wanting?"

"No, my lady," he responded rapidly in a harsh whisper. "I beg you not to think there is anything wrong with you." His grip on my waist tightened, and he drew me imperceptibly closer so that I could almost hear the pounding of his heart-beat. "The more I've gotten to know you, the more I admire you." The confession fell from his lips.

"I know I still have much to learn—"

"Yes. We all do," he said as his dance steps slowed almost to a halt. "But I cannot fault you, though I have tried."

"Then what?" I asked too quickly. "What prevents you from seeking my heart?"

"'Tis me." The muscles in his jaw flexed. "I'm a poor, land-less knight with naught to offer you. I have no wealth, no power, no prestige, and ..." His voice dropped so that I had to silence my breathing to hear him. "I have no family name and no family honor."

His last words were spoken with such loathing that I knew I couldn't argue with him. Instead I squeezed his tense arm. "Perhaps I have need of none of those things."

He shook his head, and I could see from the determination in his eyes that he'd already made up his mind. "My friends are good men. The best in all the land. And they are much more deserving of you than I could ever be."

Even as he spoke the words, I could sense Sir Collin watching me from a side table where he stood sipping ale with the duke. I could also sense Sir Bennet's eyes on me from the opposite side of the room where he'd gone to admire the castle's artwork, which I'd requested be put on display for the dance.

They were both fine men. I'd do very well to fall in love with either one of them. But did they have the qualities I most needed in a husband? I wasn't exactly sure what those qualities were, but I realized that I coveted deeper sharing, honest relating, and common passion for the same causes.

I hadn't experienced that yet ... except perhaps with Derrick.

I focused on Derrick's chest, lest he see the truth in my eyes and it scare him away from me even more. What could I do to change his mind, especially when he was already decided against wooing me? Would I need to woo him instead? And if so, how?

A sudden scream rent the air. The music trailed to a discordant halt, and a woman's distraught voice cried out, "My husband! He's been poisoned!"

Chapter
14

I CROUCHED BESIDE THE NOBLEMAN SPRAWLED ON THE floor. A dark stain had formed around the man's mouth. His eyes rolled back into his head, and each breath was deep and labored.

The woman who kneeled next to the nobleman wept openly, her cries mingling with the gasps and anxious murmurings of the other guests.

Lady Rosemarie started to kneel next to me, but I caught the eye of the duke. One look was all it took for the older knight to guide Rosemarie a safe distance away.

I began to loosen the mantle and shirt of the nobleman, hoping to make the man's breathing easier. "Tell the cook to bring me a decoction of black hellebore to purge this man's stomach," I called to a nearby servant, who immediately ran off to do my bidding.

"Can he be saved?" Sir Bennet asked, lowering to one knee. His features creased with worry.

"It depends on how much poison he consumed and how quickly it reaches his blood." I began to roll up the nobleman's shirtsleeve, knowing I would need to do the bloodletting myself because the physician wouldn't be able to arrive in time. I'd done it before on the battlefield and the thought of doing so again didn't scare me. "Do we know the source of the poison yet?"

Sir Bennet nodded toward a silver goblet lying on the floor surrounded by a pool of strange-colored ale.

"The ale was poisoned?" I surveyed the room and the numerous cups of ale that many of the guests were still holding. Cold fear slithered through me. How many more people would suffer?

"Take away the ale," I ordered another servant standing nearby. "Dump every last drop into the moat."

"I don't think that will be necessary," Sir Bennet said gravely. "I don't believe anyone else is at risk."

But already the guests were abandoning their goblets, their faces drawn with worry.

Sir Bennet held a goblet in his own hand. He glanced inside to the spicy liquid and then swirled it in a circular motion. When he raised his eyes, they were as dark and murky as the ale. "I have already sipped from this goblet," he said in a low, almost dazed voice.

"Are you ill?" I appraised my friend, checking for signs of poisoning.

"I'm perfectly fine." Sir Bennet stared at the spilled goblet on the floor nearby. "But it should be me lying on the floor at death's door."

"No one should be lying on the floor." My keen gaze penetrated the crowd, searching for signs that anyone else was suffering.

"Yes," Sir Bennet insisted. "The poison was meant for me."

"How can you be sure?"

Sir Bennet stared back and forth between the two goblets again, before his gaze came to rest on the one that had spilled. "That one was mine." It did indeed have a special crest of small jewels around the base, the same as the other goblets given to those seated at the head table.

My pulse slowed to a crawl as I tried to make sense of my friend's words.

"I was looking at the artwork with Baron York. We set our goblets down together on the table, and when we came back I must have grabbed the wrong one. We were talking. And neither of us were paying much heed."

"Then apparently someone put the poison in your cup while your back was turned?"

Sir Bennet's normally sun-browned face had turned pale. "It would seem that someone intended to murder me."

My nerves were suddenly on edge, my senses on high alert. If someone had intended to murder Sir Bennet, then that person was likely still in the Great Hall. Was it one of the servants mingling among the guests? A disgruntled nobleman? An enemy disguised as a friend?

My mind rapidly assessed all the possibilities. Who would have motivation to kill Bennet?

A sudden unsettling thought barreled into me. Was it possible that someone wanted to murder the three of us so that Lady Rosemarie would have no choice but to enter the convent?

I glanced to the head table, where the abbot had sat all evening without moving from his chair. Even now with all the commotion, the abbot remained in his spot. His forehead was creased with worry, and he'd pushed his goblet of ale away, obviously no longer interested in drinking the beverage for fear of the poisoning.

I leaned back on my heels and peered around the room, searching for the culprit. Nevertheless, my gaze came to rest again on the abbot's tonsured head.

From the start, I'd sensed the abbot's reticence to our arrival. But surely he wasn't so strongly against Lady Rosemarie getting married that he would resort to murdering her only prospects.

It was a ludicrous idea.

Of course honoring the Ancient Vow was important. And of course becoming a nun was a sacred and valuable service to God. But surely the abbot couldn't begrudge Lady Rosemarie the chance to test whether that was truly God's will for her or not.

Unless he had something more to gain by her entering the convent.

I could only shake my head. I couldn't—wouldn't—allow myself to think that the abbot was connected in any way with the attempted murders. As a knight, I was bound to believe the best about someone until proven otherwise.

I let the abbot's gentle hands smooth my hair back. But neither the abbot's comforting gesture, the cool night air, nor the glorious fragrance from my roses could soothe my troubled heart.

"I'm sorry, my child," the abbot said again, as he had many times since I'd kneeled before him in the garden.

The physician had finally arrived at the castle, and the knights had helped move the poisoned nobleman to his chamber. But no one held out much hope that Baron York would live through the night.

While the other guests had retired to their rooms, I'd fled to my garden for solace. Abbot Francis Michael had been kind enough to follow me, but I wasn't sure anything—not even his meditations about life and death—could take away the pain of knowing a man was dying in my home ... on account of me.

I'd overheard Sir Bennet's confession that he'd accidentally picked up the wrong goblet, that the poison had been intended for him.

If only I'd never agreed to the dance. If only I'd refused to have the guests. If only I'd decided against the duke's plans in the first place ... then the nobleman wouldn't be lying on his bed in agony and gasping his last breath.

"There you are, dear one," came the duke's voice from behind me. The flicker of torchlight illuminated the nook of my garden. "I've been looking for you everywhere and was beginning to get worried that someone had kidnapped you."

At the duke's presence, I raised my head and straightened my shoulders, hoping I appeared more controlled than I felt.

"How's Baron York?" I asked of the duke, only to find that his three knights stood behind him along with the sheriff and bailiff.

"He's still alive." The duke drew closer, the torchlight causing my red dress to shimmer like dancing flames of fire.

I breathed in the night air, praying as I had for the past hour that God would spare the man's life. "Have we discovered any clues as to who might be responsible for these murder attempts?"

My gaze flitted over Sir Bennet, with his dark, chiseled handsomeness, and Sir Collin, with his carefree, windswept attractiveness. Both of their faces were hard, all traces of the usual flattery and humor gone. I was sure they were both thinking just as I was how close they'd come to losing their lives. And even though I didn't want Baron York to lose his life, I would have been inconsolable had the murderer hit his target with either of the knights. I'd only known them two weeks, but it was long enough that I'd grown to care about them. Maybe I hadn't fallen in love with them, but I couldn't bear to think of either one dying.

Sir Derrick stepped out of the shadows, and my attention flew to him like a moth to light. My pulse ceased to beat. What if the murderer struck again? Would Sir Derrick be the next target?

The very thought pierced my heart.

"We've already scoured the kitchen," the sheriff said, stepping forward. "But I'm planning to search each of the guest rooms tonight."

"Surely we don't suspect any of the nobles?"

"I'm not ruling out any possibilities." The sheriff glanced with narrowed eyes at Sir Derrick.

"Then, until we can locate the murderer," I said, "I think we should cancel the festivities."

"But we're running out of time," the duke said. "After the other delays, we have only two weeks left until your eighteenth birthday."

In the darkness of the garden with the expanse of stars overhead, I glanced up at the abbot. I'd expected him to readily agree with my assessment to cancel the activities. But instead of acquiescence, he shook his head. "I may not agree with the worldliness of these affairs, but now that you're almost halfway through the month, I don't want to encourage you to stop. If by some chance love has blossomed inside you already, I would not want to be the one to pluck the bloom."

Was two additional weeks enough? The very thought of so little time left was disheartening.

"I wouldn't want you to resent me for the rest of your life," he continued, "for stopping you from at least seeing what might happen."

If I ceased now, would I always wonder what might have happened?

My attention flickered to Derrick. His face was taut, his expression unreadable.

If I was completely honest with myself, I knew I didn't want to stop. Not yet. Not until I'd had the chance to explore the strange feelings I'd felt lately.

"But what of the safety of the knights and my guests? What if the murderer strikes again? What if next time he succeeds?"

The abbot glanced at the young knights with narrowed brow. "If these men are the three strongest and most valiant knights in the land, then they'll be able to protect themselves now that the threat is known."

"What of my guests?"

"We shall post extra guards," the duke suggested. "And for the remainder of the festivities we'll use extra caution and vigilance, especially for Lady Rosemarie."

I wanted to contradict both men. If the murderer had struck twice with such ease, what would prevent him from doing so again?

Through the flickering torchlight, I met Sir Derrick's gaze. I studied the clouded depths of his eyes, surprised that I wished for his advice in the matter. I could count on him to be honest with me. He spoke what was on his mind without thought of flattery. And I valued that quality.

What do you think I should do?

As if sensing my question, he lifted his chin, his hard expression admonishing me to be brave and face the danger.

"Very well," I said slowly. "We shall continue with our plans."

I'd pray for courage to keep going in spite of the threats that hung over us. But perhaps I'd also pray that somehow I could convince Sir Derrick to fight to win my heart.

Chapter
15

"All three knights are incredibly handsome," said one of the young ladies near me.

I sat at the center of the ladies in my grand chair, which had been placed under the shade of the splendid tent along the side of the field. We'd gathered to watch the jousting tournament, all dressed in beautiful gowns with flowing headpieces.

"You're so lucky to have their attention, my lady," the young woman spoke again, staring into the list — the fenced-off area where the knights were preparing for the first joust. Most of the young noblewomen were married, but a few single daughters had come to join the festivities with their parents.

I watched the proceedings with fascination. I hadn't witnessed a jousting tournament since my parents had died. Yet even if the proceedings were grander than what I remembered, I was aware of what was expected of me. As the queen of the tournament, I'd need to bestow my favor upon one of the knights. And even though I wanted to be fair to all three of my suitors, I'd already determined to reward that favor to the knight who wore the coat of arms with the red dragon. I must properly thank him for his rescue of the criminals that day in the marketplace. He deserved it, and my townspeople would expect it.

After getting to know the three men, I was convinced the red dragon knight and Sir Derrick were one and the same. Today, I would discover for certain.

The few unattached women around me were giggling and making eyes at the knights who had begun to assemble in front of us. Upon their snorting mounts and decked in their gleaming armor, they were indeed a sight to behold. And yet I didn't see the fire-breathing dragon among the coats of arms displayed by the various noblemen participating in the tournament.

Maybe a part of me hoped that by awarding Sir Derrick my favor for the tournament, he'd change his mind and decide to try to win me after all. But what if he didn't? How could I gain his interest in participating with Sir Collin and Sir Bennet?

I took a deep breath and turned to the lady closest to me. I forced out the question before I lost my nerve. "What kinds of things do you do when you wish to show a man that you're interested in him?"

The ladies around me tittered.

Heat rushed into my face, and I wished I could take back my question.

"Oh it's easy, my lady," said one of the married ladies.

'Twould not be easy for me, not in the least. But I bit back the words.

"You must smile at him a lot," said one pretty young woman.

"And ask him questions about himself," said another.

"Make sure to compliment him for his brave deeds."

"If possible, single him out for a conversation."

"Sit next to him."

"Always laugh at his jokes."

The suggestions overwhelmed me. How would I ever accomplish such things, especially with Sir Derrick? But what other choice did I have? He'd made it clear at the dance last evening that he was determined not to pursue me, even if he wanted to. That he'd stood back to allow his noble friends to win my heart.

I gave a soft sigh.

Of all three knights, why was I most drawn to the one who wanted me the least? Why couldn't my heart react to Sir Collin or Sir Bennet with the same measure it did to Sir Derrick? I'd spent the least time with him, and yet I found myself thinking about him the most.

The ladies grew suddenly silent. At the sight of the duke in his brilliantly polished armor approaching the list with his three knights riding behind him, my body tensed in anticipation. The sound of trumpeters heralded their appearance. They trotted gallantly toward me, and the knights who were already waiting parted to let them approach. When the men were lined up in front of me on their warhorses, my heart finally resumed its beating, albeit at twice the pace.

"Lady Rosemarie," the duke greeted me once the trumpets had faded. He held his helmet under his arm. "We're ready for the tournament to begin."

The sunshine poured down on the three noble knights decked in their best plate armor, their helmets concealing their faces. I couldn't keep my gaze from straying to the one wearing the emblem of the red dragon. From the stiff but bold way the knight sat on his steed, I now had no doubt it was Sir Derrick.

"Before you begin your day of fighting ..." I stood and spoke the words expected of me. "I would like to bestow my favor upon one of the knights."

"Would you like the men to remove their helmets, Lady Rosemarie?" the duke asked.

I shook my head. "There's no need, your Grace."

His brow quirked. He was correct in assuming that I didn't know for sure which man sat behind each helmet. But for me, it didn't matter.

Along the opposite side of the list, dangling along the makeshift fences and congregating on benches that had been erected, the town—at least those not quarantined and dying from the sudden outbreak of disease—had come out to witness the tournament. My people already were murmuring, clearly recognizing the red dragon emblem. Honoring the bearer of that emblem would send the message that I would reward kindness and bravery and that I wouldn't tolerate torture.

I slid my gauzy scarf out from around my neck. It was pale blue, the color of the gown I'd worn, and it matched the cloudless blue sky overhead. As I held it out, the silk fluttered in the gentle summer breeze.

"I wish you all good health and fortune this day." I glanced at each man, including the other noblemen who'd gathered to participate in the jousting. "I pray the best man will win."

Only then did I let my gaze land upon the knight with the red dragon. "But although I wish you all my favor, I must bestow a special blessing upon only one."

The crowd grew silent.

I pointed the scarf toward Sir Derrick—or at least I believed it to be him. "Sir, this is for you."

As the red dragon knight bowed upon his steed, the townspeople erupted into clapping and cheering. The knight spurred his horse toward me, pulling it alongside the tent in front of where I stood. I had to bend to hand him the scarf, and as I did so I caught a glimpse of gray eyes through the slit in his helmet.

It was indeed Sir Derrick.

The intensity in his eyes sent a shimmer of anticipation through my chest and into my heart.

He reached for the scarf, but for an instant I clung to it, suddenly needing to do something more that would let him know my favor went deeper than mere gratefulness for his daring deed with the criminals in the marketplace.

The advice of the women rushed back through my mind. This was neither the place nor the time to begin a conversation with him or ask him questions. But I could smile at him, couldn't I? And compliment him?

"I wish you well today," I whispered, giving him what I hoped was my prettiest smile. "I'm sure you'll be glorious."

When I released my grip on the scarf, he didn't budge. Instead he leaned in closer. "And when I win the tournament, my lady, what shall you bestow upon me then?"

"What will make you happy, sir?" I repeated the words I'd spoken to him that day in town when he'd accompanied me with my deliveries to the poor.

His eyes crinkled at the corners, the sign of his smile and his remembrance of the question I'd asked. "I shall think on it."

"Then I'll be anxiously awaiting your answer."

His gaze dropped to my lips. His eyes darkened, and the crinkles disappeared. "Perhaps I'll lay claim to my reward at the day's end."

My heart gave an unexpected flip. I didn't know quite what to make of his words, except that perhaps he might claim a kiss from me.

He started to back away. I couldn't let him ride away without encouraging him further. "If you wish to lay claim, sir, then make sure you win."

The crinkles returned to his eyes and merriment danced to life there. He said nothing more as he rode away. But he lifted my scarf high into the air toward the townspeople, earning more cheers and whistles.

My spirit stayed high the rest of the day. I found myself enjoying the company of the other ladies, even if their banter was inconsequential and about matters that hardly interested me. As the day progressed and my servants brought me news that the poisoned nobleman still lived and was recovering, I found myself appreciating the tournament even more.

The knights took turns charging at each other, gradually eliminating all but the best. Of course, the three noble knights were among the men left unseated for the final rounds. Yet, I was more than a little relieved when Sir Collin and Sir Bennet were finally bested, leaving Sir Derrick in the last joust of the day with one of the other noblemen. How would I have chosen whom to cheer for without stirring more angst between them? I supposed it was inevitable that I would have to single one of them out for more attention. If I was to have any chance of getting married in less than two weeks, I couldn't dawdle in making a decision. And that meant narrowing down the prospects to one.

Was Sir Derrick that one? Even though he didn't choose to be?

Throughout the day, I'd learned that Sir Derrick had apparently already gained a reputation throughout the realm for his jousting skills. Even so, I couldn't mask my nervousness when he took his place at the end of the long list and positioned his lance in one arm for the charge.

The herald finished recounting their great deeds and then sounded the trumpet. The loud blare pushed me to the edge of my chair, and I gripped the armrests until my knuckles turned white.

Sir Derrick dug his spurs into his warhorse and jolted forward. Dust from the hot afternoon swirled around the horse's thundering hooves. Sir Derrick picked up momentum, aiming his lance at the crest of his opponent's shield. The other knight had done likewise, and they galloped at full speed toward one another.

My fear rose, almost as palpable as the stench of horseflesh and sweat.

Sir Derrick rode straight and tall, the tail of my scarf gliding in the wind from his helmet, where he'd tied it. The strength in his arm didn't waver. His lance was unswerving. The power of his body matched that of his beast.

Even so, I had to keep from closing my eyes in a grimace at the moment of impact between the two knights. Their lances cracked against each other's shields with deafening booms. The impact jarred both of them, and Sir Derrick struggled to stay atop his horse, gripping the beast with his thighs and righting himself just in time. But his opponent was not so fortunate. He wobbled and then slipped off, falling to the ground with a thud that surely knocked the wind from him.

My breath whooshed out too—containing more relief than I'd realized.

The crowd broke into wild cheering. Sir Derrick had been their favorite all day, just as he'd been mine, even though I'd done my best to cheer all the knights equally.

When he reached the other end of the list and reined his horse, he turned. At the sight of his opponent still on the ground, unmoving, Sir Derrick spurred his horse back toward the knight, jumped off, tore of his helmet, and threw himself on the ground next to the man. He'd already loosened the man's headgear by the time the squires reached their master.

I watched, each of my breaths tight with worry. A jousting tournament was likely to be riddled with danger and injuries. I'd been thankful that so far the day had been uneventful. Except for the usual scrapes and bruises, no one had been injured.

After several tense moments, the knight on the ground finally lifted an arm, allowing Sir Derrick to help him to a sitting position. After a few more minutes, Sir Derrick positioned his arm around the nobleman's waist and helped him to his feet.

"'Twould appear Sir Derrick is the champion," said one of the young ladies sitting nearby.

"Why am I not surprised?" laughed another of the women.

"What will you reward him, Lady Rosemarie?"

The questions and chatter flowed around me, bringing back the memory of my promise to him earlier in the day and sending warmth into my stomach. What would he request of me? I didn't dare think he might actually ask for a kiss.

And if he did . . . would I give it?

I shivered, but not from cold.

"He'll likely want a full purse of silver," said one of the ladies. "After all, he owns nothing and has no prospects, unless the duke or High King is yet planning to reward him for his service to the country."

"He has no family estates awaiting his return?" I couldn't keep the question from escaping, although the moment it left my lips, I regretted asking. I ought not ask for information that Sir Derrick had not willingly given me.

Of course he'd told me he had no wealth or family honor, but I hadn't supposed that meant he was completely landless.

"I don't know Sir Derrick's entire background," said the woman next to me. "But I've heard rumors that his father once ruled lands far to the north. When Sir Derrick was but a lad, his father's castle was attacked by a rival lord who massacred the entire family. If not for a nursemaid who escaped with Sir Derrick, he would have been killed too."

"Oh my," I whispered, horrified to think of the pain Sir Derrick had suffered at losing his entire family in such a brutal manner. My gaze chased after him as he assisted the injured nobleman to his tent.

Even when he made his way back to the list a few minutes

later, amidst the wild cheering of the crowd, a strange ache had wrapped around my heart and wouldn't let go.

Sir Collin and Sir Bennet surrounded Sir Derrick, along with his squires, patting him on the back and congratulating him in high fashion. They guided him toward my tent and didn't stop until they'd congregated below me. Sir Derrick's hair was plastered to his head, his forehead grazed with several cuts, and his cheeks coasted with the dust of the field. Even so, my pulse raced forward with unusual speed at the sight of his face angled up at me, with his grin wide with pride and his eyes bright with victory.

"Lady Rosemarie," he called with a gallant bow. "As the champion of this tournament, I have come to dedicate my victories to you."

With a smile, I rose. A servant proffered a red velvet pillow with a crown of laurels resting upon it. I lifted the crown. "Sir, I accept your dedication, and in return I bestow upon you this crown. You have fought valiantly, and we honor you."

I had to lean over the edge of the gallery to place the crown upon his bent head. And when he straightened, I found my gaze colliding with his bold one, reminding me that I owed him much more than a wreath of greens.

Chapter
16

I neared the head table, my hand resting on the duke's arm. The warm summer breeze teased my hair, which Trudy had arranged in long, dangling curls. My steps were light and my heart sang in tune to the lutes the minstrels were playing.

At my approach, the guests had risen from their tables, which were arranged in a U shape around a center stage where everyone would enjoy the play-actors' open-air performance after the feast. As I climbed the steps of the raised dais where the guests of honor sat, I could feel Derrick's attention on me from the end of the head table. In fact, I'd sensed him watching me from the moment I'd started across the field and toward the tables the servants had arranged for the feast.

I hadn't dared to look at him for fear he'd see the anticipation that had been building within me all the while Trudy and the other servants had been bathing and dressing me, ridding me of the dust of the tournament.

The scent of roasted boar turning on spits in the nearby fire pits was tantalizing. It was extra work for my kitchen staff to prepare the feast outdoors near the tournament site, but I was hoping the leftovers would be easier to distribute to the townspeople, who sat on blankets nearby. And I hoped my servants would also be able to enjoy some of the festivities and play-acting.

When I reached the edge of the table, I was near enough to Derrick to catch a whiff of his soapy, clean scent. Like the other knights, he'd shed the armor and grime of the day and was now dressed in his feasting attire.

I trembled under the intensity of his stare and peeked at him out of the corner of my eyes as I passed. The tiny glimpse was my undoing. Even though he stared at me boldly, there was a nonchalance about his stance that gave me pause. He was positioned farthest away from me again, and yet he didn't seem to mind.

Would the dinner and theater production afterward be a repeat of the dance? Would he ignore me all evening, even while I longed to be near him and speak with him?

The thought sent a cloud through my cheerfulness, and I stopped. At my halt, the duke peered down at me with concern. "Is everything all right, dear one?"

If Derrick was determined to ignore me, then I must find a way to engage his attention, especially now that I knew why he was giving in so easily to his companions. My thoughts returned to all the suggestions the noblewomen had given during the tournament. I inwardly cringed at the thought of trying some of the things they'd mentioned.

I didn't know quite how to formulate my response to the duke—especially without appearing too forward. My conscience urged me to pass by, to go to my spot at the center of the table without saying more. After all, if Derrick was determined to keep his distance, who was I to interfere with his resolve? I already had the devotion of Sir Collin and Sir Bennet. That should be enough.

But strangely, it wasn't.

The duke waited for my response.

"Your Grace," I whispered, standing on tiptoe to reach his ear. I swallowed the nervousness that threatened to prevent me from saying anything. "I should like to honor the winner of the tournament by giving him the seat next to me during dinner."

The duke pulled back and studied my face. A sparkle sprang to life in his eyes and his lips twitched with a smile. "I'm glad to hear it, Rosemarie," he whispered in return. "He's a good man, and he deserves the honor."

I bowed my head in agreement and also to hide the burning in my cheeks.

The duke faced the gathering. "Lady Rosemarie would like to honor the winner of today's joust by giving him the highest seat of honor at the table."

The guests clapped at the announcement. Derrick hesitated and glanced at Sir Collin and Sir Bennet. The other two knights' smiles and laughter faded. Derrick nodded at them almost apologetically before finally rising from his spot. He bowed to me and then took the duke's place at my side, offering me his arm. I took hold of him, certain I was now blushing furiously.

"Thank you, my lady," he said as we moved toward the table. "You're most kind."

"You're most deserving, sir."

"I would have supposed you anxious to avoid my presence for fear of what prize I might claim from you for my win today." The low sultriness of his tone made my insides quiver.

"Quite the opposite, sir." I forced myself to banter even though his nearness made it difficult for me to concentrate on formulating a coherent response. "I've been curious to see what you have in mind."

I wanted to duck under the table at the boldness of my words, but I walked as regally as I could to my place. And I kept my focus straight ahead as he pulled out my chair and helped me into my seat before taking the chair at my side. He didn't say anything, and ere long I couldn't resist peeking at him. He was smiling and there was a hint of admiration in his eyes, as if he'd appreciated our witty exchange.

I took a sip of ale from my goblet. Perhaps I didn't have to be afraid of speaking to him and getting to know him better after all. Perhaps I could practice more of the noblewomen's suggestions than I'd believed possible.

What ought I do first from their list?

I swiveled in my seat, deciding it wouldn't hurt to compliment him. "You were quite talented today, sir. I'm quite in awe of your fighting skills."

He was in the middle of taking a swallow of his ale. At my words of praise, he choked. "Thank you, my lady," he finally said after sputtering through a cough. "I don't deserve your ... awe."

"Don't listen to him," Sir Collin called from his spot down the table. He and Sir Bennet still brooded, but Sir Collin put on a brave smile. "Derrick handles the lance and the halberd better than any other knight in the land."

Sir Bennet pushed away from the table and stood so abruptly that the platters and goblets rattled. He glared at Derrick, his brows coming together in a dark scowl. Next to me, I could feel Derrick stiffen as though anticipating a battle with his friend.

For a long moment the two locked eyes, and the chatter of the other guests came to a halt. Then finally Sir Bennet raised his goblet. "I'd like to propose a toast to the champion of to-day's joust." He pointed his cup at Derrick and everyone else did likewise before taking a sip.

As the conversations resumed, Sir Bennet sat down but gave Derrick a low parting comment. "You may have won the tournament, but that doesn't mean you've yet won Lady Rosemarie's heart."

For a long moment the two men seemed to be waging a silent war, until finally Sir Collin elbowed Sir Bennet and muttered something in his ear.

Derrick was silent as the servants placed the steaming platters of boar upon the table, along with meat pies, fish tarts, and cow's tongue.

I wanted to apologize for any tension I was causing between the men, but before I could formulate the words, Derrick spoke. "Have no fear, my lady. No matter our squabbles, we shall always remain the closest of companions." I raised my brow in skepticism.

"They're the best friends a man could ever ask for." Derrick spoke as though to convince himself as he speared a piece of pork on his trencher with the tip of his knife and took a bite.

I twisted my spoon above my bowl of thick Bukkenade soup. I ought to let him eat in peace. He was likely famished after the day of jousting. But a whisper in the back of my mind reminded me that I had no time to wait, that the month was already half over, and that if I wasn't more forthright, I might very well forfeit this beautiful thing I was beginning to feel.

And it was indeed beautiful.

I glanced sideways, as subtly as possible, at Derrick. The outline of his strong features alone was enough to warm my stomach in a sweet but aching way. I couldn't let his reticence or my own shyness stop me from exploring the feelings further, could I?

With a resolute breath, I turned in my chair and faced him. "Have you been friends with Sir Collin and Sir Bennet for a long time?"

He swallowed his bite of food. "We've known each other forever—or at least since the day we all arrived at Rivenshire to begin our training."

"Ah, then you were pages together?" I smiled at the picture

I conjured of the three as little boys running around, wrestling together, and swinging their blunt swords in practice. I could imagine they were handsome even as wild urchins.

He grinned as if he too were remembering them together as boys. "We were quite the handful."

"The duke was daring to take you all under his care at one time."

Derrick's smile faded. "I don't know what would have become of me, if not for him."

I couldn't keep from thinking back to the rumors I'd heard about him that afternoon. My own mood sobered. "Is it true then that your family was murdered?"

My question was a gentle whisper, but his gaze jumped to mine as though I'd slapped him.

"I'm sorry." Without thinking, I lightly touched his arm. His muscles rippled beneath my fingers. "The question is much too personal. I shouldn't have asked it. Please forgive me."

On the opposite side of Derrick, the abbot paused his eating at the sight of my contact with the knight. I quickly withdrew. I expected the abbot's rebuke and was relieved when he glanced away without a word.

For a long moment, Derrick stared darkly at the pork on the tip of his knife. Had I ruined my opportunity to talk to him? Would he despise me now for probing into his past?

"There's nothing to forgive, my lady," he finally said. The depths of his eyes were haunted. But he leaned in and dropped his voice. "Yes. My family was murdered. But it was completely unnecessary."

I had to bend closer to hear him.

"When my father's enemy surrounded the castle, instead of attempting to withstand the siege or go out onto the field to fight against his enemy with courage, my father decided to surrender." The lines in Derrick's face were drawn tightly, and his jaw flexed. "If my father had been braver," he whispered hoarsely, "he could have saved his family and his lands."

A siege against a castle was never easy to resist. Even with the best-laid stores of food and deep wells inside the inner bailey, most sieges ended in disaster for the castle under attack. Surely Derrick knew that. "Perhaps your father only sought a peaceful end."

"He should have known his enemy wouldn't be satisfied unless blood was shed."

"The rules of engagement allow for surrender under a white flag—"

"It didn't matter. Even with the white flag flying, my father was forced to watch the enemy chop off the heads of my mother and two little sisters . . ."

"No . . ."

His eyes were dark pits of pain. "He displayed them on spikes on the drawbridge, where he then proceeded to torture my father to death."

I swallowed the bile that rose in my throat. "And how did you escape?"

"My nursemaid disguised me as her child. After several weeks of harrowing travel and evasion, she delivered me to the Duke of Rivenshire."

"Oh, sir, I feel your pain," I whispered, uncaring that my head was almost touching his.

Shadows flickered across his face as if he fought the demons of his past. His breathing was labored. Was he reliving the nightmare? I reached out and squeezed his hand atop the table. I tried to ignore that my guests were witnessing the intimate gesture. The urge to offer Derrick a measure of comfort was too strong to resist.

He stared at my fingers upon his hand. A war waged across

his features, and I was afraid he would pull away, that he would retreat into himself and resist my comfort.

But after a long moment, he flipped his hand over and surprised me by capturing my fingers. He laced his fingers through mine, enveloping me with his strength. His weathered skin contrasted against my paleness, and the warmth made my chest hitch.

"Thank you for your kindness, my lady," he whispered.

"I shouldn't have made you relive such things."

"And I shouldn't have shared such gruesome details at dinner."

I had seen much worse the day I'd encountered the rat cages, but I didn't want to bring up my inner demons now as well.

He stared at our fingers laced together. "At least now you can understand why I'm a knight without family honor."

"It doesn't matter—"

"It does to me."

He was shutting me out of his life again. And I couldn't let that happen. "But your father only did what he thought was safest for your family—"

"He gave way to fear," Derrick said sadly. "And in the end, his lack of courage cost him everything."

"Courage can be displayed in many forms, my lord," I said gently. "Sometimes it's evident in the knight charging forward with the lance on his steed. But perhaps it can also take the form of a head bowed before the enemy."

Derrick didn't say anything for an eternal moment. When he finally lifted his head, the gray of his eyes had lightened considerably. "And perhaps it takes courage to face the unknown rather than to run and hide from it."

I knew he was referring to me. I'd put aside the safe course in my life. I'd braved my doubts and taken the chance at finding true love.

Had I found it?

I examined his face, the strong, handsome lines, the layer of scruff that lent him a rough edge, and the steel of his eyes. I couldn't deny that I found him attractive. And being near him always did strange things to my insides. But what else did I like about him? Was there something more that set him apart from Sir Collin and Sir Bennet?

The abbot cleared his throat loudly and frowned directly at Derrick's hold on my hand.

Rapidly, I tugged free, only to earn a grin from Derrick.

"I suppose it's a good thing we have such devoted chaperones." His gaze skimmed my lips. His voice was so low that no one else around could hear it. "If not for the abbot watching every move I make, I would most certainly claim that prize you owe me."

I felt my blood rise to my face, and I focused on my trencher and the untouched food.

I'd never kissed a man before. And although the thought of Derrick pulling me close and pressing his lips against mine sent a welcome shiver through me, I also knew I must be careful. I didn't want to lead him on to believe I cared about him— unless I truly did. For all his whispers and hints about kissing me, he was much too honorable to casually do so.

Nevertheless, his words did speak of his desire. And even though he'd denied his willingness to win my heart, he couldn't deny that he was interested in me and found me attractive, could he?

If I proved to him that his past didn't matter, would he be willing to let these new feelings between us develop and grow?

Throughout dinner, I did my best to engage Derrick in further conversation. I discovered that he was easy to talk with, that he shared openly on a variety of topics, and that he sought my opinions on matters too. When other noblemen came past the head table to congratulate him on his win and his place of honor, he conversed with them with ease and authority. He included me in the discussion of the strange outbreaks of fever and the increasing number of poor who were dying. We were all thankful that, so far, the illness in town hadn't spread.

I could see he was knowledgeable and that the men respected him. And after listening to him, I couldn't help but give him my own respect.

As the play-actors put on their stage production, I could feel his gaze on me more than on the play. And when I turned to smile at him, his eyes lit with appreciation, as if he respected me too.

Afterward, when the sky was streaked with pinks and purples and the stars were beginning to make their faint appearances, he leaned close. "It's been a very fine evening. With you."

Underneath the cover of the table, he reached for my hand in my lap. Without breaking eye contact, he laced his fingers together with mine. I didn't resist.

He glanced at the abbot, who was in a deep conversation with the nobleman next to him, then offered me a secretive smile. I returned it, suddenly happier than I could remember having ever been in my life. Was this what love felt like?

Had I fallen in love with Derrick?

I sucked in a quick breath at the thought. His eyes darkened, almost as if he'd read my question. But I glanced away, too confused to let him see the truth in my eyes—a truth I wasn't sure I was ready to admit.

"I see you've monopolized Lady Rosemarie's attention all evening," came Sir Collin's voice from down the table. Even though he laughed, there was the hint of challenge in his words.

Sir Bennet nodded at Derrick with the same brooding

glower he'd had earlier. "Sir Collin and I were just saying that since you've had Lady Rosemarie to yourself all evening, each of us deserves the same chance on the morrow."

Derrick stiffened. His fingers tightened against mine almost possessively.

"The duke has agreed," Sir Collin said. "I shall have the chance to spend the morning with Lady Rosemarie. And Bennet will have her undivided attention all afternoon. 'Tis only fair, is it not?"

I couldn't deny Sir Collin's rationalization. But it didn't stop me from wishing I could spend the entire day with Derrick instead.

Derrick hesitated answering, and when he pulled my hand closer to him under the table, my heart did a fast twirl. Had he changed his mind about sitting back and letting his friends win me? Was he going to fight for me after all?

The muscles in his face tightened before he forced a smile at Sir Collin, one that was decidedly cool. "If the duke has agreed to the plans, then who am I to stop him?"

I wanted to reassure Derrick that I'd rather spend the day with him, but I refrained. Perhaps I needed another opportunity to be with both Sir Collin and Sir Bennet, to test my feelings. They were good men too. And I couldn't dismiss their affection without giving them at least one more chance.

An outing with each of them would surely help ease my confusion.

The minstrel's tune mingled with the laughter of the guests. In the distance came the music and dancing of my townspeople, who were now enjoying the leftovers of the feast.

Derrick released my hand and pushed away from the table. His expression had turned as dark as the deepening twilight.

I wanted to whisper to Derrick that he had nothing to worry about, that he'd already won my heart. But the words stuck in my throat. He deserved much more than my platitudes. I couldn't lead him on in any way. I couldn't tell him those words until I knew for certain they were true.

Surely after tomorrow, after more time in the presence of the other two men, I would know. And then I would be able to decide who was the right man for me.

Chapter
17

The next morning, Sir Collin held an archery contest in my honor. I quickly realized he was as skilled with the bow and arrow as Derrick was with a lance and halberd. Although I was impressed by the display of his skill, I found that the contest was not nearly as exciting as the jousting tournament the previous day.

When Sir Collin stood behind me and put his hands on mine to give me tips on archery skills, I found that his touch failed to elicit the same reaction Derrick's had the previous evening when he'd held my hand. I also had been unable to keep my attention from drifting to the sidelines, where Derrick stood. My heart had pattered faster at the glimpse of jealousy that had clouded his face when Sir Collin had touched me.

I wasn't too disappointed when Sir Collin's tent collapsed on him in between events. And although I was concerned about the deep gash he suffered on his head when he'd been hit with one of the poles, I was secretly relieved I didn't have to pretend to be having a good time any longer.

During the afternoon with Sir Bennet, I was distracted as well. After demonstrating his superior skill with the long sword in a mock fight with one of his squires, he then took me riding. During the leisurely outing, he quoted beautiful poetry to me.

But all the while he spoke the verses, I had thoughts of what it might be like if Derrick were the one bestowing the eloquent lines upon me.

Halfway through our ride, Sir Bennet's horse lost a shoe and tossed him from his saddle. A bruise the size of an egg began to form above his eye, so we made our way back to the castle grounds so his servants could attend him.

Even though I fretted over Sir Collin's and Sir Bennet's injuries, I released a happy sigh when the events were finally over. But soon after I changed from my riding outfit, the abbot informed me he believed the mishaps could be part of the murderer's scheme and had thus called in the sheriff to investigate further. Although I wanted to believe the harm to both knights had been coincidental, I couldn't deny that something more seemed amiss.

It didn't help matters that the sheriff singled Derrick out for questioning. I was concerned that perhaps the sheriff would frustrate Derrick. After all, Derrick hadn't endeared himself to the sheriff by breaking into the man's estate. I chose to put my worries aside, however, when I received a note from Derrick later saying that he'd finally planned his special day with me for the morrow, and although he couldn't tell me what the day would entail, he promised it would be special.

I awoke the next morning with an excitement that thrummed through my pulse. I would get to spend an entire day with Derrick, and I couldn't think of anything more I wanted to do.

"How do I know when I'm in love?" I asked Trudy, who was finishing pinning my veil in place over my braided hair.

"In love?" My nursemaid clucked her tongue and then stepped back to stare at me in the looking glass. "Are you in love with one of the knights, then?"

"I don't know." I absently tugged on the edge of the veil. "I think I might be, but how do I know for sure?"

"My lady, I wouldn't know. I've never been in love myself. But surely if you feel it, then it must be so."

"Is it just a feeling?"

Trudy pursed her lips at the turn of the conversation. She was silent for a moment as she fidgeted with the laces of my bodice. "Heavens, moon, and stars above, I do wish your mother was here to answer your questions. She would know exactly what to tell you. I, on the other hand, know nothing about love."

"But my parents were deeply in love, weren't they?" I thought back to the last hunting party I'd gone on with them, the final time I'd seen them together. I could still picture the way they'd held hands when they'd ridden their horses side by side, their fingers laced much the same way Derrick had laced his with mine.

Trudy paused and stared into space as if looking back into the past. A smile hovered on her lips. "They were indeed in love, my lady. The thing I remember most about them was that they truly enjoyed spending time together."

"What did they like to do?"

"Riding, taking long walks, and reading together in front of the fire." Her smile widened. "And if they disappeared, I always knew I could find them up on the turret, looking at the stars."

I warmed at the thought of my parents snuggled together at the top of the tower, stargazing.

"They were always talking, discussing history or other important matters," Trudy continued. "And whenever your mother talked, your father listened and respected her opinions."

The way Derrick had included me in his discussions.

"They were there for each other during the difficult times

too." Trudy's smile turned sad. "I've seen difficulties rip other families apart. But not them. Somehow they each had the inner strength the other lacked. They could provide what the other needed."

Did Derrick have what I lacked? And likewise? Could my strengths hold him up in his weakness?

"As I said, I'm no expert in love, my lady." Trudy turned to me and cupped my cheeks. "I don't know if what you're feeling is true love. But I do see that you're happier now than you've been in a very long time."

I could only nod in agreement. I was happier. I felt more alive than I ever had before.

"Then you don't think it would be wrong for me to get married instead of entering the convent?" There was still part of me that wondered if God would be displeased if I chose to pursue the love of a man.

"Oh, Rose." Trudy patted my cheek. "Even though I'm still tempted to carry you off to the convent for your safe-keeping, I can't deny you this chance to experience what your mother did."

I'd once resigned myself to the safety, peace, and quiet of the convent. But after the past two weeks of companionship, I again had to ask myself: Could I be satisfied with solitude the rest of my life? How would I be able to face the loneliness after having experienced the joy of relationships?

"If one of those knights has made you happy, then you have two weeks left to discover if it's love."

"Ten days."

Trudy chuckled and then turned to pick up a scarf from the floor. I smiled, and my entire body felt invigorated. If I spent not just today, but the next ten days with Derrick, I would surely learn if I loved him enough to marry him.

What excuse might I offer so that I could spend every minute with him the rest of the month?

When I finally made my way outside onto the upper landing, I was breathless with anticipation. Even though it was still morning, the sunshine was warm and held the promise of a glorious summer day. Derrick was holding the reins of both his horse and mine while conversing with a servant who was seated on a cart near the stables.

As the duke escorted me down into the inner courtyard, speaking with me as we descended the stairs, I could feel Derrick's attention turn on me and follow each step I took. The intensity felt as if it was burning through me, until finally I couldn't keep from looking over at him. His gray eyes smoldered with something I couldn't begin to understand. And when he smiled at me—a smile meant for me alone—my knees went weak. He started across the bailey toward us.

"I can see that the two of you are looking forward to this special day together," the duke murmured with a hint of humor.

I quickly averted my gaze from Derrick and focused instead on Pup, who followed closely behind Derrick. "I was hoping it wasn't quite so obvious," I muttered back.

The duke chuckled. "It's a very good thing that Derrick finally planned something. I was afraid of what he might do if he had to watch you with the other two knights again."

"I don't wish to harm their friendships with each other."

"Of course not." The duke squeezed my hand, which was curled into the crook of his arm. "But they all knew when coming into the contest that they must fight fair."

"I did my best to give Sir Collin and Sir Bennet a chance yesterday," I said quickly. "But I wish only to spend time with one man now."

The duke's eyes brightened. "Then we shall make that happen."

I knew my words were bold—much bolder than I would have used under different circumstances. But always at the back of my mind there was an urgency prodding me, reminding me that time was short. With each minute that ticked away, so did my chance of finding true love. I had to make the most of every second.

When Derrick met us, however, I was at a loss for words. What did I say to a man whose presence overwhelmed me?

"My lady." He held out his arm to me and his brow quirked, almost as if he knew the effect he was having on me and was enjoying it. "Are you ready for what's in store?"

Of course I was ready, but I couldn't tell him that, not when he already knew it. Instead I tipped my head and gave him what I hoped was a coy look. "I think you take too much pleasure in surprising me, sir."

He grinned. "Life is always a little more enjoyable with a few surprises, don't you think, my lady?"

I smiled in return and tucked my fingers into his arm, letting him guide me the rest of the way to my horse. At his nearness, my heart thudded against my chest like a wild drumbeat. How was it that the merest contact with him could affect me so much?

As we passed Sir Collin and Sir Bennet, who stood near the stables as well, I nodded at them and prayed they could see an apology in my eyes, an apology for favoring Derrick above them. Sir Collin's head was covered with a bandage from the cut he'd sustained yesterday, and the bruise above Sir Bennet's eye was black and blue. They'd battled for me, but I suspected they had lost, even if they didn't realize it yet. Although, from the resigned look in their eyes, perhaps they did. At the very least, I was relieved that their anger toward Derrick seemed gone from their countenances, at least for now.

Later, I would need to speak with both of them privately and thank them for their kindness and efforts during the past month. I owed them that much.

"How did you enjoy the festivities yesterday?" I asked Derrick after we were mounted and on our way.

He leaned toward me. "It was the worst day of my life, my lady."

"The worst?" I tried to feign nonchalance by studying the open field ahead, where many of my peasants were hard at work reaping the wheat with hand sickles.

"I couldn't bear knowing you were with Collin and Bennet." He spoke the words I'd longed to hear. "I hope you're not planning to spend any more time with them."

"And why is that?" I asked, trying to keep my voice innocent.

"I cannot guarantee their safety should you keep their company."

"Then I suppose I shall have to avoid them."

He grinned.

"And if you insist," I said softly, "I shall plan to spend every day henceforth in your company."

"I insist." His voice was low. I didn't dare glance at him for fear that he would see straight inside to my heart, which was tapping too fast. Instead, I focused on what his plans for the day might be. A cart rumbled behind us. A leather covering spread across the contents prevented me from speculating what he was bringing along.

"I cannot fault your noble friends for the fun they showed me during their special days," I said. "Do you think you'll be able to impress me with more than Sir Collin's garden banquet or Sir Derrick's art fair?"

"Do I need to impress you, my lady?" He rode with a confidant, almost purposeful posture, one that reminded me of the strength I'd noticed in him the first day I'd met him in the market square. He glanced at me only briefly before scanning the fields and the peasants bent at work. Although his eyes were kind, there was a censure there that I was learning to appreciate.

"You have no need to impress me, sir," I admitted. "But you do with your honesty nonetheless."

He turned to me again, and this time his eyes sparkled with pleasure from my declaration. "I can guarantee that this day will far surpass anything my friends have done."

Though several guards flanked us and the duke rode at the rear, it felt as though we were completely alone. We traveled for some time, our conversation soon turning into an easy sharing of our pasts. He talked about the many years he'd spent fighting with the duke and the escapades he'd taken part in with his friends. And I shared more about my childhood, especially the fond memories I had of my parents.

When we finally arrived at one of the small towns on my land, I was surprised when he led me to the poor area of town that was fenced off from the rest. From the crudely painted sign, I knew this had been one of the areas hit by the recent illness. It was eerily quiet and deserted, lacking the usual barking of dogs, laughter of children, and shouts of housewives. Derrick helped me dismount, and I followed him cautiously as he crossed past the fence. The doors on the huts stood ajar, the floors barren, the streets strangely clean of the usual refuse.

As we walked, Derrick informed me that only one small group of destitute men had lived through the illness, and the sheriff had assigned them the task of clearing out and burning the once-infected area. Derrick called the men over so that we could speak with them and give them provisions, which I soon realized he had packed in the back of the cart.

We repeated the process in two other towns, and by the end of the afternoon I was disturbed by all that I had seen and learned.

"So many poor have lost their lives," I said as we rode side by side in the shade of a glen. Slants of sunlight filtered through the canopy of branches overhead. A soft breeze brushed my heated cheeks. But nothing could soothe the ache in my chest—an ache that had grown larger as the day had passed. "Entire sections of each town have been wiped out."

"I thought my squire was exaggerating when he brought back his reports," Derrick admitted. "But his claims are entirely true." I'd learned earlier that Derrick had sent his squire ahead yesterday to discover how many carts of provisions we would need to bring. Sadly, we'd only needed one.

"If I had to guess, I would have to say nearly three quarters of the poor population on my land has died."

Derrick nodded thoughtfully. His forehead was marked with lines of concern.

"Don't you find it strange that the illness isn't spreading in a usual manner?" I asked. "Did you notice it only seemed to affect the poor districts?"

"That same question has been troubling me since I first heard the reports from my squire yesterday."

As I rode along, I began to think deeper on the matter. Why did this particular illness affect only the poor? My parents' death attested to the fact that illnesses like plagues usually feasted on rich and poor alike. I'd also found it strange that the survivors had all said the same thing, that the outbreak started after the sheriff and his men had visited.

Of course, the sheriff had visited only to collect the usual taxes, as he did at certain times throughout the year. But nevertheless, the fact bothered me. "Do you think the sheriff or one of his men is a carrier of the disease?"

Derrick frowned as if he too had been puzzling over the connection. "If so, then why didn't the disease spread wherever those men went? Why just in certain areas?"

We were nearing the gates of Ashby, and the tall towers of

JODY HEDLUND

my castle rose to welcome us back. The only problem was that I wasn't sure I was ready to be home and to end the day with Derrick.

As if sensing the close of our time together, Derrick shifted in his saddle. His expression filled with sudden uncertainty. "Perhaps I should have planned a more light-hearted activity for the day."

"No," I assured him. "The day was perfect. And you were right. It far surpassed anything else I've done this month."

The uncertainty lingered in his eyes. I wanted to reach out and span the distance between us, but instead I smiled and hoped it conveyed the depth of my appreciation for our day together. He hadn't sought to amaze me with riches or beauty. He hadn't tried to entertain or woo me. Instead, he'd taken me to the filthiest, poorest places to mingle among my people and help them. He'd shown compassion and insight. And he'd pushed me to do the same.

Derrick seemed as genuinely concerned about the plight of the poor as I was.

As we passed through the city gates, Derrick glanced to the duke and the guards, who'd fallen behind us. Then with a half smile, he drew his horse nearer so that his foot within the stirrup almost brushed me.

He reached for my hand and slipped his fingers through mine. The tender hold made me exhale in contentment. I resisted glancing back to the duke to check for his approval. Surely this linking of our hands wouldn't displease him even if it was rather bold.

"You're a strong woman, my lady." His voice was pitched for only me. "You have earned my deepest respect for facing all that you did today with such dignity."

Before I could think of a response that would vocalize all I was feeling, we broke into the town square and found ourselves on the outskirts of a gathering in the market green. To my dismay, in the center the sheriff stood before a man tied to a post. The man was stretched taut, and the sheriff was in the process of pressing a hot iron against the man's bare back. Several bright red welts already dotted his flesh.

The instant the hot iron seared the man's skin, his hoarse screams rose above the clamor of the townspeople who'd gathered to watch the display.

Nausea immediately welled in my chest, but anger rose just as swiftly. "Release him this instant!" I called. And without a moment to lose, I pulled away from Derrick and charged forward on my horse.

At the pressure of my horse bearing down on them, the townspeople couldn't ignore my presence as they had the last time I'd tried to stop public torture. With silent fury spurring me on, I urged my horse onward until I crashed into the center green. I didn't stop until I stood before the sheriff.

I jerked my riding whip toward the sheriff's outstretched arm and slashed at the hot iron. The snap and power of the coil forced him to let go of the torture instrument and drop it to the ground.

As I worked to calm my emotions, I sat stiffly in my saddle. I sensed more than saw that Derrick had followed and was beside me. The crowd behind us had grown silent, so that the only sound was the labored breathing of the man tied to the post.

"What is the meaning of this, sheriff?" I demanded. "You know my laws forbid public torture."

The sheriff's eyes narrowed on me, and he wiped his hand across his dark beard and mustache, grumbling something behind his hand.

"Watch what you say, sheriff." Derrick's voice was hard. "You'd do well not to insult Lady Rosemarie unless you wish to pay for it."

"And what are you going to do?" The sheriff's expression turned derisory. "Are you going to cut out my tongue?"

"As tempting as the prospect is," Derrick said, "I respect Lady Rosemarie's decision not to inflict torture."

"Oh, but yes," the sheriff said with a thin smile. "You wouldn't dare disobey Lady Rosemarie, would you? Not when you hope to win her into your bed."

With a growl, Derrick slid from his horse, unsheathed his dagger, and had the blade pressed against the sheriff's heart before he could blink.

I sucked in a sharp breath of panic, especially at the sight of the blood that pooled around the sharp edges of the blade.

"Sir Derrick! Please take care," I urged. I didn't want him to do anything rash that he might later regret.

At my words of caution, Derrick loosened his grip on the sheriff's cloak. But the muscles in his arms and back were rounded with strength and anger. He bent in so that he was almost spitting in the sheriff's face. "Your blatant disregard for Lady Rosemarie's wishes disgusts me."

Derrick thrust the sheriff away with a force that sent the man stumbling backward only to land on his backside. Derrick then strode to his horse and in one swift motion was astride again. He glared down at the sheriff, who stared back just as darkly. "Be certain of this, sheriff. If you ever speak ill of Lady Rosemarie again, I will not cut out your tongue." Derrick's steely voice carried over the gathering. "For I shall cut out your heart instead."

Chapter
18

The nightmares came again that night, unbidden, unwanted, but certainly not unexpected.

Restless, not only from the terrible dreams but also from all that I'd witnessed during my day with Derrick, first thing in the morning I met with Abbot Francis Michael in the chapel to pray. As much as I dreaded what I must do, I also knew it was past time to exert my authority as master and ruler over the lands of Ashby. My first act would be to discipline the sheriff. Although he'd once earned my father's gratitude for protecting me, I had to make an example of him by taking away his esteemed position—perhaps even putting him in the dungeon for a time. With only a week until my eighteenth birthday, I had to let him and all my people know that I was to be obeyed.

If I did nothing—as I had the last time—then I would prove how weak I truly was.

Thankfully, the abbot agreed. And after prayers for strength and guidance, the abbot promised to send his messengers to retrieve the sheriff.

As I waited in my golden chair in the Great Hall, my mind replayed all of the conversations Derrick and I had with the peasants the previous day. I realized I must not only discipline the sheriff for his disobedience, I must also question him about the outbreaks of the strange illness. After sharing my concerns with the abbot, he'd been the first to suggest that perhaps the sheriff was more sinister than he'd believed.

The weight of my responsibility sank like heavy stones onto my shoulders. Why did becoming a leader and an adult have to be so difficult?

The knights and their squires were seated at the side tables breaking their fasts, but I had no appetite. My stomach was wound into too many tangles. I kept my focus on the wide double doors, awaiting the sheriff's presence, mentally trying to plan what I would say to him.

I half-jumped when my porter, James, entered. But I sat back once I realized he wasn't ushering in the sheriff but rather one of the hired laborers who worked at the monastery. The man approached the abbot, who was breaking his fast down the table from where I sat. After several moments of speaking to the abbot in low, urgent tones, the abbot sprang from his chair with such speed that it toppled over behind him, hitting the floor with a reverberating bang. The abbot's eyes were round with horror. "Are you certain?"

The hired laborer nodded gravely.

"Do we know who the murderer is?" the abbot asked, his face pinched and pale.

At the mention of murder, silence descended over the Great Hall and all eyes came to rest on the monastery worker.

The laborer glanced around the Great Hall, his gaze only stopping when he reached Derrick, who stood with the duke and his two companions near the double doors. They'd obviously anticipated some resistance from the sheriff and had planned to support my efforts to confront him.

Derrick's handsome face was unshaven, and dark circles had formed under his eyes. But he stood as straight and strong as befitted a knight of his rank.

The laborer tore his attention from Derrick, shook his head, and then whispered in the abbot's ear.

The abbot's eyes narrowed and the creases in his face deepened.

"What is it, Father Abbot?" I asked.

He turned his kind eyes on me, and there was a sadness in them that sent warning bells ringing inside. Something dreadful must have happened.

I prayed it wasn't another outbreak of the illness.

"I regret to inform you, my child," the abbot said gently, "that the sheriff was found murdered in his bed this morning."

"Murdered?" I rose rapidly from my chair, unable to believe that such a thing could happen. Who would have done it? Not with the fortifications the sheriff put into place around his estate. Not with his vicious dogs. Of course, I had reason to dismiss and discipline him. But murder? I shook my head.

The abbot glanced at Derrick with a sharpness that sent a sudden tremor through my heart.

No! The silent protest screamed through my mind. Not Derrick!

But when the abbot turned to face me again, I trembled so that my knees almost gave way. "The sheriff's servants found their master in his bed this morning ... with his heart cut from his chest. They informed my messenger, here, of what happened."

I shook my head, too dismayed to respond.

"The heart was found nailed to the post in the middle of the town square."

I collapsed into my chair.

"I'm sorry, your ladyship," the abbot said.

"That doesn't mean—" I couldn't bring myself to accuse Derrick.

"Several servants saw Sir Derrick inside the sheriff's estate last night."

All eyes turned on Derrick, who stood frozen next to the duke, his face a stony mask. I silently begged him to explain himself, to tell us that he hadn't broken in to the sheriff's house again, that he hadn't sought revenge against the sheriff for the altercation in the market square yesterday.

But he remained silent.

To my relief, the duke spoke. "There must be some mistake. Sir Derrick never made any mention of going out last night—"

"I did go there last night, your Grace," Derrick said. "But I only went to investigate. I have my suspicions that the recent outbreaks of illness in Lady Rosemarie's lands are related to the sheriff somehow, and I only wished to find evidence of such."

"And so while you were there, you got into another fight?" the abbot asked.

"I didn't seek out the sheriff," Derrick said, shaking his head. "I had no wish to fight him."

The abbot's eyes narrowed. "Only to murder him—"

"Please refrain from accusing my knight until you have solid evidence." The duke's voice was low and edged with anger.

"I think we have plenty of evidence," the abbot said in an equally hard tone. "Everyone in town heard Sir Derrick tell the sheriff yesterday that he would cut his heart out. Even I have learned of it. And if that's not enough, we have Sir Derrick's own admission he broke into the sheriff's estate last night. What more do we need?"

"We need more than assumptions," the duke said.

"You know as well as I do that Sir Derrick is already close to censure for all of the accidents regarding his friends Sir Bennet and Sir Collin," the abbot replied.

I sat forward to the edge of my seat in surprise. I'd known

the sheriff had questioned Derrick, but I hadn't known the law-man was seriously considering Derrick as a suspect.

"He's in no way to blame for the murder attempts," the duke countered calmly, although his eyes and nose flared with barely concealed anger. "He's one of my most trusted men. I would put my life into his hands. And I know they would do so for each other. They aren't capable of perpetrating what you say."

I glanced to where Sir Bennet and Sir Collin stood. Their faces were as hard as their leader's, eyes flashing with resentment directed at the abbot. They obviously didn't accuse Sir Derrick either.

"But the circumstances are quite unusual, are they not?" The abbot's brow lifted and crinkled against the ring of hair that surrounded his bald head. "Since when have your men had to compete against one another for the most desirable woman in the land?"

"We may be competing with each other"—Sir Collin pushed away from the wall—"but we would never seek to harm one another."

"I've seen the discord between you," the abbot said. "We all have."

I thought back to the dance, when the men had almost come to blows with one another.

"No matter the tensions we've experienced this month," Sir Collin spoke again, "we aren't murderers."

"Perhaps that's true of you and Sir Bennet, who both have land and wealth to speak of," the abbot said. "But since Sir Derrick has none, he has much more to gain in the union."

Derrick stood immobile, his back stiff, his chin held high. Why would he not rise to his own defense? Surely he could say something to deflect the abbot's condemnation . . .

Unless he was guilty.

As soon as the thought came, I thrust it aside. I cared about him too much to think him guilty even if all the evidence said otherwise.

"My knight would never harm his friends," the duke insisted. "They're like his brothers. And he has no reason to hurt them, not when he's capable of winning Lady Rosemarie's heart without resorting to such methods."

The abbot shook his head. "One of my servants overheard Sir Derrick telling her ladyship that he didn't consider himself worthy enough for her. Perhaps he thought his only hope was to eliminate his competition."

I couldn't keep from thinking back to the innocent comments both the duke and Derrick had made concerning his jealousy. Derrick had said he couldn't guarantee the safety of the other two knights if I spent any more time with them. And the duke had said he was glad I'd chosen Derrick because he was afraid Derrick would harm his friends with his jealousy.

I'd believed them to be jesting. But what if Sir Derrick was more reckless than I'd imagined?

The abbot cleared his throat and spoke again. "Can you explain why these unfortunate accidents have happened only to Sir Collin and Sir Bennet—first the shooting and poisoning, and then the fallen tent and the horse losing its shoe? Why have both of them suffered such attempts and not Sir Derrick?"

Sir Bennet had stepped next to Sir Collin, and his dark gaze narrowed on the abbot. "Perhaps Sir Derrick is being set up by one who doesn't wish him to win Lady Rosemarie's heart, especially since he appears to be succeeding at it."

The abbot's eyebrow rose again. "Are you laying claim to the misdeeds then, Sir Bennet?"

"You know that I'm not." His voice was rigid and his glare narrow. "I believe there is one who has greater motivation—"

The duke stopped Sir Bennet with a touch to his arm.

Sir Bennet clamped his lips closed, but his chest was puffed with the words he apparently wanted to speak.

"Of course you'll want to defend your friend," the abbot said in the measured, calm tone he always used. "But now, with all the evidence of the sheriff's murder pointing directly at Sir Derrick, we have no choice but to lock him up."

Sir Collin's and Sir Bennet's protests echoed through the Great Hall.

"If not for your safety, sirs," the abbot said, "then for her ladyship's? You surely would not wish to see any harm befall her? Would you?"

Suddenly, Derrick stepped forward, his gray eyes blazing like the white heat of a hearth fire. "She had better not get hurt." His voice was ragged.

Only then did the abbot look at Derrick, holding his gaze for a long moment. "If you wish your friends and her ladyship to be free of danger, then I think it best that you hand yourself over. Don't you agree?"

Beneath the layers of my gown, my legs trembled in fear for Derrick, of what would befall him. He was being accused of murdering the sheriff and treachery against his companions. And there seemed no way to refute the evidence.

As if coming to the same conclusion, the duke finally nodded at Derrick, as though trying to reassure him, before turning to the abbot. "Very well, Father Abbot. If you must lock up Sir Derrick, I ask that it be in one of the chambers."

"I concur," I said. "We can post a guard outside his door."

The abbot didn't turn to acknowledge me, but instead continued to direct his conversation to the duke. "If he's not in the dungeon, what's to prevent him from trying to escape?"

"Because he's a man of honor," the duke replied.

The abbot only shook his head, his face filled with scorn.

"In the meantime," the duke continued, "Sir Collin and

Sir Bennet and I will commence a thorough investigation to find evidence that he's innocent."

"He deserves death by hanging for taking the life of the sheriff," the abbot said bluntly. "The law demands it. The people will expect it. And justice must be served. If not, I cannot guarantee what may happen."

The abbot's words dripped with a foreboding and an undercurrent of threat.

"If I hand myself over and allow you to lock me in the dungeon," Derrick said, "then you'll guarantee Lady Rosemarie's safety?"

Surely he didn't think I was in danger.

"You don't have to do this, Derrick." Sir Collin's harsh whisper echoed in the silent hall. "We'll find another way."

Derrick spun and glared at his friends. His face was carved granite, his eyes iron. Their expressions pleaded with him.

I didn't want to meet Derrick's gaze, but when he turned his on me, I had no choice. He studied my face and something within his eyes pleaded with me to believe him, to trust him.

I wanted to. I didn't think him capable of murdering the sheriff or harming his friends. But with so much evidence against him, I knew I couldn't ignore it. I had to get to the bottom of all that had happened too. "Rest assured, I shall start my own investigation into all the recent happenings as well."

But as I spoke, disappointment filled Derrick's eyes, as if he'd expected more from me than what I'd given him. "Call the guards," he said in a hard voice to the abbot, "and you may lock me up."

Even as he spoke the words, my heart gave a thump of protest. I knew I should have added my objection to that of Sir Collin and Sir Bennet. But how could I proclaim him innocent until I found the real culprit?

As the guards came forward reluctantly and bound

Derrick's hands, I turned to the abbot. "I don't want him in the dungeon."

"I know how disappointing this is to you, my child," he said while starting down the steps of the dais. "But 'tis best you learn of his true nature before it is too late."

Disappointment didn't quite encompass my feelings. It was much more complicated than that. Something about the situation wasn't right. I couldn't put my finger on it at the moment, but knew I wouldn't rest until I learned what was going on.

"Don't worry," Sir Bennet called as the guards led Derrick away. "We'll discover who's really behind all the murder attempts. And we'll set you free."

His words echoed my thoughts exactly. I willed Derrick to turn around and see the determination in my face and eyes, but his head was bent and his shoulders slumped, and as my guards ushered him through the Great Hall, he didn't glance my way again.

I pressed my face into my hands as I knelt at the prayer altar. Except for the abbot's soft murmurs in Latin, the chapel was silent.

In fact, the entire castle was silent, as if in mourning with me for all I'd lost.

The truth was I'd grown to care about Derrick more than I'd ever dreamed possible. But now with all the accusations, especially one as serious as murder, there didn't seem any way possible that I would be able to finish discovering if Derrick had fallen in love with me and I with him.

Maybe God was sending me a sign that I was destined for a life in the convent after all.

"Oh God," my heart cried out. "Then why did you allow

me to care about Derrick so much? Why did you let me experience the love of an earthly man if I'm destined for a life with only you as my bridegroom?"

Had the whole month been simply a test to show me my true destiny? The anguish in my heart spread to every limb, every nerve, every muscle in my body.

"He played you falsely, your ladyship," the abbot said, standing above me, dangling a long wooden cross on a golden thread from his hand. "He knew if he withheld himself from you, if he was more aloof and acted unworthy of your attention, you would be drawn to him."

My chest constricted. Was that what Derrick had intended? If so, it had worked. I'd most certainly been attracted to him.

"He was crafty." The abbot's voice contained an unusual edge. "But I suppose he decided he'd safeguard his claim on you by scaring away — or killing — the other two men."

I still couldn't believe Derrick was capable of harming his friends. I'd immediately sent guards to begin an investigation. Even so, my time was running out. I'd had so little to begin with. And even if I could find a way to prove his innocence, I doubted there would be enough hours left to finish getting to know one another and truly decide if our affections were indeed love.

"He's not worth the sorrow, your ladyship," the abbot said more gently.

At a clearing throat at the back of the chapel, I finally lifted my face and tried to pull myself out of my pit of despair.

"Excuse me, Lady Rosemarie," came the duke's voice.

I rose from my prayer cushion and tugged my veil over my face. I was in mourning and I didn't care who knew about it.

"I've sent the guests home as you requested," he said, coming down the aisle toward me. He was dressed in his suit of armor, his helmet tucked under one arm, his sword sheathed at his side.

"Thank you, your Grace."

Faint light poured through a round stained glass window above the altar. The candles in the wall sconces had been lit. Even so, the duke's face was dark.

"My men and I are ready to depart."

I nodded. "I wish you Godspeed in your searches." Even if any of us found enough evidence to clear Derrick's name, I doubted he'd want to proceed with our courtship, not after the humiliation of his arrest. Any respect I gained from him had certainly been lost when I'd failed to take better charge of the situation. I'd proven myself a weak leader once again.

With only a week until my eighteenth birthday, the odds of getting married seemed suddenly insurmountable.

In some ways, it seemed wiser to resign myself once again to entering the convent. I couldn't hold back a sigh of disappointment. Perhaps I needed to begin the move to the monastery guesthouse, even though my heart resisted the thought.

The duke reached for my hands and folded them between his. "I know you're confused and hurt. And I never meant for that to happen."

"This is exactly what I was afraid would happen," started the abbot.

The duke cut him off with a sharp look. "Will you promise me two things?" he asked me gently.

"Anything."

"I know it's tempting to think that the situation is hopeless and that the contest ended in failure. You might even think it's in your best interest to go to the convent now."

I nodded. He'd read my mind.

"But there may yet be hope," he said. "Will you wait the full week before you go?"

The abbot released an exasperated breath. But the duke continued before I could add my protest. "I just need one week," he pleaded. "Please?"

What good will come of one more week? Except that it would drag out my heartache and postpone having to accept my fate.

The expression on the abbot's face echoed my thought. But I nodded anyway. How could I deny my old friend his request? "If you wish it, I shall wait one more week."

"And one more promise, dear one." The duke squeezed my hands. "Please see that Derrick doesn't come to any harm."

The guards had taken him down into the dungeon underneath the castle. I hadn't been to the dark underground hovel in years. In fact, I'd only gone once, and the scurry of rat claws against the stones had awakened my nightmares. I'd been unable to sleep for many nights after the visit.

"Is it really necessary for him to be in the dungeon?" I asked the abbot again. "Are you sure he cannot be locked into one of the chambers instead?"

"I've already made an announcement to the townspeople that the criminal responsible for the sheriff's death has been caught and is locked in the dungeon. If you set him free, what will the people think about your leadership? Would you have them know you as fair and just or as someone moved by every whim of your heart?"

The duke gave the abbot a sharp sidelong glance. "I have a feeling the solitude of the dungeon will be the safest place for Derrick during my short absence."

"The safest place for Derrick?" I repeated. The duke made it sound like Derrick needed protecting.

"I'll be leaving his squire to keep watch over him," the duke continued, "but nevertheless, I ask that you make Sir Derrick as comfortable as possible while I'm gone."

"I'll make sure my guards know they're to treat him with the utmost kindness." It was the least I could do for the duke and for Derrick.

The abbot pursed his lips and caressed the wooden cross in his hands. "I hope you don't think you're going to set Sir Derrick free when you return, unless, of course, you have the proper proof that he's innocent."

The duke's hand stiffened around mine, but his composure remained the same. "We shall speak of the terms of release once I return."

Even if the duke's test for true love had failed, I still trusted and believed in him. I was confident he would do the just and right thing where Derrick was concerned.

"Don't forget your promises to me." He bent and kissed the top of my head.

"I won't."

Then with a final, sad smile, he spun on his heels and left the chapel. Even before he'd had the chance to ride away, I was already wishing for his return.

Chapter
19

I froze on the first landing of the dark passageway that led to the dungeon. A waft of dank, sour air sifted over me, making my nose wrinkle.

"My lady?" whispered Bartholomew, my faithful old guard. He was already halfway down the first set of winding steps. He peered at me over his shoulder, his eyebrows raised. When he lifted his torch, the flickers cast ghoulish shadows on the stone walls.

"Do you want to go back?" he hissed through the gap where he was missing his top front teeth.

I shook my head and took a step forward. My slippers were soundless, and I wrapped my cloak tighter around my night gown. I'd come this far. I couldn't turn back now. Even if everything within me longed to retreat.

I'd promised the duke that I'd make sure Derrick was treated kindly. After more than a day of doing nothing but imagining him shivering and hurt in his dark cell, I'd decided I needed to go down and discover for myself how he fared.

Bartholomew started forward again. His shuffling footsteps echoed too loudly as he continued his descent into the bowels of the castle.

My legs trembled, and I could only stare into the dark

abyss that awaited, as the nightmares flared to life in my mind: rats in the bottomless cage, digging frantically and hungrily through human flesh.

My gaze flew back to the door at the top of the stairway, where the abbot had positioned two guards. I didn't have to go. I could send Bartholomew down to bring back a report.

Besides, I doubted Abbot Francis Michael would approve of me descending into the dungeon to speak with Derrick. But since the abbot had returned to the convent that afternoon to make preparations for my move, I didn't have to worry about earning his censure.

I knew Trudy wouldn't agree to my descent into the dungeon, which was another reason why I'd waited until the darkest hours of the night to make the trip, after my nursemaid's snores filled my chamber.

Bartholomew disappeared around the winding steps, taking the light with him, thereby leaving me in growing blackness. I stumbled after the old guard before I let fear keep me from doing what I knew I must.

As much as I wanted to turn around and run back to fresh air and the safety of the upper levels, there was something driving me that I couldn't ignore. I had to see Derrick.

And if I was honest with myself, I knew my desire to see him went beyond my promise to the duke.

I cared about him. And I'd believed he'd begun to feel the same way about me. I had a driving need to discover the truth before I moved to the convent.

Even if it didn't change the outcome of becoming a nun and fulfilling the Ancient Vow, at least I would have peace in knowing the answer.

I leaned my head back against the stone wall, heedless of the webs and dust that caught in the dirty strands of my hair. I rubbed my hands over my arms, attempting to bring warmth to my chilled flesh.

Even though it was mid-summer, the heat didn't reach into the underground pit. And it certainly couldn't touch the cold emptiness of my heart—a coldness that had gripped me since the moment I'd looked into Rosemarie's eyes and seen her mistrust and confusion.

I wasn't sure what pained me more: the knowledge that she could believe me capable of the misdeeds, or the fact that I'd lost her.

Of course, maybe I'd never really had her to begin with . . .

I released a pent-up breath, the foul, dank air swirling around me.

If only I'd stayed true to my earlier conviction that I didn't have the right to win her heart. If only I'd worked harder to keep my distance from her.

But even as the thought pushed through me, anger chased it away. It wouldn't have mattered which of us had won her heart, as the outcome would have been the same. One of us would have ended up in chains.

I wasn't quite sure who had murdered the sheriff and who had threatened Bennet and Collin, but I had a suspicion that somehow the abbot was behind it all. His last threat had been clear—if I wanted to keep Rosemarie from getting hurt next, I needed to willingly hand myself over.

I'd been afraid the duke would resist, that he'd force the abbot to free me. But thankfully he hadn't protested too strongly. The duke knew me too well. He realized I'd do anything to ensure Rosemarie's safety and that there was no way he'd stop me from handing myself over to the abbot if it meant I'd protect her.

What wasn't clear was why the abbot wanted to keep Rosemarie from getting married. For whatever reason, the man of God seemed to think Rosemarie would be better off spending her life in the convent.

Maybe she would. At least there, she'd be safe.

But what did the abbot have to gain from her living there? The question wouldn't leave my mind. Certainly he stood to gain something. Otherwise, why bring the competition to an end?

A scuffling sounded in the hallway outside my cell. Other than the jailer who brought me food several times a day, and the visits from my squire when the guards would allow, the rats were my only companions in the deserted dungeon.

I could at least count my blessings I was being fed. And that the jailer had scraped the muck from the cell and strewn the floor with fresh straw. Even though he'd been a gruff man, he hadn't abused me, at least not yet.

A creak at the far end of the hallway pushed me up from my spot on the floor. I stared in the direction of the doorway as it began to open, letting in the light that had become all too rare over the past two days. Wariness quickly sprang to life and my muscles tensed.

I knew it was night based on the delivery of my last meal and the fact that the jailor hadn't visited me again. Anyone else coming in the middle of the night would surely only bring trouble.

The door opened completely, and the light of a torch spilled into the dungeon, illuminating my cell and the empty one across from me. I flattened myself against the damp wall and wiped my grimy hands across my eyes. When I looked again, I saw an angel.

It was Rosemarie following behind her guard. Her hair was

loose and floated around her head like a halo. The glint of the flame turned the strands to pure gold.

My chest tightened with a sudden surge of desire to hear her voice, to stand near her, and to know she was safe.

"Derrick," she whispered, searching the opposite cell.

Although my noble self prodded me to stay hidden in the shadows, to let her go once and for all, I couldn't resist pushing away from the wall and moving to the center of my cell. All I wanted to do was see her face one last time.

At my movement, she gasped and spun. "Derrick." Her voice had a breathless quality, and did I detect just a tiny amount of joy? Was she glad to see me?

She crossed to the rusted bars and peered inside.

The guard raised his torch so that the light fell upon me, revealing my filth and the state to which I'd fallen. I was tempted to shrink back. I didn't want her to see me this way. But the eagerness in her eyes sent another wave of need into my blood, stirring it faster. I took a step toward the bars, wanting to reach for her and draw her close.

She glanced over her shoulder then and visibly shuddered. "I haven't been down here in years," she said, looking around again and drawing near enough to the bars that she almost touched them.

"Why have you come now?"

In the light of the torch her beautiful blue eyes were filled with honesty. "I've been worried about you, and I had to see for myself how you were."

"I've been better."

Her face crumpled in distress. "I shall have you moved to a chamber upstairs immediately."

With a sudden lurch of anxiety, I shook my head. If I allowed her to move me, what would the abbot do next? To her? His threat may have been subtle, but it had spoken loud enough to me. "I must stay here, my lady. I dare say you have the nicest guards and the finest prison I've ever been in." I gave her a wry grin, hoping to ease her discomfort.

"You're sure you're well?"

I nodded, and in spite of how I smelled and looked, I bent closer to her. I caught the sweet scent of roses that was uniquely hers. "And you? Are you well and safe?"

"I'm well in body. But disquieted in spirit." When her gaze met mine, I saw fear radiating from deep in her eyes.

My muscles tensed. "What's wrong?" Was she in some kind of trouble?

I couldn't stop myself from slipping my hand through the bars and taking hold of hers. Her fingers were cold but soft. And I was relieved when she didn't pull away, but instead gripped me tightly, as if I was her only hope.

"Tell me what ails you," I demanded, my chest swelling with the need to burst out of prison and defend her against whatever enemy she was facing. It didn't matter anymore that she'd not risen to my defense in the Great Hall.

How could I blame her for remaining silent? She hadn't known me long. She was wise to show caution when faced with the kind of evidence that had been brought against me. If anything, I should be angry with her for searching me out down in the dungeon, especially because of the possible danger she could bring on herself if the abbot were to learn of her visit.

She glanced around again and shuddered so violently it rippled through my hand all the way to my heart, piercing me with a fear I'd never believed possible. I looked to the guard who had accompanied her to the dungeon, and he seemed concerned for Rosemarie as well. "Is someone trying to harm you, my lady?"

"No," she said with a faint smile. "It's just my past coming to haunt me."

"What of your past?" I asked, trying to keep my voice gentle.

"'Tis silly, really." She ducked her head. "Only the nightmares of a torture I once witnessed by chance. I should have forgotten the scene by now. But there are times when I cannot ..."

"Like when you saw the man in the boiling water?"

She nodded. "Or when I see rats."

"Rats?"

Her voice dropped. "They'd put cages upon the stomachs of the men, bottomless cages, with starving rats inside."

"Speak no more of it," I urged softly. I knew well enough the method of torture—that the frenzied rats would gnaw and dig through the human's flesh until they reached the entrails. It was a slow and excruciating way to die. "I've witnessed it once myself. As a matter of fact, I saw it here the day of your parents' funeral."

Surprise flitted across her delicate features. "Then perhaps we witnessed the same scene."

My muscles tensed as I thought back to the men's agonized screams as they lay dying. "I took pity on the men and hastened their death."

Her eyes widened and she studied my face.

"The duke had given his approval," I explained, hoping the darkness of the dungeon kept the grime on my face hidden. "He would likely have done it himself if I hadn't spoken first."

"I've always wondered who showed those poor men compassion." A small smile graced her lips. "And now it would appear that you are the one to whom I owe my deepest gratitude."

"No, my lady—"

"Now it would appear that I'm indebted to you again." Her smile inched higher.

In spite of the grave circumstances, I couldn't resist teasing her. "Shall I start to keep a tally of your debts to me? I wouldn't want you to forget to give me my rewards."

She ducked her head, and I was sure if there had been enough light I would have seen a pretty flush on her cheeks.

I grinned, even as my insides flared with the thought of the kind of reward I truly longed for from her, though I would never ask for it now.

Standing next to the door, the old hunched guard gave a slight cough.

"Is it true what I've heard?" I asked, quickly changing the subject. "Are you making plans to enter the convent?"

"Yes. It's true." Her voice had a note of resignation. "I have only five days left. The abbot has gone to make ready my rooms. What other choice do I have?"

I wanted to argue with her but forced myself to respond rationally. "Have you thought about how you'll guarantee the safety of your people when you're in the convent? How will you protect them from there?"

"I don't lose my ability to rule after I fulfill my vow."

"Will the abbot allow it?"

"Of course he will. I'll be eighteen and ruler in my own right."

I shrugged, but wariness wormed into my stomach, turning it sour. Did the abbot think that by keeping Rosemarie cloistered, he'd still be able to control her? Was he opposed to her marrying because he knew he'd lose his influence over her?

"Perhaps you should speak further with the abbot about how you'll continue your reign from inside the convent's walls."

She peered at me, her eyes thoughtful, her lips pursed.

"My lady," whispered the guard. "I think we should be going now."

She moved as if to go, then pressed even closer to the bars of my cell, gripping my hand harder. "Did you do it, Derrick? Tell me the truth. I need to know." Her voice was low and anguished.

I knew what she was referring to. I knew she wanted me to deny any involvement in the crimes. But it hurt that she could believe, even for one minute, I'd stoop so low.

"Do you really think I'm capable?" I whispered back, unable to keep the harshness from my tone.

"No." Her whisper was still troubled but her answer took away the sting of her question nevertheless. Her brows furrowed and she peered into my eyes as if attempting to see into my soul. "If you didn't do it, then why won't you defend yourself?"

The reckless, heedless part of me had longed to rise to my own defense when the abbot had leveled the accusations against me. I'd wanted to shout out that I had nothing to do with any of the incidents, especially when I'd seen the disappointment in Rosemarie's eyes.

But the self-restraint the duke had taught me over the years had been in good stead. I'd held back the words of defense. I'd humbled myself. And I'd taken the brunt of the abbot's accusations without a fight, so that no one else would incur such needless blame.

"Remember, we show courage in many ways," I said.

Even as the words left my lips, the truth of the statement pounded me. I'd always believed my father was a coward. But what if my father had refused to fight because he'd hoped to keep his family from dying of starvation? Perhaps he'd believed that handing himself over would at least save the lives of his wife and children. And it likely would have, under normal circumstances.

Rosemarie continued to study my face as if searching for the truth there.

"Sometimes courage can even take the form of a head bowed before the enemy," I said softly, repeating the words Rosemarie had once spoken to me. Maybe I'd been wrong

191

about my father all this time. What if my father had shown more courage in humbling himself rather than fighting?

"But if you're innocent, why didn't you say so?"

"Would it have done any good? With all the evidence pointing toward my guilt, who would have believed me?"

"I would have believed you," she whispered. "I do believe you."

I leaned against the bars. We were less than a hand's span apart. Her warmth and life radiated into me, and once again I inhaled the fragrance of roses that surrounded her. Before I thought to stop myself, I slipped my fingers through the bars and touched her cheek. I knew I should resist. I had no right to win her affection, especially now.

Even so, I caressed her soft, unblemished skin. When she leaned into my touch, my heart gave a hard knock against my chest.

"I want you to believe me too," I said softly. "I want you to trust that I would never, ever do anything intentionally that would bring you harm. In fact, I would lay down my very life for you."

She released a sigh that brushed my wrist and sent my pulse into a thundering gallop.

The old guard nearby lifted his torch, exposing my intimate touch on her face. "We really need to go, my lady."

She took a step back, breaking our contact. "If not you, then who?"

"I cannot say." I'd spoken briefly with the duke as well as Collin and Bennet about my suspicions. But they couldn't bring forward any accusations until they had solid proof. "I'm hoping when the duke returns, he'll bring news of the true criminal that will set me free."

"Unless my servants can uncover the truth first." She drew

her cloak about her. "I won't let them rest until they've questioned every person in the land."

Her declaration sent warmth pouring over me and I almost reached for her again. But she spun away, following her guard back down the passageway.

I pushed against the bars, the cold rusted iron bruising me. I wanted to call out after her not to leave me, that I couldn't bear to be away from her again, that I didn't see how I could go on in life without her.

The truth was, I loved her. Deeply and truly.

I hadn't meant to fall in love with her, had tried not to, hadn't thought I was worthy. But somehow, over the past month, it had happened anyway. Maybe I'd even fallen in love that first day I'd ridden through Ashby and watched her frantic efforts to stop the torture in the town square.

Whatever the case, I couldn't deny the truth any longer. "My lady," I called after her.

Already in the doorway, she stopped. In the faint glow of the guard's light, she was achingly beautiful. In fact, she was so much more than I'd ever imagined she'd be—intelligent, kind, thoughtful.

Her bright blue eyes regarded me with expectation.

I swallowed hard but couldn't get out the words I wanted to say, that I loved her more than life itself, that I didn't want her to enter the convent.

But what good would it do to tell her when I was locked in the dungeon, with only five days left until her eighteenth birthday, only five days to make her fall in love with me, only five days within which to be married.

"My lady," came the old guard's voice, more urgent.

She lifted her brow at me, clearly waiting for me to speak.

"Stay safe," I managed.

She nodded and then turned once more. In an instant, the

dungeon door squeaked closed, taking the torchlight and all hope with it.

I released a frustrated groan that echoed against the stone walls of my cell. Then, weary, I rested my head against the bars, letting blackness settle over me.

Perhaps this was exactly what the abbot had wanted. Unable to prevent the duke's courtship plan, and unable to keep Rosemarie from being attracted to the three suitors—to me—perhaps the abbot figured the next step was locking me away to keep me from winning her heart.

And with so little time left until her birthday, it looked as if the plan would work.

I could only pray the duke would bring back evidence that could set me free before it was too late.

Chapter 20

"I don't like this one bit, my lady." Trudy's voice echoed through the deserted Great Hall. She smoothed out the wrinkles in my gown and draped it around my chair.

"We'll be fine," I said for the hundredth time since I'd awakened Trudy and dragged her from her pallet. "Everyone else is asleep. No one has to know except you and Bartholomew and the night jailer."

"I say we should be abed."

"But I can't sleep." Not only had the nightmares returned after my visit to the dungeon the previous night, but I couldn't stop thinking of Derrick down in his dark, cold cell all alone. My heart ached every time I thought about him there.

Trudy's graying hair poked out from the plain veil she'd hastily draped over her head. Her cheeks were splotched and red stained her throat, the sign of her frustration with me. "This is much too dangerous. What if he tries to harm you?"

"He would never hurt me." Warmth wrapped around me at the remembrance of the words he'd whispered when I'd visited him — that he would never let any harm come to me, that he would lay down his life for me.

"Besides, we won't be alone," I continued, nodding to the

chair placed a discreet distance from the hearth. "You'll be here watching us. And so will Bartholomew."

The side door leading to the kitchen opened a crack, and my heart flew forward at double speed. "Here he comes," I whispered, twirling a long curl around my finger one last time before straightening in my chair and doing my best to look stately and beautiful.

"For the love of earth, rivers, and sky," Trudy muttered under her breath. But thankfully, my faithful nursemaid took several steps back from where I sat at the table positioned in front of the hearth.

Bartholomew's craggy face peeked through the door. He checked both ways before stepping into the Great Hall. He then tugged on the chains he held, and Derrick stumbled into the Hall after him, his wrists bound with the heavy links.

I gave a soft gasp. "You needn't have chained him."

"The jailer wouldn't let me do it any other way."

At the sound of my voice and sight of me, Derrick stood taller. Across the distance and darkness of the room, his gaze sought and found me, landing on me with an intensity that as usual took my breath away.

With his shuffling steps, my old guard brought him nearer.

"I should say that I'm sorry to appear before you without first cleaning up, my lady," Derrick said, stopping several feet away. "But that would be a lie, because the truth is I'm just happy to see you."

I took in his wrinkled apparel, his smudged face, and the scruff on his chin and cheeks from several days without grooming. He was every bit as handsome as he'd always been.

"I thought I would go crazy if I had to spend another day without seeing you," he said in a low voice that did funny things to my stomach.

Before I could think of how to respond, Pup rose from his

spot next to my chair and bounded over to Derrick. The dog's tail flapped back and forth in delight, and he licked at Derrick's hands, which were bound in front of him.

"I guess both of us are happy to see you as well," I said with a smile.

Derrick managed to awkwardly scratch Pup's head through his chains.

"Can you not remove the restraints?" I pleaded with Bartholomew, who stood next to Derrick.

Bartholomew hesitated, and from her chair in the corner Trudy clucked a loud warning.

"Please?" I gave my guard what I hoped was my most winsome smile. "How can he play chess with me if his hands are bound?"

For the first time Derrick seemed to notice the table next to me with the chessboard atop it. His eyes lit up and a grin played at the corners of his lips.

"I don't want you to get in trouble, my lady," my guard said, his kind eyes pleading with me to listen to reason.

"As much as I want to spend time with you, my lady," Derrick said, "I agree with your guard. I don't want you to bring any trouble to yourself."

"Why would I get in trouble?" I asked, dismissing the abbot's warning about my people trusting me to be a strong leader. "No one need know."

Bartholomew studied his prisoner for a long moment.

"Please, Bartholomew." I meant the words with all my heart. "If anyone else awakes, I give you my permission to take Sir Derrick back immediately."

"But Abbot Francis Michael told us he would flay us alive if the prisoner escaped."

The harshness of the abbot's stipulation took me by surprise. Why would the abbot say such a thing? He wasn't in charge of my servants. "Surely he was jesting," I started, although I'd never known the abbot to say anything he hadn't meant.

"If I'd wanted to escape, I would have done so by now," Derrick added. "But if it makes you feel better, then why don't you chain my legs instead of my hands?"

With both of our reassurances, Bartholomew relented. And in a matter of minutes Derrick was sitting across the table from me, his legs chained beneath him but his hands free. Bartholomew stood only a few feet away, and Trudy had settled in her chair nearby. Even so, I perched on the edge of my seat, nervous and excited to spend time with Derrick again.

Pup sat by Derrick's side, his tongue lolling from his mouth, his adoring eyes beaming up at the knight. I could only smile at the dog's devotion to the man. "I see you still claim Pup's undying affection."

Derrick ran his fingers through the dog's thick white fur. "If only I might say the same of you." Although his words were playful, there was something in the depths of his eyes that took my breath away.

Under his scrutiny, I ducked my head and waved at the chess game spread out between us. "I decided I must see for myself what kind of chess player you really are."

"Oh, I see." His tone hinted at humor. "You hoped that in my vulnerable state you might discover my secrets of success at chess."

"Why, sir." I sat up in surprise. "I thought I was the one with the secrets regarding chess. And that you were in need of my tutelage?"

A crooked grin tugged at one corner of his mouth. "I guess we shall have to see who is in need of whose tutelage."

"I've witnessed the recklessness of your playing." I leaned forward. "And I have no doubt you are in need of my help."

"I've no doubt, either." His voice dipped for my ears alone. "I am most certainly in need of you."

A thrill spread rapidly through me all the way to my toes and fingers. I didn't dare meet his gaze. Instead, I focused on the chessboard and moved my first piece, my knight.

What could he mean? Did he think there was hope for us after all?

With only four days left and with only the chance of secret meetings, even if we cared for one another, how could we manage to arrange a marriage?

He moved one of his pawns, then sprawled back in his chair and scratched behind Pup's ear.

I studied the board, trying to anticipate Derrick's strategy and where he might move next. I was thankful my old tutor had enjoyed playing chess with me over the years and that he'd taught me all he'd known. After several minutes of analyzing the various possibilities, I finally moved one of my pawns.

Derrick responded without any thought, swung his horse into an L, and took my pawn.

"That was too quick."

He grinned in response and sat back.

I peered at his pieces, attempting to determine why he'd taken my pawn and what moves he might be planning next. "Have you no strategy, sir?"

"I have no need for any."

"Then you won't make it far against those who do." I positioned another pawn in a place where I could tempt him into taking it so that I might then kill his rook.

He fell prey to my tactic, and with a smile I swiped the piece.

"You're quite skilled, my lady."

"Thank you." I placed his piece in front of me. "Instead of merely reacting, perhaps you'd be wiser if you took the time to think through each move."

"I've never had reason to think ahead." Once again he moved a piece haphazardly and then focused on Pup and rubbed his neck.

"It's never too late to start." Somehow I had the feeling we weren't talking about chess anymore. And when the warmth of his gaze fell back upon me, I couldn't keep from shifting my attention away from the board and onto him.

"What will you do with your future?" I asked with a boldness that came out of need. "That is, after the duke returns and wins your freedom?"

By the light of the lone candle on the table, the gray in his eyes turned sterling silver. "Then you're confident he'll win my freedom?"

"I believe the truth will eventually make itself known." I only wished the duke would return soon and make things right, before it was too late. "And once you're free, what will you do? Where will you go?"

He shrugged. "I suppose I always thought I'd fight in tournaments for a while so that I could save up a fortune for myself. And the duke will reward me with land for my service to him ..."

"Have you ever thought of trying to reclaim what once belonged to your father?"

"No. 'Tis not mine to claim anymore. The lands, the castle, the wealth has changed hands many times over the years. And to go in now and try to win back what once belonged to my family would mean ripping away the livelihoods and homes of innocent people who now live and work there."

"I respect you for your decision."

The lines in his face had hardened. "So you see why I haven't had reason to plan ahead. I have no future—at least not one that is worthy."

I could sense from the darkness settling over him that I was losing him again to his past. "But you have such good ideas. I've listened to the way you've spoken with my noblemen. And all of your ideas for improvement have great merit. In fact, I should like to hear more of them, especially since you've aptly pointed out to me that I could help the poor of my kingdom in more efficient ways."

I was relieved when his passion for the topic chased away his melancholy. The chess game lay untouched between us as I found myself enveloped in a conversation about the various ways I could promote prosperity and health among my people, the new farming techniques he proposed, the better methods for distributing help to those in need, the creation of better jobs and pay, and the ways to control illness.

I was swept so deeply into the discussion, I was startled when Bartholomew approached the table. "It's nearly dawn, my lady. We need to get the prisoner back into his cell before the servants awake."

Reluctantly, Derrick pushed away from the table and stood. As Bartholomew worked on switching the chains from Derrick's feet back to his hands, I stifled a tired but satisfied yawn.

"Since we weren't able to finish our chess game," I said with a smile at him. "I propose a rematch on the coming night."

"Yes, I propose the same," he said with a wink, "as you still need the benefit of my chess expertise."

I laughed softly. And as Bartholomew led him away, my heart filled with happiness and also an exquisite longing that I couldn't explain or deny.

I fidgeted all day, my discontent growing until I thought I would fairly burst from the need to see him again. The next two days were filled with the same—waiting all day, my impatience growing until Trudy found me unbearable. My only outlet was in the ongoing investigation I was doing with the help of James, my porter. I'd sent him to scour the sheriff's estate and to interview each of his servants. Not only did I hope to gain a clue about the identity of the true murderer, but I also hoped to find some evidence that might link the sheriff with the outbreaks, although I didn't know what.

Even so, I couldn't rest or find release from my inner torment until the dark hours of the night, when Bartholomew snuck Derrick into the Great Hall to the table in front of the hearth where we could talk for endless hours with the chess game between us.

Of course, the chess game never proceeded more than a play or two before a new conversation diverted our attention.

With only two nights left until my eighteenth birthday, a panic started to form in the pit of my stomach. James hadn't discovered anything. And I couldn't put aside the thought that the duke should have returned by now, that he should have found evidence to free Derrick and absolve him of his crimes. But we'd had no word from the duke or Sir Collin and Sir Bennet. My weeklong promise to my dear friend was ending, and my birthday was fast approaching, the day when I'd have no choice but to leave the castle and enter the convent to fulfill the Ancient Vow.

Most of my chests had already been transported to my new living quarters, and I knew the abbot was patiently awaiting my arrival.

But with each passing day, my uncertainty about entering the convent only grew. I'd prayed harder and more fervently that God would show me what he wanted me to do. I didn't know how I could bear to leave Derrick. But I didn't know what other choice I had.

I'd considered going against the abbot's wise counsel and

releasing Derrick. But if I did so, what kind of message would I send to my people about justice?

And what if I married him even though he was my prisoner? The problem was that even if I was agreeable to having Derrick for my husband, he'd never made any mention of wanting to marry me.

Certainly, I'd felt his attraction. And he'd hinted at wanting to be with me. But he hadn't mentioned any plans. It was almost as if he were approaching our relationship the same way he played a game of chess—without any thought or strategy. Perhaps he didn't know what he really wanted.

What if he didn't love me enough to want to overcome the odds standing between us? Maybe he didn't really love me at all. Maybe his feelings for me didn't run as deeply as mine.

And what exactly did I feel for him? Was I really in love with him?

It was the same confusing question whose answer had eluded me before. I wasn't sure how to tell if I was in love with Derrick. I cared about him—a great deal. But did I love him enough to risk forsaking the Ancient Vow? Enough to spend the rest of my life with him as my husband?

Perhaps it was time to take a more direct approach with Derrick. We'd grown comfortable enough with each other over the past several nights of talking. Could I not simply ask him what he thought we should do?

Maybe if I looked my best, if I made myself completely irresistible, then he'd have no choice but to bring up the matter himself.

With my heart thudding in anticipation, I made Trudy take extra care with my hair. And when I positioned myself in the chair in front of the great fireplace, I tucked rose petals under my hem, hoping he'd find me especially fetching that night.

I'd worn the crimson gown that the duke had given me on the night of the big dance. The diamonds and pearls sparkled in the candlelight. A few dangling curls hung loose from the mound of curls Trudy had arranged on top of my head.

I prayed that he would be the one to initiate a conversation about love and marriage and what chance the two of us might have for a future together. The mere thought of bringing up such matters heated my cheeks and made me stare at the pieces arranged in perfect rows on the chessboard, ready for another game we'd yet to finish.

The side door of the room rattled, signaling Bartholomew's approach with Derrick. Trudy already sat in her corner chair, her chin resting on her rotund chest, her eyes closed in slumber. Thankfully, my nursemaid had lost her objection to the meetings with Derrick. It was easy to see why. Derrick was so noble, kind, and considerate that he'd easily won my nursemaid over.

Even though Bartholomew didn't prevent my meetings with Derrick, he used extra caution to make sure that no one saw Derrick coming in and out of the Great Hall. When he brought up the abbot's objection, I assured him that I could do what I wanted without the abbot's permission, especially now that I was only days away from my eighteenth year.

An impatient sigh escaped, and I kept my hands folded in my lap and my eyes trained on them as I waited for Derrick to enter the room.

My heart gave an unexpected lurch at the thought of seeing him. Even though he carried with him the grime of the dungeon, I especially liked the dark stubble on his face, making him more rugged and handsome than he'd been before.

"My lady." A voice nearby startled me. It wasn't the expected voice of Bartholomew or Derrick.

I lifted my gaze, confused by the appearance of James and an unfamiliar man behind him. "Why, James," I said, embarrassment coursing through me at having been caught in my secret meetings with Derrick. How had James discovered my doings? Why wasn't he asleep with everyone else?

I glanced over to the side door. Though it stood wide open, there was no sign of Bartholomew or Derrick.

"Whatever are you doing up at this hour?" I asked, hoping to divert the men from the room before Bartholomew showed up. "Did you bring me any news regarding the investigation?"

James came several steps closer but eyed the shadows of the room as though he would like to disappear into them. "I'm sorry, my lady." His large forehead was crinkled in distress. It was then that I noticed another man creeping up on Trudy with an empty grain sack opened wide.

I glanced to the man who stood behind James. He too carried a grain sack. And when he stepped around James and came nearer, something inside me froze. He was one of the hired laborers from the convent, the same one who'd delivered the news about the sheriff's death.

"James, why are these men here?" I tried to keep my voice from quavering with a sudden burst of fear.

But James had stepped several paces back and dropped his gaze to the rushes strewn about the floor. His broad shoulders shrank inward. "I'm sorry, my lady," he said softly. "I didn't want to let them in. But I had no choice."

My mind struggled to make sense of what was happening. I could only watch with horror as the laborer slipped his bag over Trudy's sleeping head and cupped his hand over her mouth to cut off any sound she might make when she awoke.

A scream welled up in my chest, but it caught in the tightness of my throat. I pushed back from my chair. But before I could move or force a sound out, the other laborer had closed in on me.

My gaze flew to James, to his hulking body. He was there

to protect me, so why wasn't he doing his job? Instead of answering the question that was surely glaring in my eyes, he slunk back farther.

The laborer grabbed my arm, yanked the bag over my head, and plunged me into frightening darkness. The grain dust lingering in the sack bathed my face and suffocated me. I jerked against him and fought to pull away, but he clamped his hand over the bag, pressing the coarse material against my mouth and nose, forcing me to breathe in the pungent fumes that saturated the sack.

Screams burned in my chest. I twisted and tried to pull free of my captor. But I could feel my body begin to weaken and reality start to fade away.

One last thought sent a rush of panic through me before black oblivion claimed me: I loved Derrick. I knew with certainty I loved him—because suddenly I couldn't imagine how I'd ever live the rest of my life without him.

Chapter 21

I PACED BACK AND FORTH ACROSS MY CELL. TEN STEPS TO the wall. Ten steps to the bars.

I'd worn a path through the straw to the point my boots now slapped the stone floor. The darkness was so black I was unable to see my outstretched hand. My skin was damp with the dankness of the cell. And my stomach rumbled.

My morning meal should have come by now. It was past time.

But the door to the dungeon hadn't been opened all night or morning—except for the one time the jailor had shoved a drunk prisoner into the cell across from mine. The man had passed out, and from the heavy sound of his breathing I could tell he was still asleep.

I stopped at the bars and listened hard again, as I had many times during the long night. I strained to hear footsteps, jingling keys, anything to signal that Rosemarie's old guard was coming.

But there was nothing. Only silence and the choppy breath of the prisoner in the opposite cell.

Why hadn't Rosemarie sent Bartholomew for me as she'd done the other nights? The question pounded through me with such force my chest ached.

When I'd left the last time, she'd jested with me as she had previously that we would have to finish our chess game the next night. Of course, I'd purposefully neglected the chess game so that I would have some excuse—any excuse—to return to her for our midnight meetings.

Perhaps she'd decided it was too risky to send for me again? And I agreed. It had been risky. I dreaded to think what the abbot would do to her if he found out she'd been spending time with me ...

I blew out a shaky breath against the cold bars, then spun and resumed my pacing.

Or what if she'd grown tired of me? But she'd seemed to enjoy our times together as much as I had. She'd laughed with me, spoken animatedly, and had been genuinely interested in my opinions. Her eyes had been alight, her expression open and eager, and her smile ...

My heartbeat pounded with the strength of my warhorse in a battle. Her smile was beautiful enough to knock me senseless and make me do whatever she wished.

I almost groaned at the vision of her sitting across the table from me, the strand of her spun gold hair waving about her face, the delicate curve of her chin, and the lovely arch of her eyebrows above her wide eyes.

I hadn't been mistaken at seeing something in those eyes whenever she looked at me, had I? Some growing affection?

She surely wouldn't have sought me out if she didn't want to be with me.

I jabbed my fingers in my hair and released a groan. I had the urge to pound the bars and break them down so that I could find her, fall on one knee in front of her, and beg her to marry me.

Although I had no right to ask for her love, although I was still a poor, landless knight with the accusations of crimes upon my shoulders, I knew I must ask her to be my wife. I'd let my past insecurities command me far too long. And I'd waited beyond endurance for the duke to return to clear my name.

Rosemarie's birthday was on the morrow, and I couldn't put off the future any longer.

With a surge of renewed will, I pounded my fists together. Yes. Today I would find a way to see her, even if I had to send a message to have her come down to the dungeon. I would tell her I loved her, that I wanted to spend the rest of my life making her happy, that I didn't want to live another day without her by my side.

We could get married today. In the dungeon. Couldn't we? Nothing in the exception clause to the Ancient Vow had said anything about where Rosemarie got married or under what circumstances—only that she did, by midnight on her eighteenth birthday.

Surely Rosemarie wouldn't care that the duke hadn't returned with the evidence to clear my name yet. I'd seen the trust in her eyes. She didn't believe I'd committed the crimes.

Even so, my muscles tightened at the thought of asking her to marry me and at what her answer would be. If by some chance she agreed to my proposal, I wanted better for her than this cell. I brushed a hand against the slimy stone wall and listened to the scratching claws of a scampering rat.

Was I a fool to believe she'd return my love?

The echo of a door opening far above the dungeon was followed by footsteps. I blew out a breath, straightened myself, and waited by the bars. Finally.

After several long moments, the footsteps sounded in the passageway outside the dungeon, keys jangled in the lock, and the door squealed open. Through the light of the torch, I squinted and could make out the shape of the day jailer.

"Brought you something to eat, Sir Derrick," the jailer said in a gruff whisper. "Even though apparently I'm not supposed to."

Something in the jailer's tone sent my nerves into a head-long charge. "What's happened? Is Lady Rosemarie safe?"

"Oh, she's safe as can be." The jailer approached and slid a steaming mug through the bars. "Heard she left last night for the convent. Guess she decided to go a day early."

Left for the convent? Every last bit of the frustration I'd been feeling since last night spilled out of me and left an eerie emptiness in its place. "So she just left. Without saying good-bye?"

"Rumor going around the castle this morn is that she thought it would be easier on everyone if she left without making a big fuss."

I stared at the thick slice of bread on top of the soup mug, my appetite suddenly gone. So that's why she hadn't called for me to join her for our midnight game of chess.

She'd left.

A blaze of searing hot pain ripped through my chest, leaving me breathless. Even my hands shook, and I had to take a quick step away from the bars so that the jailer wouldn't see my reaction and brand me as a weakling.

She hadn't loved me enough to stay. She'd chosen a life in the convent over a life with me.

"Sure do wish we could have said good-bye to the lady," the jailer said, moving back to the door.

"Yes," I replied. She could have at the very least come to me and told me of her decision. I would have expected no less of her.

"I know she would have wanted us to continue treating you kindly, sir." The jailer paused before the door. "She was clear on that."

"Thank you. I appreciate your kindness," I managed, even though my chest was caving in and I could hardly think straight to get the words out.

"I don't care what Father Abbot's orders are," the jailer

tossed over his shoulder. "If Lady Rosemarie insisted we feed you and keep you comfortable, that's what I'm going to do."

"What do you mean, the abbot's orders?" I called after him.

The jailer shrugged. "He said he's the one who'll be making the rules from now on."

So I'd been right. The abbot had wanted Lady Rosemarie to enter the convent so he could continue to control her, perhaps gain even more power.

As the door closed and darkness fell around me, I leaned back against the cold wall and sank to the floor. The mug of soup fell to the ground next to me, spilling the precious drops of liquid. But I didn't care. I didn't care that it was likely the last bit of food I'd be given. As kind as the jailer had been, I knew no one in the castle would be able to defy the abbot's orders for long. He wielded a strong power.

I leaned my head back and stared at the black nothingness above me. My heart pulsed in painful spurts, and my chest ached so deeply I felt as if a lance had been thrust through my body.

She'd left.

She hadn't loved me enough to stay. Maybe she hadn't ever loved me at all.

My head dropped and my shoulders sagged. I'd lost her.

I closed my eyes and let the last bit of hope seep from me. Without Rosemarie in my life, it no longer mattered what fate befell me.

I rubbed the fog from my eyes and darted up, my hands making contact with a hard bed.

A scratchy wool blanket slipped off and fell onto Trudy, who was sprawled on a pallet on the floor. My nursemaid snorted once in her sleep and then stirred.

From the light coming in a high barred window, I could

see that I was in a small, narrow room. The walls were white-washed and barren, except a wooden cross hanging opposite of the tiny bed where I sat.

There was nothing else in the room, save a chamber pot in one corner.

"Trudy," I whispered, glancing at the thick planks of the door. "Wake up."

Where were we?

Trudy rolled over, muttered something under her breath, and went back to snoring.

I slipped my feet over the edge of the bed and smoothed down my crimson gown, which seemed out of place in the unadorned, colorless room.

How long had I been asleep?

My heart jolted at the remembrance of what had happened, of how I'd been waiting for Bartholomew to bring Derrick, of the men sneaking up on Trudy and me, throwing sacks over our heads. Then everything had gone black.

I stood, tiptoed around Trudy, and padded straight to the door. With a silent, desperate plea, I yanked on the handle, only to fall back a step.

It was firmly locked.

I glanced again at the window. It was too high and the bars too narrow to even consider escaping through it.

"Trudy," I whispered again, louder. "We need to get out of here."

I rattled the door, studying the lock and praying I could somehow miraculously open it.

"My lady," Trudy said from behind me, finally sitting up and yawning. "You're up early this morning."

Had my eighteenth birthday come and gone? Had I missed my chance to speak with Derrick and discover if we had a chance at happiness?

A strange panic beset my limbs. I lunged at the door, yanking on the handle and pulling against it.

"Derrick!" I cried. I needed to find Derrick.

"My lady," Trudy said, blinking hard. Her voice rose with a note of anxiety. "Wherever in the world are we?"

"We've been kidnapped." I stood back and appraised the room again.

"Holy Father, Son, and Spirit," Trudy unfolded her portly form from her pallet and rose to her knees. Her prayer echoed against the barren walls. "Looks to me like we're at the convent. This room reminds me of one of the chambers they use for the ill."

The clamoring inside me came to an abrupt halt. "The convent?" I gave a shaky laugh. But as I took in the room, I recognized it too, from the time my parents had sent me to the hilltop monastery to protect me from the Plague. I'd been restless and had wanted to help, so I'd sneaked into the infirmary to assist the monks in caring for the diseased.

"We shall call for the abbot," I said, drawing in a calming breath. "He'll be able to get us out of this strange situation in no time."

Trudy climbed to her feet and pursed her lips together.

I leaned against the door and listened to the sounds in the hallway outside our room. There were distinct steps coming nearer, slow and measured. And when the footsteps finally stopped in front of the door, I stepped back.

A key grated in the lock, and then the door swung open to reveal the abbot. He stood before me, tall and thin in his plain brown habit.

"Father Abbot," I said, relief pouring through me and chasing away all my fears. I wanted to fall into his arms and let him caress the hair off my forehead as he often did. But at the sight of the two laborers behind him, I froze.

They were the same men who had followed James into the Great Hall. The men who'd captured Trudy and me.

"There you are, your ladyship," the abbot spoke gently. "I've been waiting for you to awaken."

"You have?"

He nodded and tucked his hands into his sleeves. "I hope you'll forgive me for scaring you, and for the rough way in which my men brought you here. I shall have them disciplined, your ladyship."

The laborer's faces had gone pale, but they didn't move, and it was only then that I noticed their wrists bound with chains, and that they were at the mercy of several guards.

I swallowed past new fear that had risen into my throat. "Why did they do such a thing?"

"It's nothing to concern yourself with, your ladyship." The abbot nodded curtly and one of the guards shoved the kidnappers down the hallway, forcing them away.

"Now that you're here and safe," the abbot continued, smiling at me, "I shall take you to the guesthouse, where you'll live until the abbey is constructed. My servants have been busy unpacking your belongings and making it home."

He nodded at me, indicating that I should exit the room ahead of him and enter the dimly lit hallway.

But I couldn't move. My entire body protested the thought of seeing the guesthouse. My heart cried out to be back with Derrick. I wanted him more than anything else.

I knew then that I'd finally made my choice: I loved him. Without a doubt. And I wanted to marry him and spend my life with him.

I couldn't enter the convent. In fact, I couldn't even begin to imagine what life would be like without him as a part of it.

"Father Abbot," I said, reaching out a hand toward him. "I think there's been a mistake."

His expression remained placid. "I realize you don't turn eighteen until tomorrow. But now that you're here, we should get you situated, don't you think?"

I shook my head. My heart squeezed painfully at the news I must give the abbot. I didn't want to disappoint him. But I loved Derrick too much to throw away my chance at being with him. "I'm not going to enter the convent. I've decided I shall marry Derrick."

If he'd have me. I suspected that he still didn't think he was worthy, especially now with the convictions hanging over his head. But I'd assure him—until I was speechless, if necessary—that none of that mattered.

The abbot said nothing. But something about his eyes sharpened.

"I ask for your pardon." I stepped toward him, hoping he wouldn't be too angry with me. "I know you thought it would be best for me to come live here. But I've fallen in love with Derrick."

Once I spoke the words, they filled the room and swelled within my heart. I couldn't keep from smiling at the truth and beauty of them. "I love him."

"I'm sorry to hear that." The abbot retreated into the hallway. "I thought once you were away from the temptation of that man, you'd see your future lies in serving God here."

"But Derrick and I can serve God together," I said, thinking of all our conversations about the changes we could make for the good of the people if we worked together.

"You belong here," the abbot said without blinking, his tone boding no argument. "I've gone along with the duke's scheming long enough. And now it's time to put an end to it."

I stared at the abbot, trying to make sense of him. "But didn't you say you wanted me to see for myself if I found love—"

"I didn't believe you'd be so foolish as to give yourself over to the lusts of the flesh." His words had a sting to them that bit into my heart and left me aching. A part of me desired peace with the abbot, to listen to him, to give in to his advice as I always had in the past. But another, deeper part of me knew that I had to step into my role as a leader. I had to be more commanding and confident as the ruler I was destined to be.

"I never imagined that I'd have the chance to fall in love," I said, keeping my voice as even and authoritative as I could. "Even when presented with the exception to the Ancient Vow, I still thought it unlikely. But despite all the odds, it's happened. I've found the love of my life. And now, if he'll have me, I'll marry him. Today."

The abbot's face pinched. "I'd hoped you would be reasonable as you have been in the past. But I can see now that your lusts have clouded your good judgment."

With that, he spun out of the room and closed the door behind him. My pulse came to a shattering halt, and I could only stare at the door with an open mouth.

When the key scraped in the lock, a burst of panic erupted inside me and moved me to action. I flung myself at the thick plank and yanked on it. "You must release me, Father Abbot."

"This is for your own good, your ladyship," he called from the other side. "You'll thank me later."

"I command you to let me out of this room," I shouted. I was the ruler of Ashby. How dare he presume to make this decision for me?

"I'm sorry, my child." His voice was that of a parent chastising an errant child. "This is the best thing for you, even if you don't realize it yet."

"No!" The abbot wasn't planning to set me free. I was his captive. The panic inside swelled and I beat my hands against the door. "Please! I love him."

"You must put him out of your thoughts once and for all. He's not worthy of you."

I flattened myself into the cool wood, and a sob clawed at my chest, nearly strangling me with its power. "I don't want to lose him!"

"You already have," the abbot retorted, his steps moving away from my room. "For all of his crimes, he's sentenced to be drawn and quartered. On the morrow. Think of it as a birthday present, your ladyship."

Chapter 22

I SAT IN THE SAME SPOT. I DIDN'T KNOW HOW MUCH TIME had passed. It could have been hours, days, or weeks. I didn't care anymore.

The only thought pounding through my head over and over was that Rosemarie had rejected me.

I didn't even move when the prisoner in the opposite cell began to stir.

"Hello," came a hoarse whisper from the prisoner, likely finally awakening from his drunken stupor.

I didn't answer, grateful for the darkness that hid me from the other man. I didn't want to talk with anyone, didn't want anyone to try to cheer me up with annoying platitudes.

"Anyone there?" the voice spoke again, this time stronger and followed by a rustling of the straw.

An ingrained code of courtesy demanded that I reply, but I couldn't make my lips form the words I knew I ought to speak.

The other prisoner released a long moan. "Father Almighty, help me."

Something about the man's voice penetrated my consciousness, and I sat forward. The movement triggered the scampering of rats.

"Hello," the man said again. "Is that you, Sir Derrick?"

I strained to see through the blackness of the dungeon, but all that met me was the usual foul air. "Yes," I said hesitantly. "It is I, Sir Derrick. Who are you?"

"'Tis me, sir. Bartholomew. Lady Rosemarie's guard."

I didn't know who I'd been expecting, but at the revelation I slumped against the wall. Bartholomew was the last person with whom I wanted to converse. The old guard's presence alone would remind me of Lady Rosemarie and the clandestine visits with her over the past week.

But again, the duke's lessons on manners and kindness demanded that I acknowledge the other man's presence. "How are you feeling?"

"Like a wild boar let loose inside my head."

I snorted. Had the old guard been celebrating Lady Rosemarie's decision to leave? "That's what happens when you imbibe too freely."

"Imbibe?" The guard's question rose a notch. "Not me, sir. This wasn't from imbibing."

"I beg your pardon—"

"I took a whack to the head. And once I catch the men who did it, they better watch their backs."

I stiffened. "You were attacked?"

"I was coming down here to fetch you for Lady Rosemarie when two men came upon me from the shadows."

My muscles sprang to life, and in an instant I was on my feet, grabbing at the bars. "You were coming to get me?"

"Aye. I was—"

"Then Lady Rosemarie wanted to spend another night with me?"

"She was dressed in her prettiest gown, sir. The red one that she wore to the dance. And she was sitting at the table waiting for you, excited as could be."

The red gown that the duke had given her? A breeze of

relief blew across my chest, loosening the chains that had been holding me prisoner since I'd heard the news from the jailer. She'd been waiting to see me. Had been excited about it. Had even donned her best dress for me.

"Then what happened?" I asked, peering through the darkness to the cell across from mine, wishing I could read Bartholomew's face. "Did she change her mind and decide to leave for the convent in the middle of the night?"

"Convent?" The guard's gap-toothed voice rang with surprise. "No, sir. She made no mention of leaving for the convent. Especially not in the middle of the night. In fact, I thought she was changing her mind about leaving at all. If you catch my meaning, sir."

My mind spun with the new information, and I worked to make sense of it. Had she intended on staying, then? If so, what would have made her change her mind? "Do you have any idea who hit you, Bartholomew? And why?"

"I don't know, sir. They came up behind me too quickly."

I released my tight grip on the bars and stalked the ten steps to the wall and then back. There was only one person who had any reason to keep Rosemarie from me: Abbot Francis Michael. Perhaps the abbot had learned of our midnight chess matches and decided to put an end to them.

Heavy footsteps sounded on the stairs leading down to the dungeon.

I yanked at my tunic and tugged it over my head. "Take off your outer garment, Bartholomew," I whispered urgently. "And twist it into a rope."

I didn't know what had happened to Rosemarie. Maybe she'd gone to the convent willingly. But maybe she hadn't. I knew I'd never be able to live with myself if I failed to at least find out. I needed to hear directly from her that she didn't love me and didn't want to be my wife. If she said so, then I'd leave and let her take her vows.

But I couldn't languish in the dungeon any longer. I'd already shown courage by humbling myself in this pit in order to keep her safe. But now it was time to rise up. Time to charge into battle.

"I want you to call the jailer over to your cell," I whispered, twisting my tunic tightly. "Then take him by surprise and shove him straight back toward me."

"And if that doesn't work, then you'll push him against my cell?"

"Exactly." Bartholomew wasn't a strong man, but we would have the element of surprise on our side. Hopefully the day jailer would have compassion on us and not put up too much of a fight.

The door scraped open, bringing a blinding light and, to my dismay, two unfamiliar guards. The day jailer was nowhere to be seen.

I hid my shirt behind my back, and my muscles tensed, ready for action.

One of the guards sauntered near me. "The abbot wanted me to inform you that since today is Lady Rosemarie's birthday, she's decided that the gift she'd like to have most is your head on a silver platter."

I gave an inward sigh. There was still time. Maybe not much, but at least her birthday hadn't passed.

"But before that," the guard continued, "she wanted to make sure you suffered for your crimes. She ordered that you be hanged, drawn, and quartered in the town square at midday."

Public torture was the last thing Rosemarie would ever order, even against her worst enemy. A burst of fury pumped through my veins. Something was wrong with Rosemarie. I knew it with certainty now.

"I would advise against taking any action against me without the consent of the Duke of Rivenshire, the brother of the High King," I said, my fingers twitching against my tunic. I didn't know how I would be able to fight against two guards with only a scrap of cloth, but I had to try.

One of the guards drew nearer, dangling the keys in one hand and holding a spear in the other. The guard by the door followed on his heels, holding the torch.

"My source says that we won't need to worry about the Duke of Rivenshire or his knights trying to rescue you from your due punishment. He's been unavoidably detained by the abbot."

I let the news bounce off my chest. I'd have to worry about my companions later. For now I'd have to fight this battle by myself—hopefully with a little aid from Bartholomew.

Through the flickering light, I caught the old man's gaze and cocked my head toward the second guard. Bartholomew gave a slight nod and set his mouth grimly.

"If you promise to be a good lad," the guard said, looming nearer, "then I'll make sure to deliver you to the town square in one piece. If not, I'll be cutting off your fingers one by one for every struggle you make."

Sunshine poured in the barred window and indicated midday. My birthday was already half over.

Trudy sat on the edge of the tiny bed, her cheeks flushed, her eyes wild. "My lady, we have to do something."

I paced back and forth. "What can we do?" I'd gone over all my options too many times to count. There was no way around it. I would have to fight if I hoped to set us free.

It would be dangerous, but throughout the past sleepless night, I'd realized that I had to show my strength as a leader.

Maybe I was late in doing so. Maybe that's why the abbot thought he could still make decisions for me.

But I had to show him once and for all that his behavior, his control over me, was completely unacceptable, that I wouldn't tolerate it.

The door rattled, and Trudy rose from the bed, her wide eyes frantically sweeping our narrow room. "This isn't right. I won't stand back and let them do this to you, my lady," she whispered fiercely.

The abbot had sent news with our morning meal that I would be taking my vows at the ringing of the afternoon bells. And now they were coming to get me.

Trudy strode to the chamber pot and picked it up. "I only want you to be happy, my lady. And I can see that's not going to happen unless you're with your knight."

The lock squeaked.

"I'll distract them." Trudy planted herself in front of the door, her feet wide, the pot drawn back. "And you run and get help."

"I can't leave you here," I whispered.

The door started to open.

Trudy pursed her lips and drew her shoulders back. "Don't worry about me, my lady. I can fend for myself."

As the door swung open and revealed the armed guard waiting to deliver us to the chapel, Trudy swung the contents of the chamber pot forward so that the sour mess fell directly upon the face of the guard.

He stumbled and cried out, dropping a once-white robe to the floor.

"Run, my lady," Trudy screamed, tossing the chamber pot itself against the guard and knocking him in the head.

Even though I didn't want to leave my nursemaid behind, I bolted forward past the confused guard, out the door, and down the hallway. My footsteps echoed in the barren hallway. And my heartbeat slammed into my ribs.

I had to get away. I wouldn't be able to help Trudy or myself if I was locked in the convent. In fact, perhaps that's what the abbot intended all along. Maybe he'd never planned to let me rule in my own right when I turned eighteen.

The long corridor ended and opened into a covered walkway that passed through the courtyard. I paused and glanced to the monk kneeling in the flowers, pulling weeds.

Shouts echoed behind me. I had to find a way out of the convent. Perhaps the secret gate I'd once used to sneak inside?

I sprinted down the covered walkway, heedless of the monk stopping to watch me with a curious stare. Ahead loomed an arched door with a stained glass window above it.

The chapel.

If I could make it through the chapel, I would find the door that allowed the public to come and go into the sanctuary. I would be able to slip outside and command someone to take me back home, to Derrick.

Chills shook me, as they did every time I allowed myself to think about what the abbot had planned for him. Drawing and quartering was one of the most gruesome of torture methods, surely invented by the devil himself. Why would the abbot do such a thing? The idea of my wise counselor purposefully planning to harm Derrick revolted me.

I'd trusted the abbot these past years, and my heart ached to think about how he'd kidnapped me and locked me up. And now he was planning to torture the man I loved? How could he? Especially when he knew exactly how I felt about using torture methods?

I reached the church door and paused, gulping down a ragged breath. The shouts coming from the dormitory echoed again and spurred me forward. I yanked the door open and stepped through.

The high arches and tall pillars of the nave rose above me along with the stained glass windows. The candelabras near the altar were lit. But the glorious building was strangely quiet and deserted.

I slipped along the wall, seeking the front double doors that would take me to freedom.

"Ah, there you are, your ladyship." The abbot's voice echoed through the sanctuary.

I halted and located him at the front of the crossing, standing in his best robes near the chancel door, the Book of Prayers open in his hands.

"I've been waiting for you." He stepped to the base of the altar and scrutinized me across the span of columns. "But why aren't you dressed in the white robe I sent to you?"

I spun away from the abbot. With a new burst of panic, I bunched up my gown and ran straight for the door. I didn't stop to think. All I knew was that I must escape. Trudy had put her life in danger for me. And now I must find Derrick. If I could get to him before it was too late, then together we could come back to rescue Trudy.

I fell against the carved door. My fingers grasped the handle, and I lunged forward only to fall short.

The door didn't budge. I rattled the handle, desperation pouring into my chest. It was locked.

With a bolt of panic, I pivoted and ran back toward the side door I'd just entered. But it opened with a resounding bang, and several breathless guards raced inside with their swords drawn.

I stopped and swiveled, searching for another escape route.

"For the love of the sun, moon, and stars," came another voice behind the guards.

Trudy.

I stared as the same guard who'd come to our cell now strode into the center of the sanctuary, dragging Trudy next to him, heedless of the foul stench that accompanied him. At the sight of his dagger pointed against Trudy's chest, I cried out, "No! Don't hurt her!"

The sanctuary echoed with my cry.

The abbot smiled, but the motion lacked any warmth. "Fetch the tongue ripper." He motioned to one of the guards. "I'm sure her ladyship will cooperate more fully with taking her vows if she sees the instrument in place inside the mouth of her beloved nursemaid."

Chapter
23

I SUCKED IN A FORTIFYING BREATH AND WHISPERED A SILENT plea of forgiveness in advance for all I was about to do.

The guard bent his head to slip the keys into the lock, and I jolted forward. Before he could react, I snaked my arms through the bars and wrapped my tunic around the man's neck, twisting him around.

The guard managed a strangled cry, but I yanked the cord tighter, enough to strangle the air from his lungs.

With a roar, the other guard lunged toward me, his sword aimed to plunge through my body.

But with the strength born of practice and endless training, I positioned my leg through the bars and leveled a swift kick into his stomach with enough strength to send him reeling back against Bartholomew's cell.

With surprising quickness, Bartholomew looped his tunic around the guard's throat and twisted it into a slipknot.

I felt a sudden plunge of burning pain rip into my leg and realized the guard I was holding had slipped his dagger out of its sheath and had swung it back, grazing my outer thigh.

The man jabbed again, and this time I darted out of the way, grabbed the guard's arm, and yanked it behind his back into a painful upward hold that forced him to drop his weapon.

From the flares of torchlight, I could see Bartholomew struggle to avoid the blade of the sword that his prisoner was swinging wildly backward in an effort to free himself from the deadly hold around his neck. But due to the length of the sword, the guard was having little success.

I knew I didn't have time to spare. If Bartholomew lost his grip on the guard, the job of freeing us would grow slightly more complicated. With a swift yank, I brought my captive's head back and banged it against the bars hard enough to knock him unconscious. As the guard slid down to the floor, I pried the keys from the man's fingers before they fell out of reach.

I made quick work of unlocking my cell, and then, before Bartholomew's prisoner could react, I leveled another sharp kick into the man's stomach and then into the arm holding the sword. The pain of the attack forced the guard to release his weapon, and it fell to the ground with a clank.

In the moment of the man's weakness, Bartholomew yanked the cord around the guard's neck tighter. At the same instant, I rammed my fist into the side of the guard's head. The man crumpled, and I rescued the torch as it fell from the man's limp hand.

Without wasting a single second, I unlocked Bartholomew's cell and dragged one of the unconscious guards behind the bars.

"Good work, sir," Bartholomew said breathlessly as he stooped to help.

Once the men were safely locked away, I unwound my tunic and slipped it back on. Then I armed myself with the weapons of both guards.

I turned to Bartholomew. "I need you to find my weapons, especially my halberd, and then show me a way out of the castle that will cause the least detection."

"You need to tend your wound." Bartholomew stared pointedly at the blood seeping into my leggings.

I grabbed the old guard's tunic. With a burst of renewed determination, I ripped a shred from the edge and wrapped it around my leg, tying it tightly to stem the flow of blood. My mind was filled with only one goal: find Rosemarie.

I'd fight to the death to find her.

"There. It's tended." I stepped toward the door. "Now, are you willing to show me a way out? Or am I going to have to fight my way out of this castle with my bare hands?"

Bartholomew peered up at me, his wizened face creased with worry. "You can't ride out to the convent alone, sir. The abbot has more armed guards."

"Point the way," I demanded.

Bartholomew hesitated for a moment. Then, with a glint of admiration in his old eyes, he shuffled forward. "Follow me."

I prayed fervently I'd be able to reach Rosemarie in time. Before the abbot could force her to do anything she'd live to regret.

Screams of horror threatened me with each breath I took. The sight of dear Trudy with the rusted iron cage fixed around her head made me nauseous. Her mouth had been forced open unnaturally wide by two jagged pieces of metal and the horrific sharp point of the torture instrument that had been thrust into her mouth.

Already, Trudy's lips were cracked and bleeding from the contraption. Her eyes rolled in her head, frantic with pain. Every time she gagged, the sharp point of the instrument cut her tongue.

"Please," I begged. "Please, start the ceremony with all haste."

The abbot stood in front of the altar methodically swinging a ball of incense. "I appreciate your cooperation, your ladyship."

A guard had positioned Trudy near enough that I was forced to see her, but far enough away that I couldn't do anything to relieve my nursemaid's condition. They'd bound my hands in front of me. So there was nothing I could do but kneel on the prayer cushion.

The abbot finally turned. "I'm sorry it's come to this." His serenity only stirred a new longing inside me—a wish to slip the torture apparatus over his head and let him experience a dose of his cruelty.

"I don't believe you're sorry, Father Abbot." My voice quavered with the effort it took to keep myself calm.

"Of course I am." He lifted the ball and swung the incense above my head. "But don't worry. I shall keep your nursemaid alive. She's not valuable to me dead."

He nodded at the guard who stood next to Trudy. The guard tightened the strap that wrapped around Trudy's head. The sharp point pressed farther into Trudy's mouth.

My nursemaid gave a strangled cry.

"No!" I screamed, and swallowed the bile that rose in my throat. "I'll do anything. Anything. Please just take that off Trudy's head. Please."

The abbot smiled. "Ah, yes. That works nicely. I figured it might, especially after evaluating your reaction to the tortures I staged in town recently."

What did he mean staged?

Seeing my unasked question, the abbot's smile became more calculated. "I needed to see for myself if you still held an aversion to torture. I knew such knowledge might become useful to me in helping to control you should you develop any willful, disobedient tendencies—as you are now."

My body shook at the sense of betrayal. "So the sheriff was just obeying your orders?"

"As he should. As you will too."

"This is my land. I'm the rightful heir and ruler."

"You are a foolish young girl who knows nothing about ruling."

His words struck me like a slap across my cheek. "My people love me." But my declaration came out weak. If the sheriff and abbot felt that I was foolish, how many others did?

"You have emptied your coffers foolishly and would have become a pauper if I'd not stepped in to eliminate the poor in your kingdom."

"You eliminated the poor?" Again his words hit me, but this time in the heart.

"If you had your way, you would have given every last possession you owned to the wretches. I decided the only way to save you from such foolishness was to get rid of those demanding much of you but giving little in return."

"Then 'twas you who started the outbreaks of the illness?" My nausea rose up again along with the keen hurt of his betrayal.

"You'll appreciate the fact that I've saved your wealth." The abbot didn't move, except to continue to slowly swing the ball of incense above me. "There will hopefully be enough now to build the abbey and the cathedral we've been planning these many years."

"That you've been planning."

"In building them, you'll leave a legacy."

"And perhaps you'll gain more power and fame?"

The abbot didn't respond. But from the gleam in his eyes, I could tell that I'd come close to the truth.

How had I not noticed his ulterior motives before now? He'd hidden them well. Or perhaps when I'd been resigned to life in the convent before knowing about the exception to the Vow, the abbot had no need to hide anything. He'd simply planned to guide me as he always had. In my insecurity, I'd turned to him all too often and made it easy for him to move me like a pawn in a game of chess.

But with the real possibility of me getting married, had he realized he'd lose the ability to control me? Had he been the one to undermine the contest, to try to murder the knights?

I lowered my head for fear he would see the revulsion roiling through every corner of my body. I wanted to ask how he'd done everything. Perhaps he and the sheriff had been working together. But what difference would it make now to know any more? I knew enough. I knew the man I'd always adored and trusted was not the man I'd believed him to be.

Anger swelled in my chest. I wanted to stand up and lash out at the abbot. But one look at the blood dribbling down Trudy's chin and I knew I could do nothing. At least at that moment. I couldn't risk bringing any more pain to my dear nursemaid. And clearly the guards were loyal to the abbot.

The abbot began to pray, in Latin, the opening lines of the ceremony that would irrevocably turn me into a nun. Once I spoke the vows, I would be bound to life in the convent. There would be nothing anyone could do to change my future, even if they wanted to.

Mingling with my anger at the abbot, my heart cried out with the pain of everything I was losing, the beauty of life and love. And Derrick.

I let my head dip lower, the weight of the sorrow and horror of all that was happening pressing down and threatening to flatten me. In some ways it was a funeral. Since it was now well past midday, I had no doubt the abbot had carried out his threat to have Derrick put to death. The merest thought about how much he'd suffered made me want to weep.

"We are gathered here to unite Rosemarie Montfort of Ashby," the abbot started, "in the solemn occasion of marriage to the God of the universe."

One of the windows near the back of the church crashed, sending shards of colored glass spraying into the nave.

I stiffened and turned in time to see a man jump through the opening. He rolled to the floor amidst the glass, and then sprang to his feet. When he straightened, I gasped.

It was Derrick, and he was still very much alive. Relief hit so swiftly that I gasped out a half cry. His hair was windswept and his chest heaved as if he'd run the distance from the castle to the convent.

Derrick's steel eyes swept around the church and came to rest on me for an instant. His gaze raked over me as though surveying my safety before he strode to the center aisle, holding his halberd with both hands, with his knight's sword holstered on one side and his dagger on the other. He spread his feet wide, and his eyes blazed with fury. The convent guards started to slowly approach him, their swords unsheathed and gleaming in the bright light that streamed from the open window.

I counted the number of guards advancing upon him. Eleven.

A new fear seized my heart. How could he possibly fight against eleven well-trained and armed soldiers?

A movement by my side and another drawn sword raised the count to twelve. The soldier that had been guarding Trudy was joining the ranks of those circling around Derrick.

He would soon be trapped in the middle of twelve soldiers.

I wanted to scream my protest. But how could I? What good would it do now?

As one of the guards lunged at Derrick, he rapidly beat him away with the axe head and then fended off another blow with the sharp spear-like tip of his weapon.

My breath caught in my chest and I turned away, unable to watch him fall to his death.

At that moment, my gaze landed on Trudy, whose agonized eyes begged for release from her pain.

One look at the abbot told me he was distracted by the skirmish. If I hoped to free Trudy, now was my chance. I couldn't delay.

Before the abbot tried to stop me, I stood and made my way to my nursemaid. Even though my hands were bound, my fingers were still free. With the grunts and cries of the battle taking place behind me, I resisted the temptation to crumple to my knees and cry out in dismay at the sight of the contraption on Trudy's face.

Instead, I found the leather strap and latch at the back of Trudy's head that held the torture instrument in place. With shaking fingers, I fumbled for it. At the barest movement, Trudy gave a guttural, animal-like cry of pain.

"Our Father who art in heaven," I whispered while swallowing screams of my own. I wanted to back away, to hide, to pretend this was all just another nightmare. I wasn't sure that I could face my fears so fully.

A roar sounding much like Derrick's voice came from the battle, jarring me and reminding me that he was facing twelve armed guards. He'd come to rescue me. If he could defy death itself and fight so valiantly, surely I could stand strong too.

Trudy's entire body shook, and I moved faster.

"You'll be fine in just a moment," I crooned, fighting back tears. "You'll be fine, my sweet, sweet Trudy." My fingers tangled with the latch as I desperately tried to loosen it.

In one last agonizing moment, the contraption slipped free and the metal fell away from Trudy's mouth. It crashed to the floor with a clang. With my bound hands, I caught her against my body and eased her to the floor. She buried her face into my chest, her body heaving with sobs.

Another cry rose above the clanking of swords.

I peered to the circle that had crowded ever closer to Derrick. From the bodies sprawled on the floor near him, he'd apparently already taken down four soldiers. But that left eight.

He wielded his halberd and spun with a deftness and sureness that showed him as the superior knight he was. I could imagine that this was how he fought on the battlefield, how he'd earned a distinction as one of the three noblest knights in all the realm.

He fought off one blow while ducking to avoid another. But how could he carry on indefinitely? He already had a bloody patch on his leg. Just at that moment, the tip of a sword grazed his arm, and in an instant a crimson spot seeped into his tunic.

"Stop!" I called, but my throat was too constricted with anxiety and my words came out breathlessly. Derrick lunged with the halberd's hook, grappling and felling one more.

Even so, the circle around him grew tighter. The guards advancing on him moved in for the kill, until he was completely helpless with seven remaining swords pressed against his body and ready to plunge.

"Drop your weapons," the abbot called to Derrick.

Through the danger of the sword tips digging into his skin, Derrick's gaze sought mine. Across the distance, the blaze in his eyes consumed me, went deep into my soul, and reassured me that he'd done this for me.

He loved me. I could see the message shining there.

"I love you too." I mouthed the words, praying that if he couldn't read my lips, he would see into my heart and know the truth of my undying affection for him. I would never love anyone else again.

As if my words had traveled the distance and entered his heart, he gave a renewed cry, ducked beneath the circle of swords, and chopped at the legs of the guards surrounding him with the halberd's axe head, causing them to fall back.

My heart surged with fresh hope, but it was immediately doused as the abbot's boney fingers circled around my neck and dragged me forward. His grip was hard and unyielding.

Trudy fell away, crumpling to a heap on the floor, her eyes dull with pain, her mouth a bloody, swollen mass.

"Drop your weapons this instant," the abbot called, "or I shall start slicing the face of her ladyship, one slice for every slash you make at my guards."

The icy steel of a knife pressed against my throat.

Immediately, Derrick pulled himself back. "Don't harm her." His voice was laced with panic.

"I like how this works," the abbot said, thrusting the knife all too close to my skin so that it pricked painfully. "In fact, I think I'm going to like my new position of power very much."

"So you freely admit you've been undermining Lady Rosemarie's efforts to find true love. That you're the one who sabotaged my companions."

The abbot chuckled. "Of course I thought she was falling in love with them first and hoped to scare them away. But then once I realized she liked you the most, it was all too easy to pin the blame for the crimes on you and make you look like the jealous friend."

After all I'd already learned about the abbot, the news didn't surprise me. Nevertheless, it stabbed me. "Father Abbot, how could you—"

The tightening pressure of the blade silenced me. "I only did it for your protection, your ladyship."

"Her protection?" Derrick called. "And I suppose you think you're protecting her now?"

"She's taking her vows very willingly, aren't you, your ladyship?" The abbot tossed a glance to Trudy and the tongue slicer lying on the floor near her.

Derrick followed his gaze, and at the sight of my tortured nursemaid, his eyes glittered as sharp as double-edged swords.

"Drop your weapons." The abbot repositioned the knife so that it finally nicked my skin. I couldn't keep a cry from slipping out, more from fright than pain.

Derrick's face turned pale and somber. He released his halberd, and the shatter of steel against stone ricocheted through the nave all the way to the arched ceiling, reverberating deep within my heart.

It was the sound of good-bye.

He unsheathed his dagger and sword and let them fall as well. And when he met my gaze this time, I knew he was saying farewell.

He was giving up his life to save mine.

Chapter
24

"No!" My scream pierced the air.

I wouldn't let him make that kind of sacrifice. But even as my scream rent the nave, a trumpet blast swallowed the sound and was followed by splintering wood.

In an instant, the church door caved in and the afternoon sunshine poured into the room. A knight ducked low upon his horse and charged through the gap, his longsword aimed and ready to thrust.

I didn't need to see the emblem on his horse blanket to know the knight was Sir Bennet. I only needed to see the deftness with which he sliced and stabbed his weapon as his steed crashed through the group of guards, his sword slashing them down.

While the guards were fending off Sir Bennet, Derrick swooped to retrieve his halberd. In one motion, he grabbed the weapon and swung it against the heels of the closest guard, sending him to the ground with a cry. Derrick spun and chopped into the swinging arm of a guard ready to stab Sir Bennet.

Sir Bennet repaid the deed by plunging into a guard who came roaring toward Derrick. Within minutes, the two knights had injured or felled the rest of the guards. When they were finally unopposed, Derrick grinned up at Sir Bennet, whose horse snorted and stamped sideways.

Another crash came from the church entrance, and two more warhorses barged into the nave—the duke and Sir Collin, who were both winded but wielding weapons and prepared for battle.

"Thanks for finally showing up," Derrick said wryly.

"You know us. We like to make things as exciting as possible whenever we can." The voice hinted at humor and belonged to Sir Collin.

"A few key bridges on the return trip had been destroyed by the abbot in an effort to keep us from returning." The refined statement came from Sir Bennet.

"Bennet was right about not needing to free you from the dungeon," Sir Collin said with a laugh. "I should have known you'd make your own way out of prison when the need arose."

The duke remained silent. He sat regally upon his horse. I could see through the eye slit in his helmet he was taking in the scene of battle in one sweep. When his gaze came on me, he stopped and stiffened.

I'd been watching the whole fight without moving. I'd hardly dared to breathe, much less speak, with the blade still pressed against my throat. Throughout the melee before us, I had waited for the abbot to strike, to punish me for the knights' actions, but the knife had not moved. I had a terrible feeling he was saving his wrath until Derrick's full attention was focused on me once more.

"Let Lady Rosemarie go," the duke called. "We've found evidence that proves you were behind the murder attempts you blamed on Sir Derrick, and have arrested the marksman you hired to shoot Sir Collin. We also have in custody a soldier who works for the neighboring Lord Witherton, who claims you paid him to kill and cut out the sheriff's heart."

"It doesn't matter anymore," the abbot said, taking a step back but keeping the knife against my throat. "I've got her ladyship now. And nothing you do will make me hand her over. There are only hours left until she's mine anyway. You might as well admit defeat when you're faced with it."

"We also found the liquid you had the sheriff pour into the ale that was distributed among the poor, a poisoned liquid that was causing everyone who drank it to fall ill. We located the man who sold it to you and have him in custody as well."

"It's my word against theirs," the abbot said.

Although my hope had been rising with each new piece of evidence against the abbot, it quickly came crashing down. The abbot would only need to perpetuate lies. All he had to do was tell my people that the duke wanted control over me and was making up the charges to keep me from fulfilling my sacred duty to the Ancient Vow. Who would dare oppose the abbot, at least without fearing for their lives?

Fresh hopelessness seeped into my chest.

The duke exchanged a pointed glance with Derrick.

"If you don't turn around, ride out of here," the abbot said, his voice ringing with the victory that was surely his, "and leave Ashby for good, I'll begin cutting her up."

Derrick shifted, and his jaw clenched with barely restrained anger.

"If you hand her over willingly," the duke replied, "we may spare your life."

The abbot's thin fingers dug into me. Who was this man? Had he ever cared for me at all? Or had he guided me out of the selfishness of his heart for the control he'd hoped to gain over my lands when I was finally locked away in the convent?

"I haven't gone to all the trouble to counsel her ladyship only to have you come in here at the last minute and steal all that's rightly mine and to take away my dreams of building a holy empire."

Now that the whole truth was out, my shoulders sagged with his betrayal. "I thought you loved me." My voice quavered but I didn't care. "I thought you truly wanted what was best for me, but this has only been about what you can gain, hasn't it?"

"And I do want what's best for your soul, my child." His voice gentled near my ear. "But at this point you're too enamored with the knights. You've become a simpering fool of a girl. And you've forced me to resort to this violence."

"Hand her over." The duke's voice boomed through the church. "This is your last chance."

A spurt of defiance rose within me. I didn't want to be known as a simpering fool of a girl. Without giving myself time to rationalize my next move, I slapped the knife away from my throat, surprising the abbot, and ducked low as I'd seen Derrick do during his fighting.

"Now!" the duke shouted. Upon the command, Derrick flung his dagger so that it flew end over end directly toward the abbot.

I sank lower and covered my head with my bound hands.

Before the abbot could move, the sharp blade punctured his chest with a thud. He gave a pained scream, fell backward, and hit his head against the altar. For a long moment, his breath gurgled in his chest. Then he wheezed a final gasp and slumped lifelessly to the floor.

It was over. The nightmare was finally over. Even so, my body trembled uncontrollably.

"Rosemarie," Derrick called, running toward me. Within seconds, he was at my side and reaching for me. I found myself being pulled against him, his arms surrounding me, his hands pressing my head against his chest.

"You were brave, my lady," he whispered against my ear. "I

don't know that I would have had the daring to throw the dagger with you standing so closely to him."

I had no doubt he would have thrown it regardless and would have made his mark. Nevertheless, I'd done something courageous. Perhaps it was an omen that I would be able to face my future the same way.

Derrick pulled me away from his chest, and his fingers found the cut on my neck.

I winced at the gentle contact. His eyes darkened into storm clouds.

I lifted my bound hands then and bravely touched the scar that ran below his eye and then his cheek. At my contact, he grasped me and swept me tight into his arms again, burying his face in my hair, which had come loose and now fell in tangled waves. He sucked in a deep breath and whispered near my ear. "I thought I'd lose you before I had the chance to tell you that I love you."

A shimmer of wonder raced through me. "Derrick," I whispered back in a thick voice.

Before I could tell him I loved him too, he burrowed his face deeper in my hair so that his lips grazed my ear. "I love you, Rosemarie. I'm just sorry I didn't tell you sooner."

I melted against him, relishing the heavy rise and fall of his chest. How was it possible to be dying inside one moment and wrapped in the arms of the man I loved the next? "Derrick," I started again, but then stopped as I realized I was using his Christian name although he'd not given me leave to do so.

He pulled back and watched me expectantly, his brow quirking with the confidence that told me he knew exactly what I was trying to tell him.

I inwardly flushed, especially when I realized the other three knights had seen our display of affection and were near enough now to hear our conversation.

"My lady?" he said, tilting his head and waiting.

I had to speak the words burning in my chest, filling me. Although I'd faced an uncertain choice these past weeks, I now knew without a doubt the course of my life. "I don't wish to be anywhere else on this earth except with you."

A slow smile spread across his lips. "Does this mean I won the competition?"

"Of course you're the winner, you foul piece of dungeon scum," Sir Collin called from where he was rounding up the wounded guards. "We never stood a chance once you actually started to make an effort."

"I think we need to get you married to Lady Rosemarie as soon as possible," Sir Bennet said from his spot next to the abbot as he pulled the dagger from the man's chest. "Since you obviously can't keep your hands off her."

I tugged away from Derrick, heat stealing into my cheeks. But before I could move too far, he grabbed the rope still binding my hands, preventing my escape. With a quick flick of his dagger, he cut the bonds loose. He pulled me back to him and cupped my cheek with a gentleness that seemed contradictory to a man of his strength and valor. His thumb swirled soft caresses against my skin while his gaze dropped to my lips as if he had every intention of kissing me.

My stomach heated in anticipation.

"Soon," he whispered, tearing his attention from my lips, his eyes alight with promise.

"The day is getting late," the duke said. "I'll find a priest and tell him to make his way to the church right away." He'd scooped Trudy up into his arms and was already striding through the church, likely taking her to the infirmary.

Derrick's brows furrowed into a scowl. "No." He stood and assisted me back to my feet.

The three knights halted their work and stared at him.

"If I'm going to do this, I'll do it properly." His voice rang with defiance, and he glared at his friends, daring them to challenge him. "We have until midnight on Rosemarie's birthday, don't we?"

"Yes," the duke said, cradling Trudy carefully. "But I think the sooner the better."

"I agree," Derrick said, turning back to me with a tender smile that made my insides flop. "But first I need to do this."

He dropped to a knee before me, took one of my hands in his, and brought it to his lips for a tender kiss that made me suddenly long for so much more.

When his eyes met mine, I could see the swirling of that same desire within his. "My lady," he said in a low voice that was raw with emotion. "I love you with all the life blood beating in my body. And I shall love you all the days of my life unto eternity."

His declaration radiated through me and chased away all the agony of the past days.

"In front of these men, the best friends a man could ever have, and in front of God as my witness, I pledge you my devotion, my heart, and my life. I only ask for yours in return." He peered up at me, his clear honest eyes beseeching me to return what I could not help but give him.

"It's already yours."

His smile broke free once again with a happiness that was uncontainable. "Then you'll marry me?"

"Without hesitation."

Sir Collin gave a whoop that echoed in the empty church, and Sir Bennet bowed his congratulations.

"You deserve better than a bridegroom covered in blood and grime," Derrick said, threading his fingers through mine.

"You need your wounds tended, sir," I agreed, frowning as I took in the spots of blood on his leg and arm.

"Only a bath and change of garments," he rushed. "You deserve that at the very least."

"What about a wedding back at the castle in my rose garden? After we've both had the chance to change?"

He hesitated, glanced at his friends, who nodded, and then tightened his grip on my hand. "As long as you guarantee it will be without any delays."

"Without any delays," I agreed, hoping my smile wasn't too eager.

The pink of eventide began to glow in the west. The color matched the roses that surrounded me.

A soft breeze tousled the sheer gown of palest rose that I'd worn on the day I'd met the knights. One of my maids had brushed my hair until it shone, and now it hung past my waist in shimmering waves.

I wore a veil over my face that flowed from a crown of roses.

"You picked well, dear one," the duke whispered as he walked me forward to the three noble knights waiting in my garden with the priest. They had cleaned up and now watched my approach with admiration on their faces.

"Did you know I'd fall in love with Sir Derrick, your Grace?" I asked.

"Yes. He's the one I chose for you. I just needed the two of you to realize how well matched you were for each other."

"We shall balance each other well, I think." My gaze strayed to the man at the front of the three knights, stocky, scarred, and strong. His attention didn't move from me as I made my way slowly toward him. "He's strong where I'm weak. And I have strength that can likewise fill in his weaknesses."

"You'll do great things together." The duke squeezed my hand.

As I neared Derrick, the first stars twinkled overhead as if God himself had sprinkled diamonds across the sky for the occasion.

"Your bride, my son," the duke said, placing my hand upon Derrick's arm.

My groom straightened his shoulders. In a clean tunic and dark jerkin, with his freshly shaven jaw and hair combed into submission, he was still rugged in a way that sent my heart into a strange pattering dance.

"My lady," he whispered. Slowly, almost reverently, he swept up my veil until he'd pushed it all the way back. "You're beautiful." He made a leisurely perusal of my face before focusing on my lips. This time there was a determination in his eyes that told me he wouldn't be swerved now or ever again.

Heat unfurled deep in my middle.

"My lady," he said again, this time raising his gaze to mine. "I've been waiting patiently to claim the prize you owe me. But today, at this moment, my patience has finally run out."

"What prize did you have in mind, sir?" I trembled, knowing full well what he wanted.

"May I show you?" he whispered, bending nearer.

I nodded.

He lifted a hand to my cheek, brushing my skin with the softness of the wind. He bent closer until his breath hovered above my lips. After an immeasurably sweet instant, his lips came against mine, claiming me as his own.

I leaned in and gave myself to him. For a long, precious moment, I was on the brink of heaven with just him.

"You don't need to rub it in," came the teasing voice of Sir Collin next to Derrick, followed by the low rumble of chuckles from the others.

I pulled back, heat radiating over my cheeks, but I met Derrick's proud grin with one of my own.

"Perhaps you shall have to claim your prize again later, sir," I whispered.

His grin widened. "Whatever you wish shall always be my command."

Epilogue

My pulse fluttered at the blaring of the trumpet signaling Derrick's return.

"He's home early," Trudy said, tying the lace on my bodice. "And I haven't even started on your hair."

"My hair will be just fine." I rose from the bench in front of my dressing table unable to contain my anticipation.

"But shouldn't we pull it up, my lady? For the evening?"

I was already halfway across the room, my hair cascading around me in wild abandon. "I couldn't bear to sit still for the time it would take to fix it."

Trudy clucked, but then her face softened. After two months, the wounds from her ordeal with the tongue-ripper were finally beginning to fade. She shook her head, gave me a secretive smile, and then waved me onward. "Be off with you, then."

I returned the smile. Although I hadn't shared the news with anyone yet, I was sure Trudy knew, especially after consulting the physician that morning.

With my heart beating louder with each passing second, I stepped into the hallway. Due to the fading light of the autumn evening, the wall sconces had already been lit.

"He's home, my lady." Bartholomew gave me one of his gaping but endearing smiles.

I wanted to reward my old guard handsomely with riches

and land for his part in helping Derrick escape from prison, but Bartholomew had resisted every reward, except one — my promise that he could continue to serve me as he'd always done.

"I didn't think he'd be gone very long," Bartholomew said, his eyes twinkling with mirth. "He just can't be away from you, my lady."

"Nor I him," I said with a widening smile. It had been the first day I hadn't traveled with him on one of his excursions into the kingdom to evaluate and plan for improvements. When I'd informed him earlier in the day that I wasn't planning to go, he'd wanted to postpone the trip.

But I'd insisted that he go without me. And he'd only done so reluctantly only after a great deal of persuasion.

I moved after Bartholomew as he led me down the winding staircase to the Great Hall. Even though Derrick had entered the castle walls, I knew it would take some time before he reached the inner bailey, dismounted his horse, and handed it over to the care of one of the stable hands.

Nevertheless, I wanted to be ready for him, wanted to be the first to greet him when he entered.

I was surprised when I made my way through the back passage of the Great Hall to hear a commotion coming from the front entry. My new porter was racing to the doors.

I'd been sad to have to send James on his way to find employment elsewhere, but after learning of his part in helping the abbot, Derrick had wanted to lock James away in the dungeon until he rotted to death.

However, I was convinced that in his heart James had only thought he was doing the best thing for me, had believed the abbot truly cared about me, the same way I had. No one had considered that the abbot was consumed with controlling me so that eventually he could control my lands.

Instead of punishing James, I'd finally persuaded Derrick to release him with the condition that he would move far away and never return.

The banging on the front doors grew more insistent until through the hallway, I could see the new porter opening doors. My breath snagged in my chest at the sight of Derrick striding into the castle, his face having grown more attractive with each passing day. He spoke tersely to the porter and then bounded toward the staircase.

"My lord," I called from the center of the Great Hall.

My call stopped him. And when he turned and caught sight of me, he started toward me with quick, firm steps that echoed with determination.

As he drew nearer, my heart pounded louder, especially when the intensity of his gaze found me. His footsteps didn't lessen. He stared directly at my lips with such purpose that I trembled with the desire rising within me.

When he reached me, he swiftly captured me, dragged me against his body, and crushed me in his arms. His lips descended upon mine with a fierceness that sent heat curling through down to my toes.

For a long moment, I lost myself in his kiss and his embrace, until finally he broke away, sucked in a deep breath, and whispered against my ear hoarsely. "I missed you today."

I smiled. "I missed you too."

"Not nearly as much as I did, I'm sure."

He brushed a soft trail of kisses across my ear, making me nearly forget reason. "I thought about you every minute of the day," I whispered.

"Just promise you won't ever do this to me again. Promise that you'll come with me every time from now on." His hands wove into my hair, combing the long strands. His lips followed, and he buried his face in my hair, drawing in a deep breath. "The people expect you. They love you."

"They love you too."

"Not as much as you."

I was grateful that when I'd assumed full leadership of my lands the people had transferred their allegiance to me eagerly. I'd already proven to them my devotion and compassion, and thankfully they respected me for it.

"I hated spending the day away from you," he whispered, pulling me closer. "Please promise I won't have to do it again."

"I can't promise that, my lord," I said coyly.

He froze.

"Although I shall be loathe to let you ride alone," I hurried, "I cannot promise to be with you every time ..."

He drew back and studied my face, his gray eyes suddenly darkening.

"At least not for the next seven months."

His eyes met mine, alight with questions and searching deeply for answers.

I slipped a hand to my abdomen, splaying it with reverence.

His gaze dropped to my hand, and when it rose again his face was alive, the weariness of the day gone. "Then you are—?"

"We are having a baby," I whispered.

He broke into a grin.

After kissing me again, twirling me around, and shouting the news for all the servants to hear, he finally pulled me into his arms.

I'd known how much he wanted a family. After so many years of grieving the one he'd lost as a boy, he was ready to move forward and to start building a legacy of his own. And I was more than a little relieved to know that I wouldn't have the same problem as my mother in conceiving.

"Thank you," he whispered, holding me tightly.

"Let's thank the One who deserves it most."

With a happy smile, he led me to the chapel, where we offered prayers of thankfulness to God for all that he'd given us. Every day, I offered him thanks for the opportunity to serve him alongside my husband, that I had the blessing of experiencing true love. I was more than grateful for the duke and his wisdom, his love, and his guidance. And I was grateful that my loneliness was truly gone, that I'd gained not only a lifelong companion, but also his friends as mine.

After praying and feasting together, we ended our day as we usually did, in front of the hearth with the chess game between us.

"Pup's behaving strangely tonight," Derrick said after one of his rash moves. Pup only lifted his head, lolled his tongue in a semblance of a smile, and then rested his head on his paws again.

I reached down and scratched the dog on his furry white head. He was lying by my side for the first time in weeks. In fact, he hadn't lain by my side since Derrick had become lord of the castle. He'd taken to his new master with a loyalty and love that mirrored mine.

Derrick grinned at the dog. "You don't suppose he knows ..."

I studied Pup, the alertness of his ears, the restlessness of his posture. "Do you think he senses we're having a baby?"

"I believe so." Derrick bent forward and gave the dog a loving pat on his back. "I think he knows how much I want to protect you and the baby and so he's just doing my bidding."

"Well, if this is what it takes to win the affection of my dog again, then I shall have to do this more often."

Derrick's grin only widened.

Just then, Pup raised his head and stared in the direction of the front hallway. Within seconds, the new porter entered. "I beg your forgiveness for the interruption, my lord. But a messenger has just arrived."

There was a subdued air about the porter's plain features that sent a shaft of worry into my heart. As if sensing the seriousness of the message, Derrick rose quickly to his feet. "Who is it?"

The porter held out a ring. Even across the distance, the cross at the center of the ring was clear. It belonged to only one man in all the land—the Noblest Knight, the Duke of Rivenshire.

Derrick's grin faded. His jaw tensed. Beneath the clean tunic he'd donned, the muscles in his arms rippled. "What message does his Grace have for me?"

The steward crossed the room and handed Derrick both the ring and a parchment. Derrick unrolled the stiff paper. As he read, his expression turned grave.

Finally, he looked up and met my anxious gaze. The seriousness in his eyes filled me with dread.

"I must ride out at the first light of dawn."

I nodded and waited for him to go on.

"Although I may be too late to help, I must do all I can to save my friend."

I didn't ask him which friend. I knew it was one of the noble knights—either Sir Bennet or Sir Collin, the most loyal and brave friends a man could ever have.

"He's to be hanged, drawn, and quartered."

I shuddered. Although I'd been facing my fears and my nightmares regarding torture methods, my heart was still tender and always would be. "Then you must go."

Derrick reached for my hand and gripped it passionately.

"Even though I will hate every second that I'm away from you, I must do this. I must fight to save his life. I can do nothing less ..."

I nodded. I knew he could do nothing less as well.

He caressed my cheek one last time and then spun and strode out of the Great Hall, his footsteps echoing their good-bye.

Want more?

Check out *The Vow*, the ebook-only prequel to *An Uncertain Choice*, available wherever ebooks are sold.

Or head over to www.JodyHedlund.com for discussion questions for *An Uncertain Choice*, as well as more books from the author!

CPSIA information can be obtained
at www.ICGtesting.com
Printed in the USA
LVOW08s2303130517
534098LV00004B/3/P